Praise for **Counting from Zero**

"Credible and believable, this story is told by a subject matter expert. I could not wait to find out what happened next."
 - **Vint Cerf**, Internet pioneer

"The threat to the Internet from worms, viruses, botnets, and zombie computers is real, and growing. *Counting from Zero* is a great way to come up to speed on the alarming state of affairs, and Johnston draws you in with his story and believable cast of characters."
 - **Phil Zimmermann**, creator of Pretty Good Privacy (PGP) the most widely used email encryption program

"*Counting from Zero* brings Dashiell Hammett and Raymond Chandler into the computer age."
 - **Diana Lutz**

ISBN-13: 978-1461064886
ISBN-10: 1461064880

Counting from Zero

Alan B. Johnston

PROLOGUE.

The exploit code compiled for the final time; it was ready to be tested.

The young man loaded the software on his computer, randomly selected a target, then hit send. He sat back to watch the results.

A world away, a single packet arrived quietly from the Internet on an unfiltered port. It utilized a rarely used protocol, and seemed an innocuous request. At the end of the request, however, was something else entirely: a carefully crafted and formatted message that would result in the automatic execution of the code that followed.

No one was using the computer – it was simply turned on and connected to the network. A mail program and a browser were running, but no one was looking at them. The screen had turned off to save power. Suddenly, a new process started up on the computer, the result of the single packet that had arrived. A binary file began downloading; when it completed, a new program began executing.

Just as a traveler to a new country looks around and explores the new place, the program began exploring. It inventoried the computer's capabilities, which were meager. The low gigahertz processor was quite a few years old. It was running a common closed-source commercial operating system. It had just enough memory. It had a small hard drive, but there was plenty of space for the download that the program initiated.

When the download had completed, the real work began. The second program went through the computer records and erased all signs of the recent activity. It sent back a report to the source. It set itself up to automatically and invisibly run every time the computer was turned on. Its entire existence would be hidden from view.

The man had been distracted by messaging on his mobile, and did not notice the first report that was sent back. He began looking through the details to see what had happened.

The first 'zombie' was not a great catch. It did not seem to contain any particularly valuable information, or belong to anyone important. Its capabilities were minimal at best – seemingly hardly worth the effort of compromising it. It was probably just sitting in someone's living room or bedroom. But it was now completely under his control!

Noting a number of others in the records, he felt some satisfaction from the success. He knew there were only a handful of people in the world who had the expertise even to detect the exploit, let alone defend against it.

He read the summary statistics to check the extent of the spread and nearly fell off his chair.

The code had already compromised 123,412 such computers, from all over the world – in just one hour! He did a little math and was amazed at the result. The things that could be done with this many computers around the world, all acting in unison…

Deciding to make a change to the code, he added one more thing. A spam email appeared on his screen; he glanced at it, deleting it without a second thought. He added his alias to the code: nØviz.

PART I.

CHAPTER Ø.

One month later...

Mick O'Malley – is feeling even more at home in Nihon than previous visits. (Ø comments)

Speed is relative, and Internet speed particularly so, mused Mick O'Malley as he traveled at 2Ø3 km/h, and accessed the Internet at 4 Mb/s. This speed was slow for an airplane, but very fast for a vehicle on the road, although Mick had gone faster on one of his Ducati motorcycles. It was also fast for a train, unless it was the Shinkansen bullet train, which Mick was currently riding out of Tokyo. He knew the train was just getting going, and it would soon be traveling much faster.

Mick finished writing a blog entry; it uploaded in a fraction of a second to his server. The speed was slow for a hard-wired local area network, but fast for a wireless mobile network. For Mick, it was just normal, as he was used to having high-speed wireless Internet on his travels around the world. He couldn't imagine life without his pentaband mobile computing device.

Mick's musing was about to veer off into the technical distinction between throughput versus goodput when he was distracted by a tingling sensation just behind his right ear; it was his wireless implanted speaker/microphone alerting him. A grad student friend at a university had given Mick the opportunity to try out this experimental subcutaneous technology, and Mick had jumped at it. The audio quality was excellent, and not having to worry about wires was heaven. It was a purely passive device, powered by his mobile only when needed. He could even use voice commands to place and answer calls using the implant, but the range was limited. Since the implant, he had never missed a call.

The alert from his social network told Mick that his friend Lars had arrived in Hiroshima and was enjoying an unidentifiable breakfast, except for the steamed rice. Mick recalled some of his own mystery meals he had enjoyed on previous visits to Nihon. Lars had posted his GPS track from the previous day that showed a top speed of 3Ø1 km/h on the train and dared anyone else to better it. Mick frowned looking at the mobile – his top speed was still only 279 km/h.

Outside the window, the countryside continued to zip by at a phenomenal speed.

Mick smiled to himself, looking forward to the exciting week ahead. He was on his way to an Internet security conference in Hiroshima; his best friends from all over the world were converging there.

Mick was considered a security 'guru' although he despised the term. He didn't argue with the knowledge part. Despite his twenty-four years, there were few that knew more about computer and Internet security than he, but enlightenment?

The train rounded a corner, and Mick was surprised not to feel the expected g-forces on his body. He surmised that the track must be banked, and he did a quick Internet search which confirmed that the track was banked at ten degrees. Mick's mobile was incredibly powerful, with more raw computational and networking power than most desktops. His desktop computer back in his apartment in the East Village in New York City was in another category entirely. It was so blazingly fast he had designed a custom liquid cooling system for his CPU – even a wind tunnel fan wouldn't be able to dissipate enough heat to prevent the multi-core processor from fusing into a smoky lump of silicon. Mick relaxed and looked out the window, enjoying the high-tech ride.

Just outside of Kyoto, the "New Track Hope", as "Shinkansen Nozomi" roughly translates, hit a top speed of 29Ø km/h, then 298 near Kobe. Passing another train barely made an additional sound or caused the train to shudder. The over 5ØØ km/h relative velocity was impressive.

Definitely the Formula 1 of trains!

He wondered how they maintained such speeds through all the tunnels that kept making his GPS lose contact with the satellites.

Just a few minutes before slowing down into Hiroshima Station, Mick's GPS registered a maximum speed of 299 km/h. While disappointed not to have eclipsed Lars' number, Mick considered alternative possibilities and made a mental note to check the calibration of Lars' device to ensure its accuracy.

The train station in Hiroshima was filled with the usual chaos and cacophony that Mick loved. He relished the challenge of navigating public transport in a country where he couldn't speak the language or even read the signs. Today he looked forward to figuring out the Hiroshima streetcar system.

Mick was making his way to the station exit when he stopped in surprise, spotting an older man sitting at a table slurping ramen.

Is that you Gunter?

Gunter Schafer had been Mick's friend for nearly five years now, and had helped establish him in business as an independent consultant after a disastrously brief stint with a startup company. Gunter also managed to get Mick invited to international conferences such as the one this week. These conferences were the perfect platform for Mick to make his case for better Internet and computer security. In his opinion, the entire industry had its head in the sand (and perhaps somewhere else, too) – seemingly no one had any idea what was out there and the types of sophisticated attacks spawning from the evolving alliance of techies and organized crime.

The good news was that there were great security tools and practices available that made the Internet safe to use. The bad news was that so few people used them. Mick's personal mission was to change that.

Gunter had been in the industry forever and was well respected. Mick figured he must be in his late thirties, and seemed to know everyone. He also had an amazing collection of antique Edison phonographs Mick had seen in his house in Munich, Germany.

"Mick! How goes it?" Gunter called out when he spotted Mick heading towards him.

Gunter was also about the only one of Mick's close friends that he could accidentally bump into. Mick's location based software told him the location of most of his friends in relation to him and warned him when he was in proximity. Gunter, however, was truly paranoid about his geoprivacy, and his mobile always reported deliberately inaccurate information – geofuzzing Gunter called it – Mick called it annoying. If he needed to meet up with Gunter somewhere, he had to run the software that Gunter himself had written – only then would he share this sensitive data. Mick couldn't really complain – he made all his friends and family encrypt their email to him using

PGP. He refused to read unencrypted email on principle. He also was meticulous about his computer and Internet security, which included secure voice and video calling over the Internet.

Mick's friends were all in the computer and security industry, and didn't think anything unusual about his somewhat eccentric habits, but the average person probably would, and generally did when Mick mistakenly tried to explain things to him or her. There was a long list of habits he had built up over many years now and couldn't shake even if he tried.

As a computer engineer and programmer, he knew all the inner operations of his computer and communications devices. As a security expert, he knew the many ways in which his computer could be compromised or taken over, information deleted or stolen. As a result, he would never consider using programs or software on his computer that he hadn't personally examined, vetted, and compiled himself. He religiously encrypted all the information on his computer, so that no one beside himself could use it. He also almost exclusively used secure voice, video, and instant messaging with his friends and colleagues. The only exception would be a short call to a new acquaintance or colleague to explain how they could download and install a secure voice application so they could talk over an encrypted channel over the Internet. Mick was meticulous about his passwords, changing them every week. Mick was fairly confident his computer and communications were secure, but his training and experience taught him to never assume this. He had been doing this for so long that to do otherwise just wouldn't allow him to sleep at night.

"Can't complain. What are you up to?" Mick asked Gunter.

"Just having a bite before I head to the hotel." Gunter replied, getting up. At the counter, the cashier handed him a plastic tray with an unreadable, but exquisitely printed document. He placed a few coins on the tray, took the receipt, and followed Mick out the door.

Together they rode a streetcar through the streets of Hiroshima.

"So how are things between you and Liz right now?" Gunter asked, referring to Mick's on-again, off-again relationship with Liz Clayton.

"Hard to say. I guess we're just friends right now." Mick replied. They had gone out a few times over the past twelve months. It was complicated, of course.

"What day are you presenting?" Gunter asked, flipping through the conference program on his mobile.

"Thursday," Mick replied. "How about you?"

"Not speaking this week – I'm just relaxing, and enjoying the sushi," Gunter replied.

Mick knew Gunter wouldn't be relaxing this week – he didn't know anyone who worked harder than Gunter. He was also one of the most talented programmers he knew and always was working on a project for a client or for himself.

"This is my stop," Mick announced, standing up.

"I'm one block further," Gunter replied. "Talk to you later!"

Exiting the streetcar, Mick crossed the street and walked into the lobby of his home for the week. He judged hotels primarily by the speed of their wireless Internet, the comfort of their beds, and the feel of the lobby. He loved hotels that had spacious lobbies with comfortable seating, good vantage points, and espresso within walking distance. This hotel appeared to not have a great lobby, but he knew it would have an awesome wireless network run by the Internet conference organizers.

A gentle chorus of greetings followed Mick, accompanied by various bowing and bobbing. He loved the sounds of Nihon including the little songs played on the train platforms and subway stations. He also enjoyed being able to not listen to everything said to him in Nihon, and instead could concentrate on the meaning based on context, gestures, and expressions. It reminded him of how much was said every day that really didn't need saying. He could travel the subways, shop, and go an entire day in Nihon without actually having a conversation with anyone.

"Checking in," Mick said after the requisite greeting and bowing was over.

"Your name?" she asked.

"Alec Robertson," he replied, getting out his passport. More correctly, he got out one of his passports – he had three of them, with different names on each. His friends and business associates knew him as Mick O'Malley, but this was a name he had made up when he turned eighteen and became a U.S. citizen. To his family, and whenever he wanted to obfuscate his trail, he was Alec Robertson, the name on his British passport.

His use of multiple names and identities had become a habit with him, a bit of an affectation. He started using his old identity Alec when checking into a hotel, as he disliked having to show his passport or other identification. In some parts of the world, he knew, hotels had to report this information to the police every night. He didn't like the privacy implications, or the paper trail of his travels and activities. It was just one of a myriad ways one's privacy was constantly undermined by interconnected databases. Mick was expert at covering his digital tracks, using encryption and anonymization; he was quite well known for putting theory into practice in his everyday life.

Of course, he knew that anyone who really wanted to track him, such as a government, would have no difficulty. His approach was also not without its risks as he found out in one country when he had been searched and both passports were found. Fortunately, he had done some work for the director of the national standards body in that particular country. A few phone calls helped him on his way a few hours later, although the suspicious looks did not go away when he was released.

"Mr. Rovertson, welcome to Hiroshima," she replied, slightly mangling the name after pulling up his information. A few minutes later he was unpacking in his room. He established a secure Internet connection, and moved some money around in his bank accounts. His pre-paid bank card was set up for this trip and would be cancelled and destroyed when the trip was over. It made his financial trail more difficult to follow, and generated some interesting bank statements each month, but it was not as difficult to manage as it sounded.

He registered at the conference and was getting ready to see which of his friends were around when the evening took a sudden change. Mick's social network lit up with postings about an attack spreading like wildfire across the Internet – it looked like a *zero day*, as no one had seen this type of attack before.

When a new vulnerability is discovered in software, there is a race between the computer programmers who try to fix the software and the attackers who try to use the bug to compromise computers using it. With enough time, the software can be fixed, or 'patched' in computer parlance, rendering the vulnerability unexploitable by malicious software such as a virus or worm. A zero day refers to the situation when the vulnerability is discovered the same day that it is actively used by attackers. In other words, there is no time (zero days) between when the attack is discovered and when it is used to infect and take over computers.

Mick checked his own website and blog and realized with a sinking feeling that they had already been attacked and compromised. Instead of his own content, there was a huge banner on the site reading 'Carbon is Poison' –

apparently a reference to the dangers of climate change. He checked a few other common sites, and more than half of them showed the same message. In particular, U.S. government sites seemed to be uniformly down. His heart raced as he realized this attack was a big one. Despite the situation, he smiled to himself, realizing what a perfect place he was in – surrounded by his colleagues. He just needed to make sure of one thing.

He sprinted to the Network Operations Center or NOC for the conference servers and wireless network. On the way, he checked the conference website and saw to his relief that it was still functioning and did not appear to be compromised. He burst through the door and saw the startled looks on the NOC help desk volunteers as he went straight for the on-site router. He spotted the cables that connected it to the Internet, grabbed them and, in one motion, ripped them out of the servers.

"WTF, man! That was our Internet!" one of them shouted at him as Mick turned and put up his hands reassuringly, hoping there wasn't a security guard just around the corner.

"I know. Sorry about that, guys, but have you heard about the web server zero day?" All but one shook their heads. He explained the situation quickly as they each looked up their favorite sites and confirmed it to themselves. "Your servers haven't been hit, yet. I needed to isolate them immediately from the Internet so we can set up a surveillance perimeter and observe the attack as it happens. I'm Mick O'Malley, by the way. Will you help?" he ended, catching his breath.

"Sure let's do it – I just need to let my supervisor know. I'll post an outage page and open a ticket to let everyone know what is going on with the network... there's going to be some pissed off people out there..." one of them replied.

"Is there some space around here somewhere where we

can work?" he asked and looked at a small room to the side of the NOC.

"Go ahead."

"I'll need all the computers you have set up in there, each on a different part of the network. We need to bait the trap so we can catch this sucker as it comes in!" he ordered and the NOC personnel began to rearrange things.

Mick sent messages to his friends explaining what he had in mind, asking them to meet him in the room in ten minutes. At times like this he appreciated his peer-to-peer messaging application, a personal open source project that he had written for his friends and family that could run even without a working connection to Internet servers.

Using his mobile, he tried to remotely log into his web server, and failed. He was able to log into another server where he stored his web server logs, the files recording the activity and moment-by-moment operations of a computer – a trail of digital breadcrumbs. He did this as a failsafe to cover situations just like this. He was relieved that he could at least access those logs – they weren't erased by the attack – although they didn't have quite as much detail as he needed. He didn't look up until about a half dozen of his closest friends and colleagues were standing in front of him looking over his shoulder. He blinked up at them, then his mind focused on the task at hand. He gave everyone directions.

"Lars, install a low layer trap in the server; do a full dump to an offline drive. Liz, configure the router to send all incoming traffic through this subnet. Someone else get into the firewall and set up the logging and intrusion analysis. We will only get one chance at this, so we need to get it right. Let's set this trap!" The group dispersed and set to work.

Lars Elvström was a friend of the creator of a popular open source computer operating system, and an expert in kernel security among other things – the kernel being the core or central part of the operating system in a computer. He hailed from Helsinki, Finland and traveled almost as much as Mick.

In the following minutes, there was very little discussion but lots of typing and occasional swearing. The local techs gave everyone the passwords they needed to work on the computers and servers and answered any questions about the network. Mick had already familiarized himself with the layout of the network and knew exactly where he wanted to spring the trap.

"What the hell is going on here?" The question came from a short man who walked into the room. A tech jumped up and looked over to Mick. Mick looked to Liz who sighed and went over to the man. Liz sometimes helped them out of awkward social situations such as this.

"Hi there! I'm Liz Clayton. And you are?" she began, smiling at him as she brushed a lock of blonde hair out of her face.

"Ned Iverson, I'm in charge of this network, or at least I was..."

"Right, Ned," Liz began, hoping to diffuse the situation quickly while Mick continued working. "Let me explain what we're doing. Your web servers haven't been compromised *yet* in this zero day, so we are setting up monitors and message loggers so we can try to see the attack as it happens. With the help of your techs, we are reconfiguring your routers and firewalls so we can learn how the attack works and how to protect against it."

"Why can't you just look at the logs of the compromised servers?" he asked.

"We've already tried – the attack wipes the logs, very thoroughly, hiding its tracks. No one has a dataset on this attack yet to analyze it," Liz explained. She could see him starting to relax, and knew the situation was diffusing.

"OK, but does my server have to be compromised? I'd just as soon avoid that."

"Hmm... we could replace your web server with a dummy one. That way, your real site will be safe. We'll just need to set it up quickly – everything else will be ready to go in a few minutes."

"And will you put everything back together again when we're done?" he continued.

"Of course we will," Liz replied, realizing she was going to be there most of the night.

"You owe me," she growled at Mick as she walked back a moment later. The only sign that Mick heard her was a slight curl in the corner of his mouth.

Less than fifteen minutes later, most people in the room were looking around and feeling pleased with themselves. Mick saw the supervisor give him a nod. Only two people were still working furiously. Gunter was typing at light speed while a dark haired woman he hadn't noticed before stood over him giving him directions in an animated way. From the look of the code scrolling across the screen, this was some complex configuration setting on the firewall. Gunter gave him the thumbs up a moment later, and the woman sat down and smiled at Mick, making him nearly lose his train of thought.

Who is that?

Mick spoke with each of the groups and confirmed their settings and configurations. They were finally ready.

"OK, let's connect back up to the Internet," Mick said, getting excited.

"Um, I can only get one link up as the other connector got busted," one tech replied. Mick would feel bad about it later, but now, he was still in fight-or-flight mode. "We're live!" the tech reported after plugging the Ethernet cable back in.

Everyone sat quietly waiting, watching the screens. It only took a minute.

"I think we've got it!" shouted Gunter as he watched information scroll on his screen. Everyone else looked to his or her screen – some showed activity, some didn't. Mick refreshed his browser which was pointed at the conference web server; he was rewarded with the 'Carbon is Poison' page. It amazed him how fast it happened.

Everyone was suddenly calling out pieces of information about what their logs showed. Mick listened to all of it, sometimes asking for a repetition. The answer started to become clear in his mind. One fact would confirm it.

"Lars, did you see any activity on port 443?" he asked, leaning toward Lars.

"Yep, an HTTPS connection came in on port 443 which coincided with the attack," he replied. Mick slapped him on the back.

Gotcha!

Looking around at his 'team', Mick grinned and said "Thank you everyone – I'll need all these logs archived on the main directory for confirmation, but I think we have found the nature of the attack. Thanks again for all your help..." he said, already starting to ignore them.

"What's next Mick?" Liz asked.

"Time to write a patch!" Mick replied, sitting down and pulling up the web server source code. He began work on writing or 'coding' the change to the program to close the vulnerability, preventing the attack from succeeding.

The others drifted off or started looking at their mobiles, as the network was back up again. Everyone was buzzing about the attack and who was hit and who wasn't.

A few hours later, Mick had the patch written. He checked it in – uploaded it to the server where people download the software – ready for approval, release, and installation across the Internet. The zero day was almost over.

"Wait a minute, you just did an anonymous check-in of that code!" someone shouted behind him. He turned and saw the woman who was working with Gunter earlier. She looked distinctively out of place among the fashion-challenged geeks around her, wearing a knit shirt, dark pencil skirt, and boots.

"That's right," he replied evenly.

"But how will you get credit for writing the patch?" she asked. Mick shrugged.

"I won't, but that's OK. Checking it in anonymously will avoid bruising anyone's ego or otherwise distracting them from stopping the spread of this thing. We just need to get this patch released so we can end this zero day."

"You don't care that no one will know that you stopped the exploit? You *are* crazy!" she responded, shaking her head.

"Thanks. And you are..." he asked, enjoying her accent. It was definitely Eastern European, maybe Serbian, but her English was excellent.

"I'm Kateryna Petrescu, with F.T.L. in San Francisco," she replied, mentioning a well-known manufacturer of firewalls. He made a mental note to not badmouth these overused security devices in front of her.

"Mick O'Malley – thanks for your help, by the way. Nice work on the firewall," he said, extending his hand.

"You are welcome," she replied, shaking it.

A few stayed behind with Mick and Liz to help put the NOC back together. When they were done, Mick spotted Kateryna across the room; she noticed him and approached.

"OK, so tell me how you did it," she began.

"You mean uncover the attack?" he asked, and when she nodded, he continued. "Well, I've seen quite a few attacks over the years, but this one was unusual. Usually these days, it is the browser that gets infected, but in this case, it was the web server that provides the web pages. The Wireshark trace we did confirmed it – it was a web browsing request from a site that had already been infected."

"And port 443?"

"Again, the speed suggested the worm was using a common, unblocked transport. Port 443 is commonly kept open for encrypted web traffic. I was happy we didn't have to wait long."

"That patch was a nice piece of code, by the way. You must have worked as a software developer at one point in your career?"

"Yes, but it's been a while," Mick replied. "Anyway, once I knew how the attack worked, it was trivial to follow it through and find the bug. Believe it or not, it was just a type of buffer overflow attack," he concluded. He changed the subject. "Have you been to Nihon... I mean Japan, before?" A few days ago, Gunter had proposed that in honor of their visit to Japan, they should all exclusively use the word that Japanese use for their country – Nihon. The usage had caught on in their social network, and was already second nature to Mick. It was now an effort for him to say Japan or Japanese.

"Just once – I was in Tokyo and Yokohama a few years back," she replied.

They discussed his previous four visits and her previous one, and which conferences they regularly attended. Mick learned that Kateryna's new role at her company meant she would be speaking at many of the same conferences he would be attending.

Liz waved to Mick as she left the room, having restored most of the NOC configurations. Mick waved back and called out "Thank you!" to her back. Kateryna looked over her shoulder at Liz.

"Liz Clayton, right?"

"Yep. We've been friends forever," Mick replied. He thought he detected a slight reaction in her to his use of the word 'friend'.

This could be quite a conference.

CHAPTER 1.

What is the difference between a virus and a worm? dieraptorzdie

This is a good question, dieraptorzdie. Viruses and worms are different kinds of 'malware', short for malicious software. Malware is usually installed on your computer without your knowledge, and might steal information, delete information, make your computer start sending spam emails or do other things you don't want it to do.

Both a virus and a worm will try to spread to other computers or replicate – the difference is how they do this. If the malware tries to replicate itself by attaching itself to another piece of software or data – the equivalent of a biological host - we then refer to it as a virus. This could be an email message that you open, or a download from a web page you visit.

If the malware is designed to be self-propagating, using the Internet to spread on its

20

own without the help of another application, it is known as a worm. The word refers to the way the malware 'worms' its way through a network. When your computer is connected to the Internet, it can receive all kinds of messages from other computers. An attacker can send out a bunch of messages (sometimes this is called 'port scanning') to your computer, trying to cause it to unwittingly install malware. This can happen anytime you are connected to the Internet, and you don't even have to be checking mail or browsing the web for this kind of attack to happen.

Both worms and viruses can spread quickly and do a lot of damage in a short time.

There are a number of things you can do to protect your computer. Virus scanning software you install on your computer can help protect against viruses: it monitors and checks everything that you download or install, and deletes it if it finds a virus. A firewall can be used to protect against some types of worms. A firewall's purpose in a network is to block unwanted Internet traffic while allowing legitimate traffic. The word 'firewall' comes from the construction industry, where it literally is a fire-proof wall between rooms or buildings. If you have a firewall in your network, it can block port scans and only let traffic that you want flow from the Internet to your computer.

But the best defense against both viruses and worms is to ensure that you run a secure operating system and that you keep up to date with patches and patches. You should also be very careful about every piece of software you install or download onto your computer. You should immediately install every software update and patch that becomes available – many of them fix known security flaws. Myself, I only install software that I have compiled myself and examined the source code. At the very least, you need to make sure that you trust whoever wrote the software, and you fully understand

what the software does. Otherwise, you might
find your computer compromised...

-> Your question not answered this week? Argue
for your vote on the Shameless Plugging area of
our discussion forum

CHAPTER 2.

"Thank you everyone for attending this meeting," the Chairman began. He looked around the room at his team. He had built this company, Cloud 8++, from nothing. The industry had grown up as well, from lone hobbyists, to a cottage industry, to today's corporations. They had enjoyed a great deal of success and ill-gotten profits over the years, but things were changing. "First, I would like a report on the progress of the new exploit."

"Everything performed as expected," was the response from one man. "There was a 100% success rate against targeted web servers."

"Impressive, but the outage didn't last very long. You had told us it would take a day or more before the servers came back up again. Did we have enough time to install our software?"

"We did have time to install our software. This particular attack was directed against an open source program that has a large and active community of developers. They mobilized very quickly and had a patch uploaded within four hours of the attack. Web servers began coming up again almost immediately after that.

Most servers were patched within twelve hours."

"Is there anything we can do to prevent this in the future?"

"Our later zero day attacks will be against commercial software, so we won't need to worry about the open source community. In addition, our consultant has some ideas on how we can fragment and divide the community, slowing their responsiveness in the future."

"And the silent exploit?" the Chairman asked.

"Also extremely effective, although we do not have exact numbers, yet," the man hesitated for a moment before continuing. "I did a reverse lookup of the target IP addresses you gave me –"

"You should not have done that!"

"Well, I did. The addresses belong to UBK corporation, the government outsourcing company. As far as I know, they do not represent a primary target for us. Why are we using our silent exploit on them?"

"This is not your concern! And you will NOT do this in the future!" the Chairman shouted, pounding the table.

"At least we are ready to move to Phase 2!" the man replied, trying to change the subject.

"No, we are not," replied the Chairman, startling everyone around the table. They looked around the table, confused. "We will continue testing the attacks. We need to fully understand the response and counter measures for each." The room was silent for a moment.

"OK, I will say what everyone is thinking – this is crazy! We know the attacks work, and we know there will be a response – so what? Why would we continue testing?"

"This is not a discussion, I am telling you what I have decided. We will continue testing until I say we are ready."

"Is this a new direction from our *benefactors*?" another man asked, stressing the word. As soon as he said it, everyone in the room knew it to be true.

"Gentlemen, times are changing. You all know the essential role our benefactors play in our business. Even with our new command and control infrastructure, we need protection against trace backs and to handle our revenue. Now, everyone must focus on the task at hand. I want regular status reports leading up to the next test. That will be all!"

The Chairman sat alone in the conference room after the others had left. He was not without his concerns, either, but he would never have shared them with his team. He did not hire idiots; soon they would all work out the new plan, and there would be more dissent. But he knew he had no choice – to do otherwise would be even more dangerous.

CHAPTER 3.

Mick O'Malley – *feels proud every time he is able to recognize Kanji using pattern matching, e.g. recognizing Tokyo as the TV set with rabbit ears and a wrapped present on a stand. (6 comments)*

The next morning, Mick found an intriguing mail in his unauthenticated folder. All of his important mail arrived signed or encrypted using PGP software. His unencrypted and unauthenticated mail tended to be spam or junk mail, messages from slight acquaintances, or clueless introductions (sometimes difficult to discern from spam). In this case, he found an invitation to lunch to discuss a potential new consulting project. The fact that Vince Della of LeydenTech did not bother to sign and encrypt his email to Mick was not good. Even a cursory bit of research on Mick would show what he expected in terms of communication and Internet security when dealing with him. Mick only checked his unencrypted folder today because he expected to hear back from a contact at a large software company in the Northwest of the U.S. whose corporate mandatory-to-use software prevented the use of

PGP encryption. Otherwise, the message might have languished for days.

He accepted the invitation and added Vince to his professional network.

Is Vince perhaps a marketing person?

Mick was extremely selective in choosing consulting jobs. He was very open about his selection criteria. He refused to work for the government – any government. He avoided patent and intellectual property work like the plague. He would not deal with anyone who did not meet his standards for ethics and privacy. And finally, the job had to be interesting and challenging. With Gunter's help, he had been gradually building up his experience, despite his selectivity.

Mick had woken up early, something easy to do while still adjusting to east to west jetlag. As a result, he had 45 minutes to read with Sam on a video link. He sent an invitation to an encrypted video session, which she accepted.

After Sam played a new song on the flute for him, they got back to reading. They each had a copy of the book – an actual, old fashioned wood pulp and ink version. Mick read electronic books and papers professionally, but when it came to pleasure, he still preferred the physical medium of paper. They alternated reading pages to each other of *The Two Towers*. The precocious ten-year-old loved her namesake in the story, while Mick most admired the swift and light-footed elf. When they had read a chapter, they relaxed and chatted a bit about the story.

"It is so sad that Saruman turned evil... And Gandalf trusted him, too..." Sam commented.

"I agree, Gandalf must have felt terribly betrayed by his friend."

"Well, sayonara, Alec-san," she replied very seriously, putting her hands together and bowing low on the screen. Mick laughed and bowed back, logging off.

Down in the lobby, he found Lars relating a story from Tokyo to a small group of people. This time of year, Lars would always seek out the sun any chance he had during the northern hemisphere winter. He could usually be found near a window as he was now.

Lars waved from across the crowded room, but Mick had no difficulty seeing him, as they both towered over the locals. Mick came over.

"Mick, you've been to one of those costume cafés right?" Lars asked.

"You mean maid cafés? With the servers dressed up like cosplay?" Mick replied, using the term used in Nihon for costume play – dressing up in costumes.

"Yeah – I was dying of curiosity, so I went to one yesterday in Akihabara – like a bloody Hooters, which I'm sure you frequent, Mick." Lars was joking, of course.

"Actually, it's not – instead of the servers being dressed and acting like girls in ninth grade gym class, they are dressed as nineteenth century maids, and act like they are nine years old... quite creepy actually," Mick replied.

"You're not wrong! I did learn a few things, including 'Moé Moé Kyun!' Course I don't know what it means... I also got some good reading done there – I'm half way through Barchester Towers."

"You were reading Trollope in a maid café? That is so..." A series of words flipped through Mick's mind like a high speed train passing by local stations, including pretentious, incongruous, ridiculous, but none conveyed the exact level of appall he was after. In the meantime, Lars continued.

"So much for my cultural exchange efforts. When is the next major release of your software project coming out?" he asked, knowing full well Mick's reaction.

"Lars, I'm working on it!" he replied, taking the bait. "If a few other developers would write some code more often, it would be much sooner," Mick said pointedly, trying to make Lars feel guilty for his recent lack of participation, but the attempt failed – Lars was already distracted, watching an attractive young woman walk across the room. It was closer to the truth that Lars, rather than Mick, would hang out at Hooters, if they had them in Helsinki.

A little later at the conference, Mick caught sight of Liz just before she spotted him. He knew the instant they locked eyes that it was going to be a long week.

She's going to want to talk for sure...

It wasn't that he didn't want to talk to her – Mick really liked Liz and enjoyed her company, but he didn't necessarily want to converse on the same set of topics. She looked like the cheerleader he never dated in high school. Of course, Mick barely went to high school, either. Mick had had some fun together with Liz, and enjoyed her company, but the spark just wasn't there for Mick, and no amount of talking could fix that.

"Mick!" she called out as she approached. He kissed her on the cheek and gave her shoulder a little squeeze. He smiled at her.

"Liz!"

"I just love Nihon – everything is so efficient here," she continued. Mick always listened closely for the start of a Texas accent in her, but fortunately she had yet to succumb, despite having lived in Dallas for nearly four years.

"Yeah, it's pretty good," Mick agreed. She caught his arm and walked him in the direction she was heading.

"Have you heard the latest from Steel Trap Computing? Ridiculous, I know!" she began as he just listened and walked with her.

After a few sessions, Mick felt that he had the lay of the land for the conference venue. He knew where to get his espressos, where the dead spots in the wireless network were located, and some quiet places for side conversations.

With his lunch approaching, Mick did a little research on LeydenTech, and discovered that not much was publicly available. He sent off a few queries to find out whether it was just privately held or if it did government work. The location just outside of Los Alamos, New Mexico, tended to suggest the latter. It was no surprise to Mick to find that the company was involved in energy storage of some kind. Another tingle made him check his mobile: Vince had left him a *voicemail* message (non-secure calls went straight to voicemail), despite his greeting (recorded about six years ago) that said that he did not check voicemail and asked the caller to use a technology from the current century to reach him.

What kind of dinosaur am I going to do business with today?

He read the text of the voicemail and discovered that Vince had moved the meeting an hour earlier (elevenses?). There was just time to make it, and yet another session he had weakly planned to listen in to was blown off.

"Dr. O'Malley, it is a pleasure to meet you – heard so much about you!" Dr. Vincent Della, Senior Vice President of Engineering at LeydenTech began after handing over his business card, doing an impressive Nihon-style two-handed handover. Mick, of course, had no cards, making him a non-entity in the business world here in Nihon. When asked for his business card, he usually mumbled something about finding his public key on the web.

"Thank you, call me Mick. May I call you Vince? So, your company makes modern day Leyden jars?" Mick began, referring to the first electrical energy storage devices, named for the town of Leiden in the Netherlands, and used by the early experimenters with electricity, including Ben Franklin. When he first heard the name of the company, Mick recalled a sketch of tall lightning rods attached by wires to a bank of enormous foil-covered glass jars. Leyden jars were the forerunner of today's electronic capacitors, and ultimately memory storage devices used by all computational devices today. Effectively, Ben Franklin worked on the first single bit RAM (Random Access Memory) storage devices.

"Yes, we do make energy storage systems. Let me give you a little background on the company." Vince began and proceeded to recite the publicly available information that Mick had already committed to memory. Vince then paused and continued. "We are very interested in getting your help with a problem that we are having. Our servers have been attacked, and some of them compromised. The signature appears to be one that others haven't seen before. A few other consultants have drawn a blank." Mick suppressed a smirk and the urge to ask if he were talking about Miles, his co-panelist. He would be able to find out later. "At your earliest convenience, we'd like you to come out to New Mexico and start work. I've had a standard contract drawn up but couldn't find a fax number or postal address for you."

Keeping his countenance, Mick asked for Vince's admin contact information so he could be in touch about establishing a secure shared document server for the contract and other legal and technical documents.

"By the way, just so you are not surprised, I'll be conducting a Level 2 background check on you." Mick began. "I will expect something similar from you, unless you have government clearance, in which case you could simply ask them about me," Mick explained. He had his own mechanism for learning when someone was investigating him, so he always was up front with his clients in case they had similar mechanisms. One couldn't be too careful these days, Mick mused, then thought of

31

some of his even more paranoid friends, and amended the thought to *generally* one couldn't be too careful.

The conversation waned and a suitable day two weeks away was chosen for Mick's visit to New Mexico, after his trip to Seattle the following week. On the walk back to the conference, Mick stopped to examine a motorcycle parked on the sidewalk. At first, he had difficulty identifying even the manufacturer, since the bike had been heavily customized as was common in Nihon. It had a new gas tank, fenders, and seat with all branding removed. Even the wheelbase had been extended in the rear swing arm. He identified a common Yamaha type of carburetor, wide profile tire, and was able to guess the model, giving him some satisfaction. He felt an itch in his right wrist, missing riding his favorite Ducati motorcycle back in New York City. During this visit he had enjoyed seeing lots of motorcycles, although few Italian. Mick was pleased to see so many bikes that weren't Harleys – his least favorite brand of motorcycle. A check of the weather forecast back home made him happy, as Saturday was forecast to be clear; he should be able to ride when he got home.

Later in the day, Mick's own presentation went well, discussing some new ideas he had been exploring lately. Even though he had done it a thousand times, Mick still felt a few butterflies just before speaking and a satisfaction when it was over and he felt he had made a connection with his audience.

CHAPTER 4.

*From the **Security and Other Lies** Blog:*

How can I make my email communication more secure? I_heart_raptorz

Email in general is completely insecure, but using encryption software such as PGP can make it much more secure, I_heart_raptorz, and I use it all the time. Using encryption, I can send an email that no one besides the recipient can read. By checking the digital signatures on emails from my friends and colleagues who also use PGP, I can verify that they sent the email, and that the message content has not been tampered with along the way. If you have ever received an email with the phrase "Begin PGP Signature" in the message, followed by a bunch of numbers and letters, then you have received a PGP signed email. Here's how PGP works.

PGP software (which, BTW, stands for Pretty Good Privacy) is an add-on to your mail application. Whenever you receive an email that has been signed or encrypted using PGP, the software automatically checks the signature and/or decrypts the message. You need to create a PGP key pair in order to digitally sign emails that you send. A key pair is the combination of two large numbers uniquely generated by you. The numbers appear to be random digits, but are in fact related mathematically. You keep one number secret (known as your private key) and you publish the other number (known as your public key) in a key directory, on a web page or key server. You can also share your public key with your friends and colleagues. As long as you keep your private key secret, you can use it to secure your email. Here's how it works:

To digitally sign an email, PGP performs a mathematical function known as a hash to produces a message digest – a fixed length representation of the contents of the message. The private key is then used on the message digest to produce the digital signature, which is then included in the email after the "Begin PGP Signature" message. The recipient of the email can verify the signature using PGP by performing a similar operation using your public key. If the operation works, the signature is validated, and the recipient knows you sent it. Or at least the recipient knows that the sender knew your private key!

Encryption works in a similar way. If someone wants to send you an encrypted email that only you can read, they fetch your public key, perform some mathematical operations on the message using the public key, then send the encrypted results instead of the message – it just looks like gibberish as it goes over the Internet. To decrypt the message, you use your private key, and voila! You, and only you, can read the message.

So to use PGP, you just need to install the application, keep your private key secret, make your public key available to those you communicate with, and then get your friends to do the same.

Good luck, I_heart_raptorz, and send me a PGP signed email when you are up and running!

-> Your question not answered this week? Argue for your vote on the Shameless Plugging area of our discussion forum.

CHAPTER 5.

__Mick O'Malley__ – enjoys slurping ramen in noodle restaurants. (2 comments)

The next morning, Mick received a response from Vince to arrange the details of their upcoming meeting. This time, Vince had managed to sign his mail properly with PGP – a good sign for the future.

Being Wednesday, it was time for Mick to change all his passwords. He thought for a few minutes then typed:

```
AllurBasesDontblong2us
```

Mick borrowed a butane lighter from a smoker and used it as a makeshift soldering iron to repair the broken Ethernet connector in the NOC, restoring full Internet connectivity and making the techs happy.

Later, he was listening to a rather dull discussion of attack classifications when someone sat down next to him. He looked over and saw it was Kateryna.

"Good morning, Mick," she said quietly.

"Good morning," he replied evenly.

"Enjoying the presentation?" she asked, leaning

towards him. Today she was wearing white jeans with a wide belt, and a denim shirt, and looked pretty good. And, he could smell her perfume, not a common thing in this country where cigarette smoke seemed to infuse everything. He flashed a mock frown at her and she smiled at him, producing an instant reaction. "I have a couple of questions I'd like to ask you – could we get a coffee?" He said yes without a moment's hesitation and followed her out of the room.

"I have overall design responsibility for our company's future firewall products," she began as they sat down with their coffees, "and I'm having trouble figuring out how they can handle new services such VoIP and video conferencing. Here's the problem." Kateryna launched into a description of the problems she was having.

Mick listened to her description, occasionally interrupting with clarifying questions. He made some suggestions that he thought were fairly obvious, but, judging by Kateryna's reaction, apparently were not. A half an hour flew by as they conversed over their coffees, and the topic wound down.

"Wow – this has been really, really helpful, Mick. Thanks a lot!" she said with feeling.

"My pleasure, Kateryna," he replied, smiling at her.

"Please, call me Kat," she responded.

"My pleasure, Kat."

They passed the next few minutes in silence, as Kateryna thought hard about her firewall problem, and Mick thought hard about her.

Then he noticed Kateryna looking past him, and turned to see Liz eyeing him with a curious look. He got to his feet.

"Liz, come over and meet Kat. Kat, this is Liz," he started.

"We met earlier this morning," Liz said as she shook hands with Kateryna. "Hi Kat."

"Nice to see you again, Liz. Mick is helping me with some firewall issues..." she began.

"Really?" Liz replied, giving Mick a look.

"Ah... why don't you join us?" Mick asked. As Liz was making up her mind, Kateryna glanced at her mobile and announced she had another meeting and had to run. She took her leave as Liz sat down and ordered her drink.

"I had no idea you were so interested in firewalls..." Liz began. Mick rolled his eyes.

"I was just helping her with a few issues – she did help us last night during the zero day..." he replied.

"Sure. Whatever. Look, Mick, I'm not going to make things difficult for you. I think I have a good idea of where things stand between us," she replied. She quickly turned the conversation to her shopping yesterday and about an industry acquisition that was announced a few hours earlier in the press.

Is that it? Maybe this week won't be so bad...

After lunch, Mick spent a few hours writing some computer code for his open source project. He did it to relax, the way others might flip channels on a TV.

Next time he checked his mail, he saw one from Kateryna thanking him for his assistance. He noticed that her PGP key had been signed by Gunter and he made a mental note to ask him about her, as he must have met her previously. She asked if he were free for dinner; he replied that he wasn't as he and Lars had plans. He almost asked Lars if she could join them but came to his senses.

Later that evening, after enjoying their meal, Lars was detailing his latest discovery.

"Did you see the woman in the men's toilet?" he announced much louder than he perhaps should have.

"You mean the cleaning woman?"

Lars nodded and continued. "I was standing there draining the lizard, and life is good, you know, when this cleaning woman walks into the men's room and right past me! She did mumble something, which might have been 'Please hide your pecker as I'm coming through' but I don't know. She cleaned the sink and worked away in the corner where there was a cabinet. When I left she was cleaning the urinal right next to some guy... What is up with that?"

"I agree – it is strange. It's a shock, like you feel when you accidentally walk into the wrong bathroom." Lars raised an eyebrow. "Or so I'm told..." Mick trailed off.

"Now she was old and ugly. If they are going to have a woman there, why not a better looking one?" Lars continued.

"Did you see the latest security vulnerability disclosure by Maddox?" Mick asked, wanting to change the subject.

"Yeah, that jerk only wants attention. It's not like he doesn't know the right way to do things..." he started. They were discussing the process whereby a security researcher first reports a newly discovered vulnerability to the affected company, giving the company time to release a patch. The general etiquette of the industry was that once the company has had time to write and deploy a patch, the researcher is free to announce the vulnerability and claim the credit. Some, such as John Maddox instead flouted the rules when it suited them, announcing vulnerabilities before the system or product could be patched or fixed. When done irresponsibly, this could result in a zero day attack, similar to the one from the previous day.

Back at the hotel, Mick and Lars were heading to the elevator when Mick spotted Kateryna in the hotel bar. He changed course, waving goodbye to Lars.

"Hey," he said sitting down next to her and was rewarded with a glimpse into her eyes.

"Mick! I was just thinking about you," she replied, "I had one or two more firewall questions... if you were still willing?"

"Sure, fire away, and that is my last pun, I promise..."

Mick admired Kateryna's methodical and analytical approach that came out in the way she asked her questions. They talked on other topics, and in almost no time, it was last call, with the staff making polite noises for the last few sharing their custom to finish up.

"Do you feel like a walk?" Mick asked her.

"OK – I could use the exercise," she replied.

They set off into the night and ended up wandering for hours through the wet streets.

"I love how safe I feel wandering around in the dark around here," she said after a few blocks. "Nihon somehow feels both foreign and familiar at the same time." Mick smiled to himself – someone had obviously clued her in on their little Nihon/Japan word game.

"I know what you mean. Are you an only child?" he asked.

"No I'm the youngest of four – two brothers and one sister. Believe it or not, I was a bit of a tomboy when I was young. Why?"

"You a tomboy? That is hard to imagine. And you are the baby of the family – I see. I have a theory that birth order plays a major role in personality. Myself I'm youngest of two with an older sister."

They waited at a pedestrian crossing for the light to change. There were no cars in sight, but this was Nihon, so they waited patiently with a few other locals.

"It's funny – you are so different from how I thought you'd be..." she began.

"Oh, and how did you expect me to be?"

"I don't know, its just you are well known for your, well..." she paused for a moment, "paranoia –"

"I'm not paranoid."

"I know bad choice of word – my English sometimes fails me. More like overly cautious and careful."

"When you know how much information is being compiled about you and by whom..."

"Sure, sure. Privacy. Opt out. Blah, blah," she said smiling.

"Did you say blah, blah? Is that a technical term, Dr. Petrescu?" he replied.   She smiled and changed the subject.

"So can you speak the language here?" she asked.

"Besides 'konichiwa' and 'arrigato'... no. And you?" he asked, but she just shook her head. Despite his own international background Mick spoke no languages besides English. It was a source of shame to him, but it wasn't for lack of trying. Over the years, he had tried to learn French (two difficult years of required classes in high school), Italian (a month of night classes to impress a girl), and Irish (listening to Gaelic sporting match commentaries and hearing his father talk and swear), but none of it lasted. He also had learned a little Latin, but that was from his interest in the origins of words, not because he expected to spend time in the Vatican. Of course, as a computer geek he 'spoke' multiple computer languages, but this didn't count.

"So what do you do when your mobile is off?"

"Hmm. Well, for fun, I ride motorcycles."

"Ah, a big American bike..." Kateryna replied and stretched her arms out in front of her, and acted as if she were clutching at the ground while dangling over a snow ledge on a glacier. Mick couldn't help laughing.

"No, no – I mainly have Ducatis – Italian works of art, although I do have a vintage Yamaha as well."

"How many bikes do you have?"

"Seven currently, could be eight depending on how an auction goes later today..."

"One for every day of the week?"

"More like one for all my moods: cruiser, sport, off road, café racer. I have a large garage and work on them myself. I have a decent machine shop as well."

"Really? I would not have pictured you as the grease monkey."

"I do like getting my hands dirty. I like working on bikes because they are so small and simple. Cars today have so much computerization and emissions control that you need a computer to work on them. I much prefer doing mechanical things such as re-jetting a carburetor or adjusting gear ratios. I've always felt the carburetor was the technological equivalent of the CPU to the Age of Petroleum or whatever they will call the twentieth century. Now that I think of it, all my bikes are from last century…"

"I'm sure I don't know anything about any of that but I could see how riding could be fun. And the clothing seems interesting..."

Mick suddenly had a vision of Kateryna wearing leathers, and shaking her long, dark hair free as she removed her helmet...

"... so do you?" she repeated.

Mick recovered, realizing she had asked about his helmet-wearing policy.

"Of course! I'm not an idiot! So what is your hobby?" he asked.

"I guess it is photography. I was crazy about it in my teens, although I haven't had as much time lately for it," she replied.

"Wow! You're a photographer? That's great! What kind?" Mick asked.

"I've done it all at one time: journalism, studio, art. I love both ends of the technology spectrum: from advanced digital imaging on the computer, to pinhole photography, just like they used to do in the nineteenth century."

"Very cool."

They had walked a long way through the streets but Mick suppressed the urge to fire up his GPS. This walk would just have to take its course.

Much later than either thought possible, they came back to the hotel.

Why can I talk for hours with this woman yet still feel as if there were so much more to talk about?

Saying good night to her in the lobby suddenly felt a little embarrassing to Mick in a ninth grade sort of way.

The next morning, on his caffeine constitutional, Mick ran into Lars, who was photographing a sign in front of a store.

"Mick, did you know that in Kanji there are the equivalent of both Serif and Sans Serif fonts? It has taken me a while, but I think I can identify the main font types now. My favorite one is the font you see on store fronts – like this one – it has rounded strokes, designed to look like the characters were drawn with a felt tip pen!"

"Yeah, it is pretty cool here, I must say," Mick replied.

Mick saw Kateryna later that day after she had finished speaking. He thought her presentation was good: concise, to the point, and with a clear message. Liz had been sitting next to him – watching him for a reaction, he suspected. At the end, she had asked Kateryna a question. Mick realized that was probably the first time Kateryna had seen him in the audience, as he knew how bright the podium lights were. It was a tricky question but she handled it with aplomb. He smiled to himself, proud of her.

That afternoon he visited the atomic bomb (or A-bomb, as they called it) museum, and Peace Park in Hiroshima. It was an emotional experience for Mick. The museum, he felt, was balanced, unlike the Yushukan War Museum he had visited in Tokyo on a previous visit. Although the museum did not discuss how the war started, it did talk about the military role of Hiroshima and about the planning for resistance against the Allied invasion of

Nihon. The museum walls also detailed the rebuffed U.S. attempts to negotiate unconditional surrender in the days leading up to the dropping of the bomb. The planning of the bombing was chillingly documented with memos from the U.S. War Department and the White House, laying out the options and decision points as if it were just another policy issue. Discussions of site selection were particularly chilling with mentions of Kyoto and Tokyo Bay that shocked Mick. Also displayed were memos about the policy of avoiding conventional bombing of candidate cities – done to maximize the accuracy of bomb damage assessment, as if it were needed. Also amazing were memos expressing concerns that the price tag of building the bomb, the Manhattan project, could become a political liability if the war ended before the bomb was finished and used in battle.

Mick wondered about the flight crew of the B-29 Flying Fortress, called Enola Gay, who dropped the bomb. He shed a couple of tears in the museum watching the film of the bombing taken from an observation B-29. A single photograph enlarged to life size conveyed what could have only been a fraction of the horror and shock of the survivors in the immediate aftermath. The second part of the museum displayed the history and technology of nuclear weapons and the efforts at arms reduction and disarmament. The third part was kind of an archaeology exhibit, with artifacts, mockups and dioramas. It reminded him of Pompeii, except instead of a natural eruption, it was the violent culmination of a bloody decade of war in the Pacific. Usually, it took centuries to produce the kind of ruins he was walking through. In this case, it took a fraction of a second, and you could meet and talk to survivors. The atomic bomb was an incredible weapon, and its use changed world history.

There were some other westerners at the museum, although most of them seemed to be Europeans judging by their accents. The museum was crowded with school kids, normally the kind of thing that annoyed him, but not here.

Bring more school kids, pack the place, see everything, know your own history!

He wandered the grounds of Peace Park. He was not very impressed with the architecture and artwork but that was OK. The famous A-bomb dome building brought back the tears, a welling that made it hard to see or swallow. The skeleton frame of the dome had survived the detonation, as few structures did. This was because the center of the blast, the hypocenter, was almost directly overhead – so close the blast forces were nearly vertical, instead of the horizontal ones that knocked down the other structures a little further away from the center. Mick couldn't photograph the dome; he just felt it would convey too little. In his mind he could only see the building against the flat plain of complete devastation in the black and white photos. He didn't begrudge others taking their photographs, or the band down by the river singing Beatles love songs. This wasn't a place he could judge anyone.

It took a bit of searching and the use of his GPS but he found the hypocenter, the spot at which some 6ØØ meters in the air, the dynamite trigger had fired a slug of uranium into a larger ball of uranium, setting off the chain reaction. He found he was able to photograph this spot because there was just a small monument covered in colorful paper cranes on a busy street next to a hospital. Nothing original remained from that day – everything had been rebuilt.

It was so hard for Mick to imagine: all those years of secret work on the other side of the world being suddenly revealed on one fateful day, and it happened right here, where he had walked all afternoon.

Later that evening he had dinner with Lars, Liz, Gunter and a few other colleagues. He didn't mention his afternoon visit. He forgot to ask Gunter about Kateryna. He retired early with his thoughts.

The conference wrapped up the next day. Mick didn't talk to Kateryna again, but he did see her a few times in various sessions. On the long flight back, he found his thoughts drifting from his book to her.

CHAPTER 6.

*From the **Security and Other Lies** Blog:*

Is it possible to make my VoIP and video calls over the Internet secure? Raptorznest

The answer to this is a definite yes if you use secure communication software and tools!

Just like your bank information, personal details, and passwords should never be sent over the Internet without being encrypted, your voice and video communication should not be sent so that anyone can listen, watch, or record you. This is especially critical for wireless communication. In the early days of analog mobile phones, anyone with a radio scanner could eavesdrop or record conversations in their vicinity. Unfortunately, many Voice over IP (VoIP) and video communication tools do not use encryption. I would absolutely NEVER use such services that have so little regard for your privacy.

Secure VoIP and video services encrypt the voice and video packets over the Internet, preventing others from listening in or recording your sessions. Personally, I only use open source programs and tools built on standard protocols and algorithms. This way, I can make sure there are no 'back doors' - hidden ways for someone to access otherwise secure communication. The only way to be sure is if the source code is verified.

With a good VoIP security protocol such as ZRTP, I can even verify myself that the call is secure and that no one is listening in or recording my call. This is done by reading out a short string that is generated for each call and displayed on the screen, such as 'Clockwork Pegasus' to the other party in the session. This string is a word representation of the encryption key used for the session, is used to secure the call. If the words on my screen match the words displayed to the other party, then we know our call is secure.

The main downside of using secure communications software is that both sides must have it. Usually, I will have a short introductory conversation with someone without it, and I will send a link to download the right software and use it for our future sessions. And of course, if your VoIP call goes into the telephone network, then any encryption will end at the gateway, and your call will be unencrypted the rest of the way.

Also, note that no security protocol or application can protect you against a bug installed on your phone, or a listening device in the room where you are talking.

So, Raptorznest, make sure your VoIP and video calling is encrypted, and encrypted using published standards. With the right software, you can have level of security on your personal conversations that until recently was only available to heads of state and spies.

-> Your question not answered this week? Argue
for your vote on the Shameless Plugging area of
our discussion forum.

CHAPTER 7.

"Can someone explain what the hell is going on here?" boomed the baritone voice. All eyes were on the man in the U.S. military uniform as he looked up and down the table, waiting for an answer.

"Sir, have you read the report?" someone ventured.

"I have! But it is so full of CYA bull that I couldn't follow it. I want someone to succinctly explain the situation, to make sure we are all on the same page. This committee needs to get to work!"

"Well, sir… during their preliminary investigation of last week's web server outage, UBK found evidence that their servers and networks were being targeted by the zero day."

"UBK, the subcontractor?"

"Yes, for years they have been subcontracting all kinds of government services including prisons, call centers, and even some postal functions. Recently, they took over the IT operation of all U.S. non-secret government computers, data centers, and security."

"Why did their infrastructure fail so completely? Why is it so vulnerable?"

"They claim that everyone in the industry was taken by surprise by the worm. It was an un-patched vulnerability that had been in the software for years, but this zero day attack exposed it."

"And we have outsourced all our IT infrastructure with them alone?"

"Yes. The transition has taken eighteen months but is essentially complete. They are currently rolling out on-premise security for all government contractors."

The General swore.

"Didn't anyone point out the risk of this kind of outsourcing of critical government functions? If UBK can't keep our IT systems up due to attacks, how will the government function? Don't tell me, some did but they were ignored in the name of cost savings and smaller government, right?" The General paused and looked around the room. He desperately wished for some sunlight; he had been underground all day. "So what do we know about the attacks?"

"Not much at all – it was a zero day targeted at web servers. We've asked UBK for their intrusion logs. It seems it was some kind of worm that spread incredibly quickly. An independent consultant named Mick O'Malley apparently found the root case and wrote a patch that fixed it. UBK claim they are currently at 97% deployment of the patch."

"Who do we think is behind the attacks?" the General asked. When no one answered, he continued. "The usual Russian groups?" No one responded. "The Chinese?" he ventured.

"I don't think so, sir, as it doesn't have their usual signature. We need to analyze all the logs to know more. I wouldn't count out the Russians, or their network of companies."

"Get logs from all the Internet Service Providers as well," the General ordered. "Get everyone working on this. I can't stand just sitting here waiting for the other shoe to drop. Dismissed!"

The room quickly emptied out, leaving the General alone with his thoughts. He was not looking forward to briefing the National Security Council, but a cyber attack of this magnitude directed against the U.S. Government was not something that could be ignored.

CHAPTER 8.

__Mick O'Malley__ – wonders when he will be finished lying awake in the single digits of the morning. Of course, he is enjoying using that time for brainstorming and general re-evaluation of his life to date. (1 comment)

Mick squeezed the clutch and downshifted into first gear as he came up the hill to his workshop. He cut the motorcycle's engine as he crossed the threshold of the garage. He put out the kickstand, turned the fuel petcock to the horizontal position and lifted his leg over the bike. His face felt a little flushed as he pulled off the helmet and placed it on the stainless steel counter top. His heart rate was slightly elevated, although still under the norm. His resting heart rate was nearly as low as a marathon runner's, and as a result he wore a tag around his neck to let emergency personnel know this fact. In short, he was very happy with his ride. He glanced at the GPS track stored on his mobile and shared it with his social network.

It was a nice ride on his 1965 Ducati 25Ø Mark 1, café racer style motorcycle. It was one of his favorite bikes because of the way it rode with its short and low handlebars, and also for the bright orange paint. It felt good to be back home in the East Village, even if his bio-clock had not yet adjusted to New York City time.

Deciding to have a shower later, he sat down in his office and swiveled in his chair. Two giant flat screens lit up and came to life. He received a message indicating that a package had arrived for him. Mick didn't have any snail mail or package deliveries to his apartment – it all went to a service in a different neighborhood. The paper mail was automatically opened, scanned, and securely emailed to him, but he still had to pick up packages. He looked over the image of the shipping label, noticing the Australian customs declaration, filled in and signed by his uncle. His uncle was a serial inventor, and was always sending his latest and greatest to Mick to try out.

Wonder what it is this time?

Mick began the next day with his usual swim. When he started sailing small dinghies as a teenager, he had taken swimming lessons. These days, he was a strong swimmer, often swimming a few kilometers in a session. On the way back from the pool, he picked up the package from his uncle. Opening the package, he carefully removed a set of small round devices. Mick found a link to the code in the device which he followed. After examining the crypto for about an hour, he was satisfied.

Not bad, Uncle, never know when I might need one of these.

Later, he was pleasantly surprised to find himself invited to join Kateryna's social network – he had been 'friended' by her. He reciprocated and was then able to peruse her profile and friends' network.

His first stop was her pictures. There were some nice ones of her and lots of other photographs, presumably that she had taken, including a few pinhole photographs. There were mainly travel pics which showed an interest in history, and an excellent eye for composition. There were very few pictures of her with other people – friends, family, etc. Mick realized this was true of his profile as well.

In her friends' network, he saw a few people he knew, including Gunter and Liz. Her postings read just like her conversation, although she seemed somewhat preoccupied with unusual combinations of foods – those postings seemed to generate the most comments and approvals.

What would she conclude looking at my profile?

Mick brought up his own profile and looked it over for a few minutes but without forming any conclusions. He was interrupted by the alerting of the secure telephone on his desk. It was his sister. They had a close relationship, and no matter how busy he was, Mick made the time to stay in touch with her.

"Hi Jocelyn!" he answered.

"Hey Alec," she replied. "How was your trip?"

Jocelyn was happy to hear a couple of stories from his trip. She made him promise to call his niece Sam again soon. When he hung up a few minutes later, he placed one more call to a local motorcycle dealer friend to make a few important arrangements for the week after next.

Early the next week, Mick snaked his way through the JFK airport security line, heading to the gate for his flight to Seattle, Washington for yet another security conference, an invitation-only event for industry insiders and select security professionals. This was the first year he had been invited to speak, so Mick was excited.

In the past, Mick had found airport security lines vaguely erotic – all that undressing, dressing, removing of belts and shoes. These days, though, the full-body searches by security personnel were well beyond erotic...

As long as he could remember, Mick had always loved airports. Everyone there is on his or her way to somewhere exciting, or heading home to family and friends, bursting with stories and souvenirs. There are welcomes and reunions by the baggage claim. Husbands and wives picking each other up; the short kiss in the car perhaps just a prelude to a longer welcome home later in the evening after the children are asleep. Even the sometime tearful goodbyes at the security checkpoints didn't get Mick down – often it is a place where normal emotional reserve is abandoned in favor of a decent public display of affection. For some, perhaps it is a rare chance to find out how someone really feels about you, albeit as they are leaving... He had all kinds of happy memories of flights between London and New York, and flights to Melbourne to visit relatives. These days, he flew all around the globe for business. This morning, he was looking forward to the cool air of the Pacific Northwest – Seattle was one of his favorite cities.

Through security, he camped out at his gate, waiting for the connecting flight to Chicago to board and take off.

Regardless of the destination, Mick looked forward to flying – the longer the flight the better. Where else could he be guaranteed a certain number of hours of reading, thinking, and relaxing? He enjoyed the lack of interruptions, unless he sat next to a talker, but then he would pretend to speak very little English. He could usually finish a book on a short flight. On his longer transatlantic or transpacific flights, he would sometimes go through a couple of books. Despite their bulk and weight, Mick still preferred paper books over electronic books for his personal reading, although his friends thought he was slightly mad. He just liked the distinction it made between his professional reading, which was exclusively online and electronic, and his personal reading.

Of course these days he always got upgraded to first or business class, but he loved flying even back when he always flew coach. His noise-canceling headphones, used to listen to music, separated him from the world.

A few minutes later, as the plane accelerated down the runway, the overhead flat screen showed the groundspeed of the plane at 188 mph in archaic units. (For Mick, these units for speed were only slightly less out of date than his favorite – 'furlongs per fortnight'.) Doing the mental math, Mick realized this was almost exactly the same as the top speed of his Shinkansen ride just ten days ago. Thinking of Nihon made Mick think of Kateryna, which made him smile to himself.

Over the next few hours, the farms of the northeast gave way to the plains of the Midwest.

The short stopover in Chicago was uneventful. Mick caught up on some technical journal reading he had been putting off. In seemingly no time, the plane was circling SeaTac Airport and preparing to land in Seattle.

Having finished his reading, Mick relaxed and shut his eyes for a few moments. He thought about the security logs from the web server zero day the previous week. Besides his personal mobile and computing devices, Mick kept a couple of his own personal servers in data centers which he used to backup his files and manage his communication and mail. Besides the 'Carbon is Poison' web server compromise, he did find another one of his servers that had been compromised and had been acting as a spambot – a spam sending robot – automatically sending out hundreds of thousands of spam emails per hour into the Internet. Mick had not yet been able to figure out how this had happened.

On the ground, he caught the light rail train to his hotel downtown. Mick very rarely rented cars – he almost exclusively used public transport, although he occasionally made other arrangements.

Mick had expected Gunter to attend the conference, but Gunter had announced he was staying in Europe this week. Liz had corporate meetings while Lars was lying on beach

in the Maldives. It would apparently just be him and
Kateryna.

For Mick, visiting Seattle was a caffeinated adventure.
He always came away wishing some other local coffee
brand had gone global instead of the one that did. Mick
checked his location software, then headed for a café near
his hotel. It was just an average coffee house for Seattle,
but it was still better than any he frequented in New York.

He found Kateryna sipping a cappuccino, and joined
her after ordering an espresso.

"Mick!" she called out, looking up at him. He really
liked her accent, and the way she said his name, making it
sound similar to 'meek'. Mick enjoyed accents, and
especially loved to listen to women speak in Nihon. He
had a definite weakness for the sound of a southern Irish
accent in a woman. And of course, the every-statement-is-
a-question intonation of Australian women also drove him
crazy. Then he wondered at this long list and whether he
had some kind of aural fixation.

"Hey Kat! Long time, no see."

"Yeah, this is getting to be a habit!"

"What are you up to?"

"Just putting the finishing touches on my presentation.
I'll show you mine if you show me yours?" she asked,
suggestively flashing the screen at Mick. He chuckled and
looked it over. It was a good presentation: clear and
concise. The views didn't exactly coincide with his own,
but they were reasonable and well argued.

"Very nice," he replied. "Here's mine." He pulled up
his own presentation, which was shorter, blunter, and
somewhat controversial. Mick was determined to make
the best of use of this platform. Besides, if he didn't speak
his own strongly held views, whose views should he
speak?

"Wow! You don't pull any punches do you?" she
asked, smiling at him as she leaned back in her chair. "I

like it!"

"Thanks!" he replied, and he meant it.

They talked for a while about industry events as the sun went down.

"Do you have any dinner plans?" Mick asked her. When she said no, he suggested a few good seafood places within walking distance, and they picked one and set off. Over the meal, Kateryna switched the conversation to more personal topics.

"I was looking over your CV the other day. Unless my math is off, you started university pretty young, didn't you?" she asked. Mick looked up from his plate.

"Yep. I was fifteen when I started at Columbia. Due to my age, I was given permission to live at home instead of a freshman dorm."

"That still doesn't quite add up – if you are twenty-four, and have three years industry experience after completing your doctorate…"

"Well, I completed my undergraduate Comp Sci degree in three years, then my PhD in another three."

"So you really were a *Wunderkind*?"

"Not really, I just found something I'm really, really good at."

"When did you move out from your parents'?"

"I didn't really. My parents died in an auto accident when I was fourteen. I was lucky that my sister was willing to be my co-guardian, so I lived with her."

"I'm so sorry – I didn't know."

"Of course you didn't. It seems like a long while ago. I'm really lucky to be so close to my sister. Even when she got married we have stayed close. We have lots of relatives in England, Ireland, and Australia, but here in the U.S. we only have each other. Are you close to your siblings?"

"Not really, one still lives in Romania, the others are in Montreal. I've been living in San Fran for nearly two years now. I saw you were the founder of a startup – how did that happen?"

"It came out of my research – my thesis advisor and I came up with some intrusion detection heuristics – basically algorithms that enable a business or government to tell if someone is attacking their network. I thought they were fairly obvious, but they weren't, so we patented them and founded a startup to commercialize them.

"We worked for nearly a year and had a product ready to ship when we were bought out. It was the CEO's idea to shop the company even before we launched – I was against it. I made a lot of money, but the software never got deployed or used."

"Why?"

"Well, two factors. There was a competing in-house product at the company that acquired us – their management made sure our software didn't steal resources from their group. And the other was a series of patent lawsuits that competitors filed. They were all bull in my opinion, and I spent six months of hell with patent attorneys, giving depositions and answering questions. The net result was that I quit and I've been consulting ever since. It has been difficult getting established, as my views are seen as somewhat 'alarmist' as you know, but I think people are starting to realize what is out there, and what they need to do to protect themselves. Oh, and I just recently landed a really good consulting job that I am hoping will be the start of many."

"Congrats!"

"Thanks! I can't wait to start it – I'm off to New Mexico for at least a week." Mick was amazed at how much he had opened up to Kateryna.

Why am I telling her all this?

"Well, I'm very impressed – our industry could use more people like you. My work must seem a bit boring and antiquated to you, but I enjoy it."

"No not really…" Mick began, then catching her eye, changed tack. "Well, a bit, yes. But your take on it is refreshing – I'm sure you are a bit of a loose cannon in your company."

"Loose cannon?"

"Yeah, an old naval analogy – one of your own cannons, not properly secured, can cause a lot of damage below decks, even sink the ship," he explained.

"I get it. Yes, in my own way, I guess I am a bit of a loose cannon," she replied happily.

The conference went quickly the next day, and both Mick and Kateryna received positive feedback on their presentations. Mick hardly had time to think about anything besides all the business contacts he was making.

"Are you OK?" Mick asked. He waited for a response from the blonde haired youngster sitting in the chair across from his. Mick was enjoying a not half bad espresso at a café when he heard the boy's head hit the table with a thunk!

"Yeah, yeah. I'm fine." the boy mumbled, looking up, unfocused.

"You don't look fine…" Mick continued. "Is there anything I can do to help?"

"I don't know… Can you turn back time?" Mick resisted the urge to bring up special relativity.

"Tell me what's up," Mick said instead, trying to encourage him.

"OK. I just got this really awesome job, and it's going great. The only thing is, my boss has this new idea that he wants to 'connect with employees using social media'…" he replied, using a funny voice as he imitated his boss.

"He *friended* you?" Mick asked.

"Yep, and he wants to know why I haven't reciprocated yet… Dude – I've been railing on him to my friends since

I started on the job. If he reads my posts, I'm doomed! Epic FAIL!" His head fell to the table again.

"Which social network?" Mick asked. He grimaced when he heard the answer. "So you've tried deleting the posts?"

"Yes, but some are comments on other posts and I just can't get rid of them all. I can't believe he thinks he can do this – he just doesn't get it!"

Mick agreed with him. He was well aware of how the intersection between social networking and the workplace was fraught with issues and pitfalls, and the etiquette for resolving these kinds of issues just wasn't there yet.

"I can help you…" Mick began.

"You can make them disappear?" For the first time, the youngster showed some signs of life.

"Yes, but I can't just delete them. You'll need to lose some other posts, too. I can make it look like database corruption in your account."

"Cool! But how?"

"I just need a prepaid wireless data card, and about twenty minutes to write a script. Here's what I need…" Mick detailed what he needed, and sent the youngster, named Seth, off to buy one from a store around the corner – with cash, Mick had warned him. He hurried off eagerly, while Mick set to work.

In a few minutes, Mick had a script ready to extract and list all Seth's comments. Then, he wrote another script that generated database exceptions inside the social network that would result in the comments being deleted. At least he was pretty sure it would – he had never actually done this before, but the concept was sound in theory.

Seth returned and Mick accessed the Internet using the prepaid device and ran the script.

"That's them!" Seth shouted, when the posts started scrolling across the screen. Mick selected them. The script then took care of them: they were all gone.

"Sweet! I can't believe you did that!" Seth said as Mick deleted the script, removed the wireless card, broke it, then threw it in the trash. He knew he was being overly cautious, but he did not want anything that could connect him to this little piece of hacking.

"Maybe you'll be a little more careful in the future?" he asked, getting up to go.

"Yeah, I definitely will… Hey, I don't even know your name –" he began. Mick put up his hands.

"It's better that way. Good luck to you Seth!" Mick replied and walked out of the coffee shop, deciding not to come back to this one again.

He had written to Gunter telling him about the conference, and received a reply a little later:

```
Mick,

You are most welcome about Seattle - I am glad
it worked out for you.

Good luck with the LeydenTech job - sounds
really interesting. Ride safely in NM.

Keep in touch, old friend.  With luck I'll see
you in Vegas... Yeah, baby!

GS
```

```
------BEGIN PGP SIGNATURE-----
wgGnrdZfSZu9Tw5BHbYwFpQCrqir5d
kSbO5lxZOuuMeFGxQgpPZ2GQlhdTRB
W9ZCQfhp7MA===vRZQhQEMA1/E8ja5
Z9JuAQf+McLh6QFG1Q8fJxbF/QbR9b
wJufkLPRlPJ7G3+AJbdzphrqIbxmlE
-------END PGP SIGNATURE------
```

Flying out of Seattle the following afternoon, Mick got an amazing look at the dormant volcano of Mt. Rainier, with the not-so dormant Mt. St. Helens smoldering in the distance. A few minutes later, the plane banked and he got a clear view of the Columbia River. He noticed what looked like a power plant near a hook-shaped bend in the river. Mick realized it was probably the Hanford Site, where the world's first large-scale nuclear reactor was built, and where the plutonium for the atomic bomb tests and the Nagasaki bomb were produced. Another piece of the puzzle of the atomic zero day attack.

CHAPTER 9.

*From the **Security and Other Lies** Blog:*

Why do programmers use strange number formats such as hexadecimal? Just to be different? raptorzhavemorfun

Humans like decimal numbers. Computers like binary numbers. Computer programmers who bridge these two worlds often use hexadecimal numbers because they are sort of a compromise. Let me explain:

Computers, in their hardware, exclusively use binary numbers, also known as base 2 numbers. Each digit is either a 1 or a Ø, and every place represents a power of 2. This is because the storage and manipulation of numbers in binary form is very easy. For example, in a memory storage device, the presence of a voltage (such as 3.3V) can represent a 1 while the absence of a voltage (ØV or ground) can represent a Ø. A single binary digit is known as a 'bit'. If you have 8 bits of binary information, you can represent numbers from ØØØØØØØØ to 11111111 or Ø to 255 in decimal form. 8 bits are also known

65

as a 'byte', or an octet, a set of 8. (Note that 'byte' is a deliberate misspelling, since 'bite' is too similar to 'bit'.) A byte is the basic unit of information in a computer, or in larger units as MB (Mega bytes or millions of bytes) or GB (Giga bytes or billions of bytes).

Now binary numbers aren't very friendly to work with for humans, but hexadecimal, or base 16, is a more convenient form. Hexadecimal uses Ø-9 then A-F as the 16 values. For example, the number 1Ø in decimal is represented by A in hexadecimal. Each byte is represented by two hexadecimal digits, making it convenient for computer programmers to use. The 8 bits of information in a byte represent the range of ØØ to FF in hexadecimal.

As another example, in decimal, there is no real distinction between the numbers 255 and 256. However, to a computer, there is a big difference. The value 255 can be represented within a byte – that is, by 8 bits - while 256 can't be represented with a byte – it requires at least 9 bits. The values of FF and 1ØØ (which are 255 and 256 in hexadecimal) make this obvious (at least to a computer programmer).

I should also point out the programmers also typically begin counting from zero, instead of starting at one like normal people. This is partly due to the use of binary numbers and the need to make the most of a limited number of bits. However, it is also due to programmers frequently using offset pointers in strings or series of data. For example, the string 'zero' has four characters or letters. We might say that 'z' is the first character; 'e' is the second character, etc. However, if the characters are referenced as an offset from the start, then 'z' is zero characters offset from the start; 'e' is one character offset from the start, etc. So the character offset would start at Ø and go up to 3 for a string of 4 characters.

Now that I have thought about it, raptorzhavemorfun, I'm starting to lean more towards your 'just to be different' explanation…

-> Your question not answered this week? Argue for your vote on the Shameless Plugging area of our discussion forum.

CHAPTER A.

Mick O'Malley – *tries to remember to be careful of what information he shares on social networks, which is kind of a strange thought to share on a social network.* *(8 comments)*

Early the next week, Mick was riding north on Highway 25 in New Mexico towards Santa Fe, enjoying the wind pressure on his body and the sun on his back. After only a few days back in New York, he was about to begin his consulting job.

From the Albuquerque airport, he had taken a short cab ride to a tumbledown motorcycle store on the outskirts of the city. One of his own Ducati motorcycles shipped from his workshop in New York had arrived at a local motorcycle shop the previous day. It had been uncrated, and was ready for him to ride. For the duration of his visit to New Mexico, he had his bright yellow 1974 Scrambler 45Ø to ride. He had chosen the Scrambler since it was a dual sport bike, with combination road/dirt tires that enabled it to be ridden both on road and off road. Mick had an idea he could find some desert trails to ride on.

Mick would often make arrangements to have one of his motorcycles crated up and shipped to a part of the country where he planned to spend a week or more. He could then enjoy riding it all week then have it shipped back to his workshop. There were advantages to owning seven motorcycles... and being independently wealthy.

The scenery was a big change from his usual, with New Mexico offering hills, mesas, and desert all around. Just over an hour later he stopped outside Santa Fe to fuel up his bike and himself. Back on the highway, he continued north until his westward turnoff to Los Alamos. Despite the scenery and the ride, his thoughts kept drifting back to the recent attacks. In the last two weeks, two of his servers had been successfully compromised... perhaps it was time to increase his vigilance?

On the smaller highway, he headed towards Los Alamos, following the sun as it receded in the sky. Approaching Los Alamos, Mick was amazed by the sight of the cliffs of the high mesas making it look more like a fortress than a city. He rode towards the small inn on the northern side of the city where he had his reservation. He drove a few extra kilometers around the outskirts of town, going past the offices of LeydenTech, and, as the sun set, he reluctantly pulled into the inn and parked his motorcycle. The Scrambler had run beautifully for him.

At a civilized hour the next morning, he sat down with Vince at LeydenTech, having breakfast and coffee and meeting the security team. Vince performed the introductions to Will and Anil who worked in the LeydenTech IT security group. Mick had switched off his mobile in the morning, since mobile phones did not work inside the LeydenTech office. Vince had told him the building was effectively a Faraday cage – a shield blocking all external electromagnetic radiation, making all wireless devices useless inside. He wondered if this was a deliberate security precaution, or just a byproduct of the building's construction.

"You really did a great job with that web server attack the other week!" Will, the manager, exclaimed as they sipped lattes.

"Ah, yes, thanks," Mick replied, feeling a little confused as to how Will found out about the incident.

Perhaps he is friends with someone in the NOC in Hiroshima?

"Yeah, pretty slick. Not sure I agree with you on the rest of it, though..." he continued.

What is he talking about?

"You brought one of your Ducatis here?" Vince asked, and when Mick nodded continued. "That's excellent. We'll try not to keep you in our datacenter for all the daylight hours..."

Mick didn't recall telling Vince about his motorcycle habits, and wondered if perhaps Vince had done a more thorough background investigation on him than he had done on Vince. Or maybe Vince had just seen him ride in. Mick wondered what else Vince knew about him.

According to Mick's investigations, Vince had been with LeydenTech for two years now, and was employee number thirteen – startups often kept track of the hiring order – whereas now the company employed over 25Ø people. His degrees in computer science and business must have made him an obvious recruitment target when he finished his Doctorate from Harvard. He was married with no kids. His wife worked at Sandia National Labs in Los Alamos – on what, Mick couldn't determine. And he had no traffic tickets or recent insurance claims.

"I also plan to maybe do a little exploring, and perhaps some camping this weekend, too. Anywhere you'd suggest?"

"Chaco Canyon is pretty cool – it is very remote and lots to see in terms of Native American history and ruins," suggested Anil.

"Are there any good trails I could ride my motorcycle off-road?" he asked.

"Tons. Just make sure you don't wander into any reservations. Its not that it isn't safe or something, but it is a different country, and our laws don't apply," Will cautioned.

"OK – I'll make sure to mark them on my GPS. Thanks for the info," Mick replied happily. "I'm really looking forward to this."

"Well, thank you for coming out here so quickly. We would like to get this wrapped up as this might be our last investigation of this type," Vince replied. Noticing Mick's confused look, he explained. "We are getting ready to turn over our IT and security services to UBK. I'm not at all happy about it, but we have no choice."

"I've read about them," Mick replied. "They subcontract a bunch of government services these days."

"Yep, they run a couple of federal prisons in this state."

"I can't remember, are they a U.S. corporation?"

"No, they are multi-national, dealing with dozens of governments world wide."

"Is it just me, or does this seem like a bad idea? Do they even have the competency to handle IT? Have their systems and software been audited?"

"Well, their systems are extremely efficient, and they take advantage of economies of scale. For example, they standardize on a single hardware platform and single set of software, then replicate it across their systems and customers."

"Hmm. That sounds like a 'monoculture', which as you know, has very bad security properties. If a vulnerability is found, it can be exploited on a massive scale."

"Maybe you should write to your congressman..." Anil replied.

Mick was shown to a workstation and given his accounts for the servers to examine the logs. He barely looked up for the next three hours until Will came to take him to lunch. After lunch, he continued poring over the logs. Intriguingly, although one of their servers had been compromised, LeydenTech had not shut it down or removed it from their network. Instead, they had carefully set up a dummy subnet or sub-network and created some other servers with fake corporate accounts. Then, they had moved the server over and redirected all other communication to another server that mimicked a failed network connection. As a result, the compromised server was still operating as it had been, but it was isolated from the real LeydenTech network and data. It was as if the server had been put in a cleverly concealed cage so it could be observed in the wild.

Currently, all the server was doing was sending spam – lots and lots of spam emails. Mick began to wonder if perhaps this server was part of a botnet, short for a robot network of computers, a collection of compromised, or hacked, computers, known as zombie computers, organized to receive commands over the Internet and operate as a group. A botnet combines the power of each of each of the individual computers. The larger the botnet, the more powerful it becomes. Mick was aware of botnets made up of thousands, some claimed millions, of zombies on the Internet used to send spam – so called spambots. Lately, however, there was evidence botnets were being put to other, more sinister purposes.

So far Mick hadn't been able to find evidence of the LeydenTech server trying to contact a botnet controller for instructions, to 'call home'. Usually, a newly compromised computer would reach out to its creator to report in and request new instructions.

Studying the compromise, he realized it was similar to the one that happened to his own server. He was still going through the data when Vince stopped by to say that everyone was going home for the day.

As he rode back to the inn, Mick shifted gears mentally, and focused back on Will's strange knowledge of Mick's work on the web server attack.

Back in his room, Mick turned on his mobile and checked his social network that he had completely neglected since the morning. Everyone was buzzing with comments about some blog article that apparently mentioned him. Mick found the blog on the Internet Security World and read with disbelief:

ISW has just learned that last month's major web server attack was uncovered by none other than Mick O'Malley, independent security consultant. In a PGP signed email to *ISW*, O'Malley claimed credit for detecting the attack and writing the patch that was widely distributed a few hours after the attack, and effectively ended the zero day. O'Malley also criticized the open source community for security complacency saying:

"... this should be a wake up call for the entire open source community. They need to do a much better job in the future or it will hurt the image of the entire movement."

O'Malley went on to claim that he has personally found and fixed multiple exploitable bugs in different packages in the past few months, and that frustration has forced him to speak out.

We will be tracking the reaction of the open source community to O'Malley's words, and we will have a complete analysis of the attack in next week's edition.

Mick had to read it a few times before he could believe it.

How could anyone believe I had written such self-serving drivel? And why in hell would I criticize the open source community? Why would ISW lie about receiving a signed email from me?

Lars had spoken to the editor of *ISW* who had shared the alleged email. Mick again read in disbelief that the signature on the email had validated.

*The forged email was signed with my **private** key!*

His private key, which he used to sign his secure email messages was only known to him. To have it stolen from one of his computers was inconceivable!

Fortunately, none of his friends seemed to believe the email was genuine, despite the signature. However, the fact that Mick hadn't weighed in himself seemed to be making them waver a little. He contacted Lars, Liz, and some other friends, confirming that he had sent no such email, nor would he make such derogatory comments.

At first, Mick was really angry with *ISW*; why would they publish his email without confirmation? Then, he realized: how would they confirm it with him – call his mobile? His phone number wasn't published anywhere. He did nearly all his business using signed email. What more proof or confirmation would they need than his digital signature generated with his own secret private key – known only to him?

My private key has been compromised.

This realization hit home and made his knees feel weak. His private key – his identity – his ability to secure communications with, well, everyone. Without any further delay, he began a key revocation, canceling the compromised private key and making it unusable by the thief, but also, unfortunately, unusable by Mick as well. Having done that, he began the laborious process of generating new private keys and their associated public keys and getting the public keys signed by his friends and published in various places on the Internet.

He then read the comments to the blog entry, and needless to say they were not at all complimentary towards him. In fact, it was fair to say his reputation with the open source community was pretty well destroyed by this forged mail, although some of his friends had posted in his defense.

It was only a few hours until sunrise when he went to bed.

The next morning he had a scheduled video call with Sam. He didn't really feel like it, and actually considered canceling it, but went ahead in the end.

"Konichiwa Uncle Alec-san!" she greeted him.

"I'm not in Nihon anymore," he reminded her.

"I know. You are deep in the Southwest. How is the riding?"

"Very good. The terrain is pretty unique here – even the sky seems somehow different," he replied.

"Pictures please! I need to decide whether New Mexico should move up on my list of places to visit."

"Where is it now?"

"I believe it is about 4Øth on the list, but if you say the sky is different, then I may have to move it up into the teens."

"Understood. Shall we read?"

"Nope. I've got a question for you, if that's OK?" she asked hopefully. Mick smiled to himself.

This girl really knows how to get to me.

"Of course, Sam. What is it?"

"I read that 'peer-to-peer' networks are a security risk. Now, I don't know what they are, but I think I've heard you mention them, and you wouldn't talk about them if they were bad for security."

"Sam, do you read Slashdot or something? Never mind. You are right: P2P isn't necessarily insecure. This is a classic piece of clueless FUD," he started, then paused when Sam raised her eyebrows as if he had said a bad word. He smiled, then continued.

"FUD stands for Fear, Uncertainty, and Doubt. In this

case, it means half-truths and falsehoods, peddled by people with an agenda to push. There is nothing inherently threatening or bad about peer-to-peer applications – in fact, they can sometimes be more secure than other applications."

She looked away from the camera for a moment, then continued. "My mother wants to say hello."

"Hi Alec," Jocelyn began, her dark wavy hair and piercing brown eyes coming into the field of view of the camera.

"Hey Jocelyn, how's it going?"

"Oh, I'm fine. Wondered if you were coming to Boston soon?"

"Yes, probably in three weeks," he replied. She smiled back at him, and he heard Sam shout "Yes!" out of view.

"OK. Let us know, brother. Take care."

"Will do," Mick replied, and went back to talking to Sam for a little while longer.

After the video call, Mick felt better, but all day he still found it difficult to concentrate on the work at LeydenTech, but he did anyway. He tried not to think about his own security compromise until the end of the day. Back in his room, he started to carefully examine his own server logs for signs of how someone had stolen his private key. He didn't find very much, but what little he did find convinced him that his server compromise was linked to the LeydenTech compromise. His own spambot was eerily similar to the one here at LeydenTech.

Now with two examples of the spambot software, he sent both to Kateryna and asked her if she could help.

He heard back from her a few hours later:

Hey Mick,

Hope the weather is good for you in NM. It has been a few years since I visited, but I recall some great archaeological sites, including some amazing petroglyphs near ABQ.

I still can't comprehend your key compromise -
you are the most careful person I know. Someone
must really have it out for you to do this to
you. Do you have any idea who?

I don't know what to tell you about the spambot
- I'm not an expert in this area, but we do have
a few guys in the office who are. I'll make
some unofficial inquiries and let you know what
I find out.

So, I have a question for you: if you were born
in England to Irish parents, grew up in London
then moved to New York, why do you have such a
generic American accent? I thought perhaps it
was just me but I asked a couple of Americans
who knew you and they agreed that there is very
little evidence of your heritage in your accent.
I only have to open my mouth and say one word
and everyone knows I'm from somewhere else (even
in Romania today as my accent and vernacular are
out of date). What is your secret? ;-)

Regards,

Kat

```
------BEGIN PGP SIGNATURE-----
ObykTa4b/eD04V+4+xcgoZmS/9Ef7p
qWVcd2m3iXMwlJenGmxoS9K0pwYO3v
vcetJs032/4dajPEq/AK8VJUzcKbF4
v4RS/5n22R8Rh7RWByBJlVMNbuaOGX
zHln0oi3tLZNhMiJXaB8ri8VMTOStK
-------END PGP SIGNATURE------
```


Mick smiled self-consciously and fired off a quick
response. In truth, what accent he had depended on who
he was talking to. Talking to his relatives in England and
Ireland, he would slip into a light Irish accent. With his
school friends, he seemed to be from New York. The only
accent he had never really picked up was from the town of
his birth, London. It didn't worry him, as in England,
accent is used as a class indicator, and any kind of English

accent would have made him categorizable, something he tried to avoid. He didn't love everything about America, but he did love that one's class had nothing to do with accent or birth.

The next few days in Los Alamos passed without incident as he continued the investigation. He received a reply from Kateryna.

Mick,

You know, something strange came up during our investigations into that piece of spamware you sent. It looks like it is from a new codebase - our guys have never seen it before. The spam pattern was also strange - they said it was almost random. That is odd because spammers usually stick with established routes that have worked well in the past. They think that this spamware has a very low success rate as a result. You'd think that a new piece of software would be better than the old ones, but that doesn't seem to be the case here.

Oh, and the second app you sent, it is virtually the same as the first one - definitely written by the same people.

I'll keep you posted. Be careful riding that bike of yours... if I'm going to see you in two weeks in Vegas, you need to stay in one piece.

Regards,

Kat

-----BEGIN PGP SIGNATURE------
h8rYbiC2eK6qDXL43TCP8jRQiK+Ou7
YIgoZ+y+O/cjT7/dMImEvea8KwLzOg
7KFb3c3XPSsKmjieKlwjFcK4Om2tsd
QcijL+HynXNiFMItRF2yqu8ppdJ2kL
Uz7Sld6EErDdLAtAE56C2bhOF1G+qK
------END PGP SIGNATURE-------

The second application or app he had sent Kateryna

was the spamware from LeydenTech. The first was the one from his own server. Saying they came from the same codebase meant they were the work of the same set of programmers or came from the same company.

Mick could feel himself getting closer to the truth.

CHAPTER B.

From the Security and Other Lies Blog:

I've read that open source software is more
secure then commercial software. Is this true?
raptors4ever

I love this question! :-) Let me start with a
good definition of open source software.
Software is the instructions that tell a
computer what to do. When a computer is turned
on, it starts running software, known as the
'operating system' or OS. When you start a
program such as a web browser, an editor, or a
mail program, you are running software. When
you use your mobile phone, you are using
software. The actual instructions interpreted
by the CPU in a computer are known as machine
language, binary files, just binaries (named
after the binary format they are stored in), or
executable code (since the CPU executes it). If
we look at them, we just see a bunch of numbers
- it is very difficult to figure out what is
happening unless you are a computer.

Source code is a human-friendly way of representing computer instructions. Computer programmers or software developers create and write source code, then that source code is turned into the executable code using a piece of software known as a compiler. Source code is written in different computer languages. They really are languages in that they have vocabulary, syntax, and grammar, and allow one to express ideas and make a computer do what you want it to. Whew! That was a bit long, but hopefully now we're all on the same page.

Normally, when you buy or install computer software, you are using the binary or executable code. You can't actually see what the computer is doing just by looking at it - you can only observe it by running it and seeing what happens. Much of computer software is closed source - that is, the source code is kept a secret. Only people working for the company that created or owns the source code are able to inspect and fix the code.

Open source is the opposite - the source code is freely available for anyone to inspect and examine - usually published on the Internet. In fact, open source is considered 'free' software, sometimes explained as 'free as in speech, not as in beer'. That means that companies can charge money for open source software, but they can't keep the source code secret. Just as free speech allows anyone to express his or her opinion and add to a discussion, anyone can take an open source program, modify it and change it. Only, per the terms of the open source license, they must also publish the changes and alterations they made to the software.

Now, having secret source code might sound great when it comes to software security. After all, bad guys can't look through the code and find the weak points and places where they can try to crash or take over the computer. While it is possible to 'reverse engineer' some binaries to get an idea of the source code, the legality of doing this on closed source software is not clear, so only the bad guys do it. Any sufficiently complex piece of software (and today's software is hugely complex) will have weaknesses and bugs, and bad guys will find them, by trial and error if nothing else. When found, they can then launch attacks using it.

Once these attacks are launched and security experts analyze them, the software will need to be fixed or patched. But only people working at that company can do this, as only they can see and change the source code. Everyone using the software is vulnerable until they fix the bug. Sometimes this can take weeks or even months!

Now, let's compare this to open source. In an open source project, many programmers and software engineers are able to look over the code. Security researchers from all over the world are able to search for vulnerabilities and possible attacks. When they are found, any programmer can write and upload a patch to fix it. With more eyes on the code, more bugs and potential attacks are found before the bad guys can find them. When an attack happens, open source programmers will immediately analyze the attack and anyone can write the patch and fix it. As a result, in many cases, security holes can be closed more quickly with open source than with closed source software.

The open source software movement is a closely-knit community on the Internet today, encompassing both volunteers and companies. I am proud to be a part of it.

So, you can make up your mind, raptors4ever, which is more secure: closed source or open source? You can probably guess where I stand on this...

-> Your question not answered this week? Argue for your vote on the Shameless Plugging area of our discussion forum.

CHAPTER C.

Mick O'Malley – *greatly appreciates his friends standing by him over the past few days. He can't put into words what it means to him. And rest assured, he will find out who is responsible for this! (19 comments)*

Mick left LeydenTech early the next afternoon to take a break and clear his thoughts. His private key compromise had left him feeling off balance, and he felt strangely vulnerable, as if anything might happen to him at any time. He recognized the feeling as illogical, as he had already changed all his passwords and was using a new private key, but the feeling remained.

With his trip to Hiroshima fresh in his mind, Mick visited the Los Alamos Museum to learn more about the Manhattan project. The museum was housed in a building from the Los Alamos Ranch School, which the government acquired to establish the laboratory in 1942. It seemed amazing to Mick that the bomb that devastated Hiroshima was designed and built in this beautiful place. The museum had a small exhibit about the work and the workers who lived there up to 1945.

The grandmother of one of Mick's friends from Columbia had grown up in Los Alamos during this period, and he recalled her stories of life in a town that didn't officially exist. Mick really wanted to visit the White Sands Missile Range, a few hundred kilometers away, where the first atomic device was detonated. He really wanted to see the desert sand fused into glass stones by the detonation (named "trinitite" after the code name for the first bomb – Trinity). However, he knew the site was still an active military base and test site, and it was only open a few times each year. The device tested there was a plutonium device, the prototype of the bomb detonated over Nagasaki. The one dropped on Hiroshima used uranium instead, despite some claims that both were uranium.

The uranium device was not tested before Hiroshima as there was not enough processed uranium for a test detonation. Mick read that some of the uranium was processed in New York, but most of it was produced and refined in Oak Ridge, Tennessee. At peak production during the Manhattan project, Oak Ridge was using about 15% of all the electricity produced in the United States – more than all of New York City!

Mick felt amazed at the amount of work and planning that led up to the detonation. So much design and engineering of the various components: the fission fuel, the detonator, the delivery vehicle. So many parts of the project worked on by different teams in different parts of the country, culminating in one history-changing day 6ØØm above Hiroshima.

Later back at LeydenTech, Mick came to a disturbing conclusion: the compromised server was definitely part of a botnet. This was surprising because all the behaviors seemed wrong; the compromised server was not trying to act stealthily at all. A computer that was a member of a botnet normally would try hard not to give away this fact until it was ready to be used – otherwise, the computer would be disconnected, cleaned, and would be lost to the botnet. Usually, this meant keeping a low profile with Internet activity. This software seemed to be using a different approach – a hiding-in-plain-sight approach, where it *pretended* to be spamware. He was sure that the spamware wasn't the main purpose of the compromise, but that it served as cover for the real activity of the botnet. One possible reason – and this thought really bounced around in his brain – was to hide with whom the malware was communicating. This was called communication 'obfuscation' in the industry, and was one security property that was usually difficult to achieve. There were common approaches for encrypting traffic to make it private, and signing communication so you could prove who sent it, but all these approaches did nothing to hide the fact that two computers on the Internet were exchanging packets and messages.

In telephone network surveillance, a so-called 'pen tap' gives law enforcement information about who called whom and for how long, but tells nothing about the contents of the communication; a 'wiretap' is needed to listen in and record the conversations. Pen tap data in the hands of a good investigator can often be used to deduce all kinds of useful information, especially when coupled with other observations and facts that can be correlated with it. Without obfuscation, the Internet equivalent of pen tap calling information – which computer is sending messages to other computers – is not difficult to collect. Mick's own calling patterns – who he communicates with and for how long could be determined despite his use of voice and video encryption software.

In this case, Mick determined that the malware was sending out large amounts of traffic in the form of meaningless spam. Buried somewhere in the spam was actual botnet communication, he believed. He hadn't found it yet, but was convinced he would. Looking at the time, Mick summarized his findings so far and prepared for an interim briefing of Vince and his managers.

After the briefing, Mick went back to work. Vince was extremely pleased with his progress. Vince had let slip that it was Mick's colleague and speaking rival Miles who had taken this job the week before the conference in Hiroshima. Miles had concluded that the compromised server was just a spambot, but Vince was not happy with that conclusion, and had sought Mick out hoping he could do better. He was happy that Vince supported his pursuing the hypothesis and continuing the investigation. If he could prove it, he was sure that it was an entirely unknown type of botnet.

Could generate a paper or two, and some interesting presentations… not to mention the satisfaction of solving a good puzzle.

He was now viewing the LeydenTech spambot and the 'Carbon is Poison' zero day as related. He had also made contact, albeit anonymously, with two other system administrators who had also been targeted in a similar way to LeydenTech on an anonymous IRC (Internet Relay Chat) channel or chatroom for Security Administrators. They had exchanged some of the spam emails that their servers had been sending out. Mick added them to the messages he had logged on his own server, and the messages sent by the LeydenTech server.

With these messages, he was starting to build a decent data set. Today he planned to combine the packet flows from these four compromises into a single database for searching and number crunching. First he looked for traffic patterns between the servers. He wrote a script, a mini computer program, to search and analyze the messages exchanged overnight, and left for the day.

Mick stayed up late that night, coding to relax. He still felt off balance, as if he were recovering from a particularly nasty illness. It reminded him of how he felt as a kid after being in a schoolyard fight.

Wednesday morning found Mick engaged in his weekly password change ritual at the keyboard. He typed:

```
Eh,quid_facis,doc?
```

He read that it just kept on raining on Lars in Helsinki. Kateryna was looking forward to visiting a new Thai restaurant in the evening, although she didn't say with whom. Gunter was suffering writer's block as he approached a deadline for a whitepaper. Mick sent some encouraging comments to Gunter as he knew what it was like, and how good it felt when one finally reached that desired word count.

Back at LeydenTech, he almost choked on his espresso as he looked over the results of the script. His script had found a number of communication exchanges, known as flows, and had created a chronology of communication in a 2D graphical representation. He was amazed to see a pattern of communication emerge out of the seemingly random spam sent between the four computers. The information flow looked familiar to him but he couldn't quite put his finger on it. His script had organized the information in a so-called 'ladder diagram' where each computer was represented as a column and the messages between them arranged like rungs on a ladder. With a flash of insight that made the hair on his neck stand up, he rearranged the four servers as nodes on a line and redrew the messages as semi-circular arcs. Now, it was clear to him: the servers were definitely running some kind of peer-to-peer protocol. He sat back in his chair, realizing the botnet used P2P routing protocols... a staggering implication for combating the botnet.

Mick found himself staring into space as he contemplated the consequences of this discovery. P2P networks were extremely difficult to shut down. And an obfuscated P2P network that hid behind volumes of spam would be difficult even to detect, let alone shut down. This was some sophisticated programming, not your usual malware composed of scripts and borrowed code. He forced his mind to focus again with the thought that he still hadn't found the communication messages that he *conjectured* were being distributed using P2P technology. Until he found and deciphered them, he didn't have a complete picture. He set about analyzing the suspicious packets between the servers.

But by the end of the day, Mick felt more confused than ever. Every message he examined was, in fact, just spam. He had expected to find some encrypted payload or messages that he then could analyze to try to determine the kind of encryption algorithm used, and get one of his crypto friends to break them. Instead, he found only spam email messages. He stared at one particular message about a one million pound lottery the recipient had apparently won. Did people really enter so many lotteries that they honestly could not remember which ones they had entered, and hence could fall for this kind of spam? He was left with that most puzzling fact about spam: some people actually read spam, some actually call or click on it, and some, amazing as it sounds, hand money over to the spammers. If they didn't, if spam ads didn't generate revenue for someone, it would end overnight, and the industry would collapse.

Mick was about to head home for the day when Vince called him over. He sat down in Vince's office, looking around the room. Vince opened his desk and passed him something. Mick turned it over in his hand and examined it. It was about the size and shape of a small bookmark: thin, but astoundingly heavy for its size, as if it were made of something much more dense than lead. Seeing two small wire terminals on one side, Mick figured it out.

"Is it –" he asked.

"Yes, this is what we make," Vince interrupted him. "Would you believe 2Ø Amp-hours at 48 Volts?" he said, giving the storage capacity of the device.

"But that's much more energy than the battery in my motorcycle!" Mick exclaimed.

"Very true."

"It is so thin!" Mick commented.

"Actually, this one is quite thick. The capacity of this device is not about the volume, it is about the *surface area*. It can be much thinner without the protective coverings."

"Wow!" Mick replied.

"Yes, wow!" Vince echoed. "So, let's get this break-in resolved so we can concentrate on developing these babies."

"Understood," Mick responded, handing it back to Vince, but Vince stopped him.

"Keep this one – just don't go flashing it around, OK?" He placed it in Mick's hand.

"Really? No way! This would make an awesome battery for a computer. I'll just need to build a charger."

"No problems – I'll send you the specs. I really like the work you're doing for us. Just get to the bottom of it, Mick."

"Will do!"

Mick remembered he had planned a video call with Kateryna for the evening. She said she had some information she didn't want to share over mail. He finished up a little earlier, took the direct route back to the inn, making a quick dinner of ramen and various vegetables and tofu he had picked up earlier in the week. For this call, he got out his best high definition camera and actually used headphones instead of his implant. The high quality of the sound was his favorite aspect of HD video calls; it made you feel as if you were there with the other person.

"Good evening, Mick," Kateryna began, pronouncing Mick's name in her signature way as her smiling face filled the screen. She was still in her office, he guessed. However, the room seemed to have good lighting: no overhead fluorescent lights that made some video calls look so awful. She was wearing a light blue blazer and a white blouse with some jewelry a geologist would likely find fascinating.

"Hey Kat. Thanks for doing this for me – it means a lot. I'll definitely owe you one," he replied, glancing at his own sent image to make sure he looked good. He had put on a fresh black T-shirt for the call.

"No problems. Actually, I think I've made some new friends in our anti-spam group. They really enjoyed going through the code you sent. You did have permission from your client to share, right?"

"Of course, but I can't say who they are or disclose it publicly."

"Sure, I understand," she said, the corner of her mouth moving as if to start a dazzling smile. Sometimes he had a hard time concentrating when he was talking to her. "So, here's what they have found: multiple layers of encryption and some clever tricks to avoid reverse engineering or monitoring of the code. The guys say they haven't seen anything as good as this since they first looked at that peer-to-peer communication stuff a few years back."

"Funny you should say that..." he began.

"Don't tell me, P2P communication patterns, too?" she asked, her eyes getting wide.

"Yes, definitely. Or, at least I'm pretty sure."

"Which is it?"

"Well, I'm pretty sure there is communication, but I haven't found the actual messages yet. They are well hidden somehow. I feel as if they are staring me in the face..." Mick paused and stared out into space as the answer came to him – steganography – the hiding of information in plain sight. He got himself together and tried to concentrate on Kateryna who was looking on somewhat bemused. Mick wasn't sure how much time had passed.

"Did you just remember you left a motorcycle running back at your garage?" she asked.

"No, no, I just realized something. Anyway, what else did they find?"

"Just that it is some of the most sophisticated spamware they've ever seen. Also, another interesting thing: this code must do more than just send spam."

"What do you mean?"

"Well, the size of the code is much too big to just be a spambot. It must have other functions. Any idea what those might be?"

"I'm beginning to... yes."

"Are all of your consulting jobs like this?" she asked, perhaps a tinge of envy in her voice.

"No, most just involve inventing cold fusion, finding Higgs-bosons, and solving world hunger. This one is actually less difficult than most," he replied, and was rewarded with a glare.

"So have you been enjoying the riding and the scenery?" she asked.

"For sure – it is so spectacular. I'm told I need to come back in the early spring and also in the summer to see all the different moods of the desert. Los Alamos is amazing, although it is pretty isolated."

They chatted for a few more minutes until Kateryna appeared to be interrupted by a phone call.

"Oh, one last thing. Buried in the code they found the name of this software: *Zed dot Kicker*. You know these attack writers – they love to name their creations. Gotta run, Mick. Take care."

"OK, thanks a bunch, Kat. Talk to you again soon," he replied as she signed off.

The next few days, he made good progress at LeydenTech, giving regular updates to Vince. Vince had agreed to ship him a hardware encryption device so he could do the rest of his work remotely. As a result, he decided not the stay for the weekend, and had made arrangements to fly back to New York on the next morning, Saturday. He also had a response published in *ISW* disavowing the email and setting the record straight. After a terrible start to the week, things were looking up.

Walking out of the LeydenTech offices, Mick pulled on his helmet and gloves and started the Ducati. Second kick, as always. For some reason, Mick enjoyed kick starting his motorcycles. When he had a choice of kick start or electric start, he always used the kick starter.

He pressed down with his left toe to select first gear, slipped the clutch and took off. He waved with his left hand to the guard at the gate who pressed the button to open it and he turned right onto the road, shifting into second. As he accelerated, he noted a car in his outside mirror; a glance to his inside mirror confirmed it. He was sure there were no cars on the road when he pulled out – very strange. Going up through the gears, he reached his cruising speed, feeling the engine revs rather than looking at the tiny gauges mounted in front of the handlebars on the bike. As he approached the first intersection, he had his first decision: most direct route or most fun?

As if it were a choice...

There were few other cars to be seen on the road in the early evening light, so he didn't even have to slow down as he cornered to the right at the intersection by pushing on the right side of his handlebars. A common misconception about high speed motorcycle cornering is that you turn the handlebars to initiate the turn. Actually, the best technique is to counter steer – to push on the handlebars in the opposite direction of the turn. The gyroscopic effect causes the bike to lean the other way, and hence initiates the turn. The harder you push, the more the bike leans, and the harder you turn. This was one of the hardest things that Mick had to learn when he first started riding motorcycles on the street after riding dirt bikes as a kid.

He completed the turn with plenty of road left, a slight smile forming on his face. Then, he noticed the same car from LeydenTech also making the turn. Mick noted the suspension roll, or lean, on the sedan as it exited the corner, suggesting that it had taken the corner without slowing down. This wiped the smile off his face as he started to ponder the possibilities.

His route took him around the outskirts of Los Alamos. Off the beaten track, but still roads that people drove. He decided to add a few more kilometers to his ride and answer the question building in his mind. A small dirt road approached on the left, and he took it, braking slightly on the pavement, and leaning less on the turn until he knew how loose the gravel was on the road. He straightened up and accelerated with the setting sun behind him. A moment later, the sedan made the same turn. Mick's pulse increased and he felt adrenaline surge through him.

That car is following me...

He decided to turn the tables on his pursuers.

At the next slight rise in the road, Mick waited until he was over the crest and hit the brakes hard with his right foot, locking the rear wheel while modulating the front break with his right hand, keeping on the edge of adhesion. He pulled behind some strategically placed scrub that hid him from view. He down shifted to first gear but didn't have long to wait for the car to come over the crest of the hill.

As the car roared past, he had a good look at the two occupants, men in their twenties or thirties, dark haired with sharp features. The passenger turned and spotted him as they roared by, but it was too late. Mick slipped the clutch at the same instant and gave the Scrambler full throttle. His rear wheel moved around but he kept it under him as he rapidly caught up. He saw the driver touch the brakes in surprise, but then take his foot off, and instead stepped on the other pedal. Mick was eating a lot of dust, and from the sound of it losing some paint on his bike, but he twisted his wrist and accelerated, keeping up with the car.

As the road started getting a little bumpier, he rose up off his seat, making his legs part of the suspension of his bike, and keeping his weight on his foot pegs, providing better control. He bent his elbows slightly, pointing them outwards, making his body a fulcrum as the bike pounded over the bumps, motocross style. The car in front of him was having a harder time, almost getting airborne on some bumps. The passenger kept turning around to glare at him. Mick's tinted full-face helmet prevented them from seeing the concentration on his face. With the cloud of dust kicked up by the car, he wasn't getting a very good view of the road.

Mick had only a fraction of a second to react to the glowing red brake lights and the resulting shower of dust and stones. He jumped on his brakes hard, locking his rear and applying his front brake as hard as he dared without washing out. The car was coming to a complete halt, and with its four wide tires, it was stopping faster than Mick's two wheels. The car slid sideways, nearly blocking the road, forcing Mick to choose between running into it or heading off the road. He chose the latter, nearly laying the bike over on its right side as he released his brakes to gain traction. The edge of the road made a jump and Mick went airborne. He would have stuck the landing if it weren't for the erosion rut that claimed his front wheel. He couldn't steer or do anything except go over on his side. Mick parted company with his bike, rolling to a stop a few meters away.

As his head cleared, he sat up and pulled off his helmet. The engine of the Scrambler was still running, the back wheel spinning in the air. He crawled over and hit the kill switch to stop the engine. He then realized he was not alone, as the two men stood over him.

"O'Malley! You should mind your own business," one of them said, kicking the dirt with his boot. This guy was not from New Mexico, or even from North America, judging from his accent. Mick said nothing, glaring at them. "If I were you, I'd forget about *Zed dot Kicker* if you know what's good for you..." The man paused and then both turned around and began walking back to the car. "Oh, and O'Malley, you should be more careful with your things, like your private keys."

Mick tried to stand up but a sharp pain in his leg made him hesitate. He tried to shout but his throat was bone dry. He watched as they climbed back in the car. Mick unzipped a sleeve pouch on his jacket, retrieved something small, and flung it towards the car.

Mick watched helplessly as the car left him behind in a gradually receding cloud of dust. He caught his breath, his heart rate returning to normal. He took a drink of water, then pulled out his mobile, firing up an application.

Bull's eye!

He smiled looking at the map of the New Mexico desert with two dots: one was his location, the other was the location of the car speeding away. His uncle's invention, a magnetic GPS tracker, had attached to the car body and was working perfectly.

He dusted himself off, righted his bike and set off following them. Fortunately nothing mechanically was broken on the bike, although the forks were slightly skewed from the handlebars. As darkness fell, he left the corrugated road and was back on the pavement again, heading south. He adjusted his speed so he stayed about five minutes behind. Mick did a quick fuel economy calculation in his head and determined that he could make it to Albuquerque, but not much further. Fortunately, they took the turnoff towards the airport and he closed on them. He could not follow them into the car rental return area, but instead parked near the terminal and waited. He positioned himself in the middle of the terminal so he could see the check-in counters. In the meantime, he made note of the rental car company, based on where the car was parked.

Mick spotted the men checking in. He ducked inside a souvenir store and purchased a baseball hat and a bulky sweatshirt that had some joke about cow tipping printed on it. He put them both on, pulling the cap over his eyes. He positioned himself near where they would walk to get to the security checkpoint. The two men walked away from the counter with their boarding passes in hand and their bags slung over their shoulder. He made for the taller of the two, keeping his eyes on the ground. As he bumped shoulders, he made sure he knocked the papers from the man's grip.

"Blin!" the man shouted.

"So sorry, y'all!" Mick mumbled in an awful southern accent, picking up the papers. The man ripped them out of his hands and caught up with his friend. When Mick looked up a moment later he had a grin on his face, and a name to go with a face.

So Pavel Michalovic, you are on your way to Atlanta today...

Back in the parking garage, he made two calls.

"Hello, yes, I'm considering making a change to my reservation... My first leg is Albuquerque to Atlanta on flight 829... Pavel Michalovic... Yes, the second leg...

Right, Frankfurt. I was wondering if there are any flights to Amsterdam... I see, that's OK. I can take a train I guess. Thank you. Oh, and could you look up my frequent flier number for me? Yes... got it. Thanks, you've been most helpful."

Mick hung up the phone. He searched another number and dialed again.

"Ah, yes. I'm hoping you can help me. I just dropped off my rental car and I think I left my car charger... Albuquerque... about twenty minutes ago. Yes... yes. Pavel Michalovic... I don't have my agreement number – can you look it up? Great thanks... OK, you'll let me know? And could I get the agreement number from you? Wait! I just found the charger – never mind. Thanks."

More good information about his pursuer... He circled back to the rental car lot and retrieved the tracker from the car. When disengaged from the metal car body, the GPS tracker went dormant again to save battery.

All the way back to Los Alamos, he thought about the men.

Who were they? Did they think that threats would make me back off?

The mention of his private keys confirmed the link between Zed.Kicker and the forged email.

How did they steal my private key?

He wondered whether he should mention it to Vince and decided against it; he didn't want to complicate his investigation. By the time he went to bed, he almost felt he had imagined the whole thing, although his ruined pants and soreness of his leg contradicted this.

The next day he awoke with an extreme soreness in his thigh. Mick rode back to Albuquerque to catch his flight. Despite his mood, Mick was determined to stop for a few hours to explore Petroglyph National Monument, on the western side of the city. It took him a few minutes to learn to recognize the petroglyphs, but once he did, he could spot them everywhere on the trails. He also spotted a few rattlesnakes sunning themselves in the late morning air. Many of the petroglyphs were recognizable as animals or geometric shapes, but others looked a lot like aliens, which made Mick wish he had time for a side trip to Roswell. He looked forward to sharing his impressions and photos with Kateryna.

Back at the motorcycle store, Mick saw the pained look on the face of the mechanic as he parked the bike. Considering what it had been through, the Scrambler was in pretty good condition, but it did have dents and scrapes, and both the front and rear fenders were deranged. The owner offered to do a little bodywork and painting on the frame before crating and shipping the bike back to New York, which Mick agreed to.

Mick mainly slept on the flight back to the city.

CHAPTER D.

*From the **Security and Other Lies** Blog:*

What is the difference between a keylogger and a Trojan? Can I protect my computer against them? BohemianRaptorD

This is a great question, BohemianRaptorD. Although often associated with each other, keyloggers and Trojans are different things. A keylogger or keystroke logger is a piece of software or hardware that records and logs the keys typed on a computer. Think of it as a keyboard 'bug' if you like. They are a great way to spy on someone, as you can find out everything he or she types, from emails, web site addresses, to credit card numbers, passwords, etc.

A Trojan is a piece of software that hides another piece of software. Usually, a Trojan appears to be something useful or benign, while the hidden software is some kind of malware. For example, you could download a piece of software that installs without your knowledge a keylogger on your computer. There was a famous

ALAN B. JOHNSTON

case of fake virus scanning software that
actually installed viruses on the unsuspecting
computer! The Trojan is named after the Trojan
horse of Homer's Iliad - the wooden horse used
to sneak soldiers inside the walls of Troy,
resulting in the destruction of the city by the
Greeks.

The best way to protect against both is to be
careful what software you install. I never
install binaries, which could contain anything.
Instead, I download the source code, inspect it
and check the signature, then compile it myself.
This way, unless there is some very, very clever
programming going on, I know everything that is
happening on my computer.

A hardware keylogger is a device that is
attached to a keyboard of a computer. To
install one requires physical access to your
computer. An attacker could open up your
computer and install the device in minutes. You
need to keep control of your computer to prevent
this. Periodic inspection also helps, as long
as the device is identifiable. For example,
I've read about keyloggers built into firmware
chips. The attacker just replaces an existing
chip with one that looks identical on the
outside but has the keylogger built in. I
suppose you could mark or put a seal on your
chips so you could notice if one has been
swapped out. Another option is to weld or seal
your computer case closed so that an attacker
cannot easily open it up.

Keyloggers and Trojans also tend to go hand-in-
hand with rootkits. A rootkit is software that
hides the fact that your computer has been
compromised. Otherwise, you might discover
right away that your computer was compromised,
and you would get the malware removed or
cleaned, and the compromise would fail.
Rootkits are particularly insidious pieces of
software. Thinking about them sometimes keeps
me up at night...

-> Your question not answered this week? Argue
for your vote on the Shameless Plugging area of
our discussion forum.

CHAPTER E.

Mick O'Malley *is having a hard time distinguishing fact from fiction. (12 comments)*

Mick was back on an airliner just over a week later, but this time no shipped motorcycle was waiting for him. Instead, he stood in what appeared to be the world's longest taxi stand line, which was, fortunately, also seemed to be the world's fastest moving taxi line.

He had spent the week back in Manhattan healing from his adventures in New Mexico. He ate healthy food, exercised, rode his motorcycles, and felt life returning to normal. Still, in the back of his mind, he was on the lookout for what would happen next.

He hadn't found out very much more about Michalovic. He had discovered he was a Serbian national, here on a tourist visa. Michalovic's destination beyond Frankfurt, Germany was unknown. Otherwise, Michalovic didn't seem to exist.

From his window on the plane, Mick had watched Las Vegas appear out of nowhere in the bleak desert. His flight circled to the north and west of the city, in the direction of the Nevada Test Site, used for atmospheric nuclear testing during most of the cold war.

Mick was only out of the jet way for a few seconds before he saw and heard the airport terminal slot machines – strategically placed for those just stopping over or those who didn't get quite enough gambling done on their visit. Despite multiple visits, Mick was always freshly amazed at the efficiency of Las Vegas – the efficiency of separating people from their money.

Much faster than he would have believed, Mick was in a taxi speeding towards his hotel on the strip. Mick was in Vegas for another Internet security conference. This conference was not his favorite, but it always had the best turnout since it was held in Vegas.

Mick was giving a tutorial at the CIO (Chief Information Officer) Expo that was co-located with Mick's security conference. He was lecturing on botnets, a topic that was becoming increasingly of interest to Mick. Up on a small stage in front of a crowd, Mick spoke with his slides projected on an enormous screen behind him. He finished his lecture with a summary:

"... So having covered the history and evolution of botnets, I want to leave you with a few sobering thoughts about their future.

"Botnet code is not written by amateurs, so-called 'script kiddies' – the stereotypical fourteen-year-olds who copy script source code from the Internet and launch attacks. Professionals write botnet code. There is an industry built around botnets: from the generation of new exploits and attacks, managing, or 'herding' of the compromised computers, known as 'zombies', to the collection and transfer of revenue. These companies often have the support and protection of foreign governments.

"The threat of botnets is like nothing else we have ever experienced on the Internet or on our corporate networks. Sophisticated botnets are harnessing the computational power of potentially millions of computers, effectively operating as a supercomputer. Their ability to wreak havoc on the global Internet should not be underestimated. Here are some of the things they could do:

"Denial of service attacks to take out entire networks, countries, or even the root servers of the Internet.

"Surveillance and espionage. Zombie computers organized in a botnet, operating *inside a corporate firewall or inside a government office* spying on you... your own computers turned against you without your knowledge. And it is not just about documents and files. Built-in microphones and cameras can be activated and made to stream information covertly to any part of the globe.

"Weapon of war. We already have documented cases of botnet cyber attacks being used as part of conventional warfare.

"Economic gain. Botnets can be used to manipulate markets, influence trading, and disrupt global supply chain management. They could be used to cause recessions or even depressions.

"A tool of organized crime. Botnets can allow criminals to extend their extortion, racketeering, and judicial influence schemes to a global scale, while completely covering their tracks.

"This might sound alarmist to you, but I assure you that each of these is already happening today, albeit on a limited scale. With sophisticated botnets, the power and destructiveness of these threats is greatly magnified. It is not a question of if these attacks will happen, but when.

"In closing, I hope this presentation has been useful to you. The best way for us to fight botnets is to prevent computers from being compromised. The only way to do this is to utilize better security tools and procedures. While the government has some responsibility, most of the compromised computers are owned by corporations and individuals, and we must take responsibility for them.

"Thank you for your attention!" Mick finished, getting his applause.

Gunter came up from the audience and gave him a big grin. "Nice job, Mick! I was going to ask you a hard question or two but then I decided to go easy on you." They walked out of the room together and off to lunch. "Hey, and I like the shirt." Gunter was once again making fun of Mick's clothes. Mick's fashion was almost invariable. He wore a black shirt, sport coat, dark khakis, and sandals. The black shirt he always wore was either a T-shirt, long sleeve mock turtleneck, or, if he wanted to really dress up, a button down collar. The sandals varied slightly with the season: open toed in the summer and closed in the winter. Under some circumstances, he even wore jeans instead of khakis. Of course, Gunter wasn't exactly a paragon of style, but at least his clothes varied, and sometimes they even matched.

They rode the elevator together and walked out towards the hotel lobby. Using Mick's criteria for evaluating hotels, Vegas strip hotels were the worst. Their lobbies were noisy, crowded, and had absolutely nowhere to sit down except in front of a slot machine or at a gaming table. He had only been in Vegas less than twelve hours, but the incessant noise of the machines was already starting to get to him. They turned and headed for the buffet Gunter had chosen for their lunch.

"So, Gunter, how did you first meet Kat?" Mick asked after they sat down with their first plateful of food.

"I guess I met her two years ago at a visit to F.T.L. She is very sharp, and a useful person to know."

"I see that. She was very helpful in Hiroshima… that's when I first met her," Mick replied as their food arrived, and the conversation paused.

"I know. She asked me a bunch of questions about you, too." he replied, winking. Mick changed the subject by asking about Gunter's latest phonograph restoration.

Gunter was one of Mick's oldest friends, both in age and how long he had known him. Gunter had worked nearly everywhere, with everyone, and had strong opinions on everything. He was in big demand on panels and conferences. He was also famous for misunderstanding questions; he would usually end up answering a different question than the one that was asked, leaving both the questioner and the audience bemused. Mick tried to avoid Gunter's restaurant choices – often he would mix up the names or the types of the food. He also often made the most dreaded suggestion for lunchtime meetings at a conference: 'Let's just eat here in the conference hotel.'

"Mick, I almost forgot... I've got a consulting job for you," Gunter began. Mick looked up and Gunter continued. "It is with JCN, Inc. They are looking for a consultant to help them analyze the security of their entire service operation. I guess it is from the new CTO they hired last month. He wants a complete audit: procedures, operations, all the way down to protocols and servers. You are the perfect man for the job!"

"Thanks for thinking of me Gunter – I really appreciate it! I'm pretty busy with a job right now, but I should have time around, say, the second half of December to start on it," Mick said.

"Hmm. I think they want someone to start right away. I told 'em I'd need a day or two to see if I could do it or recommend someone else. You wouldn't walk away from JCN, would you?" he asked.

"Of course I don't *want* to turn it down. It sounds like a great gig, but I also have to finish what I started. And my current contract is more involved than I would have anticipated. If they need someone right now, I'll have to pass," he concluded.

"Really, Mick? What if I finish that other job for you?"

"No, I'm not comfortable with that. I just can't take it... but thanks again for thinking of me."

Gunter looked as if he were going to argue more but then changed his mind. A few minutes later, Mick raised the issue that had been consuming his waking hours.

"Gunter, you've studied steganography, right?" Mick asked, remembering his botnet puzzle.

"Sure, I once broke a cipher that used it – boy was that tough!"

"Tell me about it."

"Well, I was called in to help build a case against a particularly clever drug dealer. The prosecutor had all these emails that the dealer had sent to others in the cartel, but couldn't find any messages in them. I eventually found hidden messages in the emails. What's your interest?" he asked.

"Might have a case of it, myself. I have all kinds of messages, but I can't find anything hidden."

"Well, you just have to go through every millimeter of every message. Look for anything out of place, strange, or odd. You'll find it if it's there."

"Right... thanks," he replied. Mick felt a tingle, and answered his mobile. It was Vince. "Gunter, could you watch my backpack?" he whispered.

"Sure thing," was the reply. Mick walked towards the exit, searching for a bit of quiet so he could answer Vince's questions.

Mick spent the rest of the afternoon in his hotel room finishing up a progress report for LeydenTech.

That evening was the social event for the conference, typically held the night before the conference started. Mick had been following the travels and arrivals of his friends in his social network. In the ballroom (named for its size, not for being fancy), Mick met up in person with Lars, Liz, Gunter, and Kateryna. They stood around a table, drinking and eating appetizers. It always amazed Mick how different the sexes reacted to dressing for these kinds of events. While the women would dress up, the men would dress down – if that were even possible. His own attire didn't change. Rightly or wrongly, Mick felt his clothes blended in with a range of formality.

Kateryna had seemingly joined their little group these days. The last to join them was Liz a year ago, and Mick recalled it took a while for her to be included by default in their plans and discussion. Then again, Kateryna wasn't completely new, as Gunter had known her for a few years. But, Gunter knew everyone in the industry, so that didn't count for too much. Mick was pleased about it, but at the same time it made him feel uneasy. He deliberately toned down his greeting to her, just nodding and shaking hands. She made no reference to their recent email exchanges, and he took her lead, doing the same. He wondered if they were hiding their relationship, whatever it might be, or if they were just being private. He was unsure, and this made him uneasy. Mick felt that he was heading into unknown territory.

"I just love Vegas!" Lars expounded.

"I can't believe you've never been here!" Gunter said to Kateryna. Her posting of this had generated a huge number of comments on their social network.

"Yep. I can't wait to see everything, although I'm only here until Wednesday," Kateryna offered.

"OK, for Kat's sake, everyone – quick – say your favorite thing about Vegas?" Lars began, looking at Mick to start.

"Ferraris parked in front of casinos," Mick began.

"Free drinks while you play," Gunter added.

"Really?" Kateryna asked and everyone nodded.

"Interesting conversations with strangers," Lars added. He looked at Liz. She paused for a moment.

"Historical and architectural accuracy," she contributed dryly.

"OK, OK, we all know how much you like Vegas.

Now, say your least favorite things about Vegas – quickly!" Lars added.

"Bathroom attendants!" Mick contributed.

"Yuck!" from Lars.

"Loosing my retirement in the slots," from Gunter. Everyone looked at him in surprise. "Not really," he added.

"Crazy skunk-hairdo dancing lady!" from Lars.

Kateryna opened her mouth but Mick preempted her, saying "Don't ask!"

"All the unhealthy behavior: everyone smoking, drinking too much, overeating –" from Liz.

"Yeah, yeah..." Lars interrupted. "So, Kat, we'll ask you on Wednesday to add to our list, OK?"

Soon, the room was clearing out as the food dwindled and the bar closed. Miles walked up to the group and made straight for Mick.

"So *Mike*, have you saved the Internet again lately?" he asked sneering. Mick just smiled back.

"Haven't had to – no one has implemented any of your security plans, lately," he replied.

"Well, I just wanted to say how much I agreed with your comments on open source security. Very brave of you." Gunter stepped between them.

"Miles, why don't you go over there – I think I see a skirt you haven't chased yet," Gunter suggested. Miles just smiled and sauntered away, seemingly in the direction of the woman.

Mick's stomach turned; he hadn't thought about his key compromise in days, but the bad feelings came back with Miles' reminder. He wondered when it would end, then answered his own question – it would end when he figured out who did this to him. He looked up from his drink and was surprised to see only Kateryna with him.

Did the others just silently wander off? How long ago? Am I missing time again? Where is Mulder when I need him?

"Well, I'm going exploring now," he said.

"Mind if I tag along? I'd love to see your favorite places here," she asked.

"Sure… that sounds great. I'll show you some good places." The thought of exploring with Kateryna got him instantly out of his bad mood. He thought through his favorites, scratched a few off the list for obvious reasons, and tried to think which of the remaining places Kateryna would most enjoy. "Shall we?"

They set off walking together.

"You like Vegas, don't you?" she asked.

"I guess I do," he replied. "It is so different. So tacky, yet so surprising."

They went down to the lobby together where Mick hailed a cab from a seemingly inexhaustible supply. As the cab stopped, Mick opened the door for Kateryna. She thanked him and sat down. He went to close the door and walk to the other side, but Kateryna slid over in the seat to make room for him. Mick quickly looked away; Kateryna was wearing a grey knit dress that was quite short… He recovered himself and climbed into the cab, telling the driver to take them to Caesar's. Mick really liked Kateryna's outfit, and her dark hair, southwestern style jewelry, and black boots completed the look.

"Do you gamble?" she asked as the cab waited at a traffic light.

"Hell no! I know way too much about probability. And if you actually try to apply probability theory to the gaming, you get thrown out!" he explained. Seeing her puzzled look, he continued, "You know, card counting. Tried it once just to verify it works."

"And does it?"

"Yep, but you have to have a lot of patience. I wonder if I'm still banned in Atlantic City?" he mused.

"Right, right. So what's so special about Caesar's?"

Kateryna asked as they pulled up in front. "Besides the obvious," she added, looking at the enormous fake columns and fountains.

"You'll see soon enough," he replied.

They climbed out into the evening, enjoying the warmth of the desert. Mick took off his jacket and slung it over his shoulder and they walked into the hotel together. They walked past the ridiculous statues, silly decorations, and ever-present slots and tables. They veered to the right and went into an area with shops.

"Are we going shopping?" Kateryna asked.

"Patience," Mick replied. They turned a corner and Mick stopped. Kateryna did the same as they both looked at the six meter tall statue of a man in front of them.

"Wow!" Kateryna said. "I've seen Michelangelo's before, but this is amazing."

"Yep, a full size copy of David, even carved out the same kind of marble." They both stood and stared for a few minutes, then slowly walked around the perimeter to get a side view, then back view. A few people stopped for a look, but most just passed by obliviously.

"Even in this setting..." Kateryna began, then paused. "Thanks for sharing that," Kateryna said when they wandered off a few minutes later. "That was so unexpected."

"You're welcome. I've seen the original, and you can't even get near it due to the crowds," he offered before continuing. "I'm used to wandering around Vegas alone, so this is a different experience for me, but a nice one."

"Don't you hang out with Lars here?" she asked. Mick looked at her, and she quickly understood. "No, I guess not."

They left the casino and walked along an outdoor path. "So, did you grow up in Romania?" Mick asked.

"I did, until I was fifteen. It was really, really different. It's hard to explain. I did well at school, in maths and science, of course, and was even in the Union of Communist Youth, would you believe?"

"Was that similar to the Komsomol in Russia?"

"Yes, exactly," she replied, surprised.

"Were your parents party members?"

"No, they weren't. I didn't want to join but I was approached by my favorite teacher when I was thirteen. She told me I could go far if I joined and applied myself. I thought my parents would try to talk me out of it, but they didn't. But, I never really got into it, the whole class struggle, thing – it never made any sense to me, none of it. Perhaps that were true of everyone, and everyone was also just playing along, giving the right answers – I don't know. It might have rubbed off on me a little; these days I find progressive politics much more appealing than the mainstream. When Ceaușescu was overthrown, my parents suddenly had an opportunity to leave, and they jumped at the chance, even though they had to leave all of their money and possessions behind."

"Wow! That's hard to imagine."

"Yes, I had hoped we would come to America, but we went to Canada instead. I wanted to go to Toronto, but we went to Montreal. So then I had two foreign languages to learn..."

"Well, you've learned one of them well, at least," Mick replied. She wrinkled her nose.

"I don't think so. I get by, but I often feel frustrated that I don't have the exact word I want. I would love to be able to talk the way you do."

"The way I do? Really? Do you mean my accent, or my expression?" It was Mick's turn to be surprised.

"Both, but especially your expressions. You know, sometimes I look up words you use later to see their full meaning."

"Really? You don't have to do that. You can just ask me."

"I know, but I like to look them up myself – just to make sure you used them correctly!"

Mick pretended to gasp and Kateryna smiled. They had stopped at the edge of a large body of water, with a huge casino hotel glowing in the distance. A number of others were also standing around.

"The Bellagio," Mick indicated with a nod of his head, then glanced at his mobile.

"You grew up in London, right?" Kateryna asked.

"Right, in Kilburn. I was born there and lived there until I was ten. My parents were born in Ireland, so we lived in a kind of Irish ghetto – it was fun! I wandered the city by myself on buses and the Tube when I was about eight years old. Can you imagine that today?"

"No, no one does that today."

"My niece, Sam, is ten and lives in Boston, but it will be quite a few years before she can even walk around the block in her neighborhood. Maybe my sister will let her ride the subway when she is twelve or thirteen." Mick paused, waiting for what would happen next.

With a loud pop and an incredibly high shot of water, the fountain started its music show. Kateryna jumped at the sound, then laughed and put her hand on her chest. She watched, mesmerized, as the illuminated jets danced across the water, waving and shaking. Mick didn't recognize the song, but it was definitely a country and western, which didn't thrill him. He noticed Kateryna tapping her toe and moving her hips to the music. When the chorus started, he noticed her singing along. He stared at her lips as she sang the lyrics "... this kiss, this kiss..." Smiling, Mick joined in singing on the second verse (it was a country and western song after all, and hence had copious repetition). Kateryna noticed, smiled back and sang along a little louder. Some Koreans standing nearby also joined in, apparently thinking this was an American custom. By the end, the whole group around them was singing along as the water played and popped. When the song ended, Kateryna applauded enthusiastically, and Mick joined her.

"Wow! That was amazing! And I love that song!" Kateryna began, turning from the fountain to Mick.

"You listen to country and western music?" Mick asked.

"Every now and then... alright, I love it, and Faith Hill is one of my favorites. You don't have to tell everyone, do you?" she asked.

"Your secret is safe with me, Ms. Petrescu!" Mick replied. "The fountain really is beautiful, isn't it?"

"Oh, yes. I'd seen videos, but it is so much better in person. And I didn't expect the sound – the pops sound like fireworks. You were expecting it to start, weren't you?"

"Yep, the shows are every fifteen minutes, so if we wait, we can watch another one."

"Yes, let's do that."

"You know, the first time I saw this fountain, it played one of my favorite songs, too."

"Which was?"

" 'Con Te Partiro' with Andrea Bocelli... I like all kinds of music, but I'm a big opera fan."

"I see."

"But I do like Shania Twain," Mick offered.

"Her music?" Kateryna asked, mostly suppressing a grin.

"No, not really... her videos."

They passed the time and watched another performance of the fountain. This time, it was a Broadway musical number, but the fountain was still fascinating. They stayed outside, watching, talking, and occasionally singing along for the next two hours before they set off walking again.

"Hey, we can go to the top of la Tour Eiffel!" Mick nearly shouted. Kateryna frowned at him.

"I already have – the real one," she replied.

"Well, so have I, but don't be a spoilsport. It would be so romantic!" he joked, then was surprised when he saw Kateryna's cheeks color.

Did she just blush?

For the first time, Mick began to think that perhaps this little... whatever it was, perhaps wasn't only on his side.

Instead, they continued walking, not noticing Jupiter's azimuth or the slow movement of the moon across the sky.

It was after four in the morning when they returned to the hotel. They paused near the elevators to say good night. Mick had a feeling that something had changed tonight. He decided to take a chance.

"Coffee? At the bar?" he asked. Kateryna considered it for a moment then smiled.

"OK, sure."

They sat down at the bar, which was almost entirely deserted at this hour and ordered their drinks. The bartender left them alone.

"It really has been a great evening," Mick began. Kateryna nodded and sipped her latte. "I can't tell you how much I enjoy spending time with you." Mick summoned his courage. "Kat, I'm attracted to you. You are such an amazing woman..." he trailed off. Mick waited a moment before he looked up into her eyes. She met his eyes for a moment, then leaned in and gave him a short kiss on the cheek. Mick had closed his eyes, and when he opened them a moment later, he was surprised to see an empty chair beside him – Kateryna had gone. He spotted her turning the corner, then she was out of sight. Confused, he replayed the last few minutes in his mind.

Am I supposed to chase after her or something?

Instead, he took another sip of his espresso, deciding that she wasn't the type to play those sort of games.

Back in his room a few minutes later, Mick had trouble sleeping, so he wrote some code until he fell asleep.

CHAPTER F.

*From the **Security and Other Lies** Blog:*

What is a 'rogue access point'? Is wireless
Internet access secure? Raptorz_8_mebrain

Wireless Internet access security is a very
important topic, and I'm glad you brought it up,
Raptorz_8_mebrain.

An 'access point' or AP, is a generic term for a
radio or wireless base station – a router with
an antenna and a wired connection to the
Internet or other network. It allows computers
to wirelessly access the Internet. It is also
an excellent place for someone to launch an
attack on a wireless device. Here's how it
works.

An attacker can create a fake or 'rogue' access
point or base station, say on his or her
computer, then can set up along the highway, or
in a car in a parking lot or street, or at a
coffee shop. When you turn on your wireless
device or move into range, your device connects
to the rogue access point instead of the real

one. The attacker is now in a perfect position to be a 'man in the middle' - an uninvited third party to your Internet activity. The attacker can, for example, listen in to your calls, monitor your data, read your mail, and potentially steal your passwords, bank account information, or credit card numbers.

Fortunately, there is something you can do. Firstly, if your Internet traffic is encrypted, then you are most likely OK. Otherwise, you can do your own encryption and authentication across the wireless link until you reach a part of the Internet that you think is secure. This is what I do. All my wireless access is tunneled back to a server that I trust (because I run it!). Only after I have established an authenticated and encrypted link from my computer back to my server will I use a wireless Internet connection. This way, if the AP goes rogue, there is nothing it can do except end my session. Sometimes this is known as a Virtual Private Network or VPN, and some companies require employees to use this when they connect outside the office.

So, I'd say that it is possible to securely access the Internet wirelessly, but you can't rely on your mobile device or service provider to provide that security - you or your company will have to do it yourself.

Also, note that I use the same thing for wired Internet access when I travel. I won't trust a network in a hotel or other location, so I establish the same secure tunnel and then encrypt all my traffic.

-> Your question not answered this week? Argue for your vote on the Shameless Plugging area of our discussion forum.

CHAPTER 1Ø.

Mick O'Malley - *step by step, little by little. (2 comments)*

Mick managed to get through the next day at the conference without dozing off. When Liz asked about his evening, he just said he wandered around and ended up at the Bellagio fountain.

He read a mail from Sam:

```
Cher Oncle Alec,

When are you coming to Boston??  I can't wait...
I hope it is on a Saturday, and when I don't
have orchestra practice.

I have a question for you, but only if you have
time...  (Mom made me write that!)

Are there any places in Manhattan that we could
visit and learn more about the 'Manhattan
Project'?  Seems like there should be.  I know
it will be a while before I can visit Hiroshima
and Los Alamos like you (and I'm going to visit
Nagasaki as well - I can't believe you skipped
it!!) but we can visit some places next time I'm
there, right?
```

```
Bye for now...

Sam

P.S.  Heard any good FUD lately? :)

-----BEGIN PGP SIGNATURE------
R5SQCflLH42orXO+prsbv3gNSwbkQV
Ybe7dbEfDYJcjXSyaQ1MfQh5axo+0K
27ZhCD/Ajb0qXGPIJ/x+CvCDur0Mcu
zuy50PaO2bM00GOSqHeikhbmunENha
x+hlyD+kpaLvipvR479eXHD3n29LiC
------END PGP SIGNATURE-------
```

It was a while before Mick had stopped laughing and smiling. He wondered how girls learnt to do this – to be so sweet, so cute, and so funny...

Mick sat in on a few sessions during the conference. He always liked to hear what questions people in the audience asked and how they reacted to the presentations; it was useful for keeping a pulse on the state of his industry.

During the last break of the day, he was cornered by an overweight man wearing a cheap suit.

"Mick O'Malley? I'm Josh Winters, from UBK."

"Hello Josh," Mick replied.

"I caught your presentation the other day on botnets. Very interesting, very informative..."

"Thanks..."

"I was wondering if you could perhaps give us seminar for us on the topic... with some pointers on defending against them?" he asked.

"Ah, don't you already run IT and security for the U.S. Government?"

"Yes, we do!"

"And you don't already have a botnet denial of service attack strategy?"

"Of course we do... but it could always use some... updating."

Mick was tiring of the conversation, and he remembered that he was missing a panel discussion involving Liz.

"Sounds great... why don't you send me a fax and we can arrange it... I'm in the phone book," he replied, trying to get rid of him. Mick wished he could see the man's face upon realizing that Mick was not in any phone books, nor did he have a facsimile number.

He cursed himself for forgetting about the session; Liz had been nervous about it for days. He hoped she hadn't noticed his absence in the audience.

"... and while I don't want to contradict my colleague, Miss Clayton, I must share with you my views." Ted Zephyr spoke at the podium, and proceeded to contradict Liz's thesis and her conclusions. Mick could see that Liz, sitting at the panel table, was fuming inside, although she covered it up pretty well; it was only because he had observed her many times under pressure that he could read the little telltale signs such as a tapping of her toe or brushing a non-existent lock of hair behind her ear.

The session was soon over. Ted had made a few weak points that Liz successfully countered. Mick was disappointed that he had missed nearly all of Liz's presentation, but had heard quite enough of the Zephyr. When Mick approached the podium, he found Liz with Gunter and Lars, discussing the presentation while the Zephyr joked with a friend just out of earshot. When Liz saw Mick, her face lit up.

"Mick, what did you think?" she asked. "I think it went badly..."

"No, you did fine," he replied.

"Really? Do you think so?" she asked, a smile broadening on her face. Mick nodded in reply, but was distracted watching Kateryna entering the back of the room. Liz noticed as well, and her smile faded and went away completely as she turned away. She started shutting down her computer.

That evening, he had dinner with Lars and Gunter only; Mick suspected Liz and Kateryna were off somewhere together, a thought that unsettled him. Mick distracted himself by listening to Lars talk about the presentations he attended during the day.

"… and that last presentation, the one given by the Spaniard. I didn't get it at all. He kept talking about 'connecting the goats'. What the hell does that mean?" Lars asked, confused. Mick burst out laughing.

"He was saying 'connecting the dots' you ponce! Why would you think he was talking about goats?" Mick replied.

"I don't know… I thought it must have been some sort of goat herding metaphor," Lars replied. "So, anyway, a little later, I was talking to these two amazing girls from some 'New' state… New Hampshire, New Jersey, I don't know."

"New York, maybe?" Mick asked.

"Could be," Lars replied, not comprehending Mick's point. "Anyway, they asked what I did for a living. I explained briefly, and you know what they said?"

"What?"

"They said 'Bull! Tell us what you really do!'"

"So what did you tell them?" Gunter asked.

"Well, I made something up, of course. I told them I was a musician in a band called 'Permanent Hardness' and that we were about to go on a tour of Kazakhstan, Turkmenistan, and possibly Uzbekistan!" Lars paused until Mick and Gunter stopped laughing. "Yep, it was a good night!"

Liz and Kateryna joined them in the booth. Kateryna asked what they were laughing at, but Mick just shook his head. They ordered coffee and swapped more respectable stories for a while. Once again, everyone else got up and left, leaving Mick and Kateryna together, still talking.

Did they do that deliberately?

Kateryna seemed hesitant to start the conversation, and began with some small talk.

"Have you done all your must-do things here in Vegas, yet?" she asked.

"Not quite, but I still have tomorrow night," he replied.

"That was so much fun the other night – thanks for showing me your places."

"My pleasure. I really enjoyed it, too. And thanks for having your anti-spam guys look over the Zed dot Kicker code, too. Really helpful."

"Not at all, Mick. It has been helpful to me too," she replied. "Any progress?" Mick instinctively glanced around, quickly deciding this wasn't the place. He inclined his head towards the door, and Kateryna got the message, nodded and stood up.

Once outside, they wound their way through the casino lobby and out to the street. There was some open space to the next casino, and they sauntered along in the moonlight.

"I am making progress, but I'm kind of stumped finding the botnet control messages," he began, keeping his voice low so they wouldn't be overheard, even by the Korean tourists nearby.

"That's assuming there are messages," Kateryna pointed out.

"I know, but I really believe they are there. I just haven't figured out the steganography yet. But I will, rest assured."

"I don't doubt it," she replied.

Mick spotted a sign outside the casino they were approaching, which gave him an idea.

"Do you like rides?" he asked.

"You mean roller coasters? Or like riding on a

motorcycle?"

"Kind of like roller coasters. I think there's a 3D simulator in here that I've heard is pretty cool. You game?"

"Game? I think I understand what you are asking, but why use this word? Does it mean play a game?"

"Hmmm. I'm not sure, actually. I think more likely it refers to game as in hunting rather than in playing a game," Mick reached for the mobile in his pocket but Kateryna put out her hand and stopped him, touching his arm lightly. Despite his sports coat, his skin seemed to burn.

"No need... but you can look it up later, if you want."

"You know me pretty well, don't you?" Mick replied, smiling. Kateryna smiled back but didn't look him in the eye. "So are you up for it, then?"

"Sure, why not?" she replied.

A few minutes later, Mick had purchased their tickets and they were in a not-too-long line for the ride. There were mostly couples in the line.

Afterwards, they walked out of the ride still wearing their 3D glasses. Kateryna went to remove hers, but Mick stopped her saying, "Look at my eyes – don't they look strange?" She peered at him.

"You are right. Why is that?"

"The 3D glasses use light polarizing filters – opposite polarization on each eye. This is the wave nature of light, as opposed to the particle nature that is shown in diffraction..." he paused, noticing that her attention was wandering. "So, when you look at my eyes, you are looking through your lens, then my lens. Close one eye now and look." Kateryna winked one eye shut as Mick did the same.

"Wow! I only see one of your eyes – the opposite one... Ah, I get it! The lenses with cross polarization block the light... that's why one of your eyes is totally dark." Mick nodded his assent.

"Here," he said holding out his hand. Kateryna handed him her glasses and he took off his own and put them together, then flipped one upside down and did the same. Kateryna nodded. Mick handed hers back, but she shook her head. He kept his on upside down. "I kind of like the look," Mick commented but could not keep a straight face for long. But he kept the glasses on as they walked.

"And did you enjoy the ride?" he asked.

"Truthfully, I had my eyes shut for most of it!" she replied. Mick laughed. "I guess I will amend my statement to say that I really don't like rides. But the 3D was neat when things weren't moving." Mick shook his head.

"So how are things at F.T.L. these days?" he asked a few minutes later.

"Oh, OK. I'm just having some problems with my boss these days. I wish I could just let things go, but when he does stupid things, I have to call him on it," she replied, running her hand through her hair.

"Glad I don't have a boss..."

"Ha, ha. I'm just glad to be out of the office for a few days so I can cool down," she replied.

They walked in the direction of the hotel but talked very little on the way back. Mick wondered how he could feel so comfortable both talking to this woman, and also just being with her in silence.

Kateryna suddenly stopped and took his hand.

"Mick, listen... I have to tell you something," she began. Mick stared at her intently. "I really like you, too. It's just... I'm married."

"You're what?"

"I'm married..." Frowning, Mick stole a glance at her ring finger, which she noticed. "I know, I don't wear a wedding ring. That actually isn't uncommon in Europe. I'm sorry I didn't tell you. I meant to a few times... I'm really, really sorry Mick." Mick moved his hand away from hers.

Is this really happening to me?

"So tell me about your husband," he asked, ignoring the hole he felt inside.

"His name is Milos. We met at university in Quebec. We've been married five years. I was so young when I got married..."

"I see," was all Mick could get out. His stomach hurt.

"Mick, I'm so sorry... I didn't mean to mislead you like this. I still want us to be friends," she continued, but Mick was hardly paying attention.

"I think we should head back to the hotel," Mick said and set off walking. The rest of the walk to the hotel was also in silence, but a different kind of silence. Mick went up to his room without saying goodnight.

Mick spent the next morning catching up on some writing, both mails and his blog. He changed all his passwords to:

```
theFuture1sntEv3nlyDistd
```

His day at the conference passed quickly without anything exceptional happening.

That evening, it being Vegas, Mick finally gave into temptation. Perhaps he had been thinking about it to try to distract his thoughts from his beautiful married colleague. Perhaps it had just been building in him since his arrival.

Everyone does this in Vegas...

This wasn't Mick's first time, so he knew where he wanted to go and gave directions to his cab driver.

He alighted the cab, stretched his legs, then entered the building, a big smile spreading across his face. It had been a long time since Mick had seen so many vintage and antique motorcycles in one place! Vegas hosted one of the largest vintage motorcycles auctions each year, and as a result there were a number of amazing dealers in town. This one, on the north side of town, was his favorite, specializing in Italian and Japanese bikes. Mick passed a few hours, filled his mobile with photos, and generally escaped from reality. He left without buying another bike, which also made him happy.

CHAPTER 11.

*From the **Security and Other Lies** Blog:*

How hard is it for someone to track my mobile phone? What can I do to prevent it? Raptorwhisperer

Raptorwhisperer, the answer to your question depends on who you mean by 'someone'. If you mean the average person, then it is difficult for them to track your mobile device, unless they manage to install some malware on it, or you accidentally leak geographic information. Governments, however, are a different story.

Many phones and mobile devices are aware of their location, either through built-in GPS radios, by triangulating mobile base station towers, or a combination of these two methods. Location tracking spyware could report this location every time you turn on your phone and at regular intervals – you would not have to actually make calls or use the phone.

Some phones also tag your geo-coordinates on every photo taken. When you post or share or email that photo, you are giving out the exact location where it was taken! You can disable this with geolocation privacy settings, but this often isn't easy to do. Also, if your application isn't open source and you haven't inspected the source code, you don't actually know what it is doing with the location information known to your phone. One approach to combat this is to use an old phone that does not have GPS or other location capabilities. If the phone doesn't know your location, it can't share it with anyone!

Now, if by someone, you mean a service provider or government, then the answer is completely different - for them, it is trivial to track your location. In addition, they can identify you using two pieces of information that your mobile device shares with mobile base stations as soon as it turns on: your subscriber identity and your phone serial number. I'll explain these in terms of GSM (Global System for Mobile communications) mobile technology, but other technologies will have an equivalent, although the name will be different.

The Subscriber Identity Module or SIM is a tiny, fingernail-sized chip plugged into your phone that contains the private key that identifies your user account on the mobile network. When you activate a phone or establish your phone service, you are creating your SIM identity. Your mobile phone number is associated with this SIM identity. (Mine isn't because I only use my mobile device for Internet access and do my calling with Voice over IP or VoIP services, but that is a different topic.) If you remove the SIM from your phone and put it in another phone, that phone will ring when someone dials your number. If you cancel your service or don't pay your bill, your SIM identity is disabled, and you won't be able to place or receive calls or use an Internet connection associated with the account.

The other piece of information is the phone's serial number, known as the IMEI number – the

International Mobile Equipment Identity number.
This number identifies the manufacturer, model,
and the individual device. This is how your
service provider knows what kind of phone you
have, and can provide some phone-specific
features. This serial number is also used to
identify stolen phones. As a result, there are
laws in many countries against changing the
serial number on a mobile phone.

So from all this, you might conclude that there
is no way to use mobile services with any sort
of privacy or anonymity. However, there are
some approaches you can use. One way is to use
a prepaid mobile phone. If you pay cash and
provide only minimal information to activate the
account, there is very little to associate your
identity with the phone or the phone number.
However, if someone knows or learns your SIM or
IMSE identity, then you can be tracked. Of
course, governments and operators can easily
work backwards if they know the phone number to
get your SIM and IMSE identity and hence
discover your location if the phone is turned
on. I have heard of some approaches that use
forwarding between multiple accounts in
different jurisdictions (e.g. countries) to make
this kind of tracking more difficult.

I would strongly advise you to be careful about
your mobile device usage, and especially with
any geolocation information your mobile device
might share.

-> Your question not answered this week? Argue
for your vote on the Shameless Plugging area of
our discussion forum.

CHAPTER 12.

Mick O'Malley hopes it is true that what happens in Vegas stays in Vegas. (3 comments)

Mick didn't stay for the entire conference in Las Vegas. After a few days, he needed a break from the incessant noise and frantic activity. And, he needed to get away from Kateryna. He was also keen to get back to his LeydenTech work, and he could only do that at his apartment with the hardware encryption device Vince had lent him.

The weather had turned cooler back in Manhattan, and on cloudy days, Mick had to wear his cool weather riding gear, including thermal gloves and leather pants and jacket. He had successfully fixed a misfire in his Ducati 75Ø Imola Desmo by replacing a spark plug lead that was apparently arcing on the frame.

Mick received an email from Kateryna:

```
Mick,

I'm so sorry about how I handled things.   I
really  never  meant  to  mislead  or  hurt  you.
```

```
Please don't let this ruin our friendship.

How    are    things    going    with    your    spambot
investigation?  Let me know if I can help in any
way at all.

Regards,

Kat

------BEGIN PGP SIGNATURE-----
nxSX5cJ38DiPub5shIPfVwJWSnvz1l
JluSV24FBgNpN3anxOO/g/bMrZlqfV
bs/p2cbOPmr0uiJ4D+icXs3CCGotFc
t1utzLUaZ2NAcudGPZDZeTGODesOWH
KgEjnEQEHfQ7TbqaE4mnCocibuvkhL
------END PGP SIGNATURE-------
```

When he finished reading it, he realized that he had
been holding his breath. He tried to feel angry with her,
but in this case he found he could not. At the same time,
he detested dishonesty, and could never deal with anyone
who wasn't truthful.

Why do I feel this way about her?

He wrote back to her immediately saying he wasn't
angry, which was mostly true, trying to put her mind at
ease. He promised to keep her abreast of his investigation.
He rationalized his response, telling himself that he might
still need her help and expertise on the botnet
investigation.

The coming Wednesday was Mick's favorite holiday of
the year: Halloween. Mick didn't grow up with this
holiday in London, but embraced it fully in New York. As
a kid he would plan his costumes for months. Later at
Columbia University, he used to visit a graveyard with a
few friends and tell ghost stories. He had more than one
difficult-to-explain event occur during these adventures.
This year he had picked out an isolated cemetery near
Newburgh, NY to visit. He planned to spend the October
afternoon at the local historical society library researching
the cemetery and those buried there, then hang out until

after midnight before riding home. During Halloween, he
always did frequent posts to his social network, and his
friends looked forward to experiencing it with him.

On All Hallow's Eve, Mick had just returned from a
short test ride on his 1993 Ducati Monster 9ØØ (a fiercely
named superbike) when he received an alert of a zero day
spreading through the Internet. Mick decided to delay
leaving while he read up on it, and the more he read, the
more interested he became. According to early reports, the
attack was hitting mail servers used to send and receive
email on the Internet. This particular attack seemed to
ignore end user's computers but instead went for the mail
infrastructure: the servers that provided service for large
groups of people. Crashing a server that provided service
to thousands of users had a much larger impact than just
going after a single user's computers.

Mick hardly noticed the passing of time as he read
more and more accounts. His own mail server seemed
unaffected. He jumped when his secure telephone alerted
– it was Lars.

"Hey! What do you think about the mail server
attack?" Lars began.

"Well, it looks like there might be some new scripts out
there that we aren't aware of."

"Mick, this isn't a script. My mail server just got hit. I
still haven't been able to regain control over the server,"
Lars explained.

"What do you mean? Cleaning and rebooting didn't
work?" Mick asked, using a term from the very early days
of computing, originating from the expression 'pull
yourself up by your bootstraps'. Early computers had only
a tiny amount of permanent program storage, known today
as firmware – the name indicating that it is somewhere
between hardware and software. As a result, when first
powered on, a user had to manually enter a short bootstrap

program that would instruct the computer to load a longer program from a tape drive or punched cards.

"No, and reinstalling the OS didn't. I tried reformatting, too. Have you read of anyone else recovering their system yet?" Lars asked. Mick thought hard, then answered.

"No... I haven't. That is very strange."

How could reinstalling the operating system not work?

"Mick, I think this attack is rewriting the firmware," Lars said.

"Is that really feasible? I know people have talked about it in theory, but I've never heard of anyone actually doing it."

"I think this is it. Would you keep searching and monitoring this? I want to know right away if anyone else does a successful cleaning. I'm going to put hardware monitors on my server and try to figure out what is happening." Lars had computers that were specially modified so he could control and slow down the system clock. A clock on a computer does not tell the time – instead, it acts more like a metronome, and provides regular 'ticks' at a particular frequency. The clock regulates and synchronizes everything a computer does. Engineers continually increase the speed or frequency of computer clocks to speed up processing. Gamers even experiment with 'over clocking' their computers – risking a complete meltdown of their computer motherboards just to make a game run faster.

Lars's setup did the reverse: slowed down the clock so he could observe, effectively in slow motion, what was happening on the computer. If anyone could figure this out, Mick was sure Lars would. He hung up a few minutes later.

So much for my Halloween plans...

Mick let his friends on his social network know so they wouldn't wonder why he wasn't sharing his nocturnal adventures with them.

He barely had time to get back to reading when his video screens lit up. It was Kateryna. He stared at his reflection for a moment before answering.

"Hey Kat... this is a surprise!" he began.

"Mick, sorry to interrupt your holiday but – hey, I like the jacket," she paused. Mick had not taken off his leather riding jacket, although he was still wearing (what else?) a black T-shirt underneath.

"No worries. What's up? You following this mail server attack?"

"Yes I am, and it's what I want to talk to you about."

"Go."

"OK, our guys have been looking at it for about five hours now. A customer shared it before it was even public – can't say who, of course. Well, one of our guys, Martin, a young kid – I mean really young – it is scary to think of him driving, that's how young he seems... Anyway, Martin had a hunch after looking at the code, and the hunch played out. He compared the Zed dot Kicker code to this code, and it has very, very strong similarities." Mick felt a tingling all over his body. Now he had a moment to study her, he could see that Kateryna looked a little agitated.

"Shut up!" he shouted.

"Pardon me?" she asked, puzzled.

"Sorry – I think I'm spending too much time with ten-year-old girls. I just meant 'Wow!'"

"Mick, I know your other job is confidential, but we need to share this. Others need to know that someone has written a sophisticated program that is being used to launch a whole bunch of different attacks, and all of them so far are zero days. I know this has happened in the past with simple scripts. But this is new code – good code – advanced stuff. What do we do? Martin and I can't tell anyone without your say so, and you probably can't say anything without your client's permission." Kateryna paused while Mick thought hard.

"Can you prove the attacks are from the same source?"

"Prove it?" Kateryna thought hard, then replied, "I'd say no. We can't prove it yet. But it is extremely probable."

"OK, then keep working on it. Your corporate handlers probably wouldn't let you announce without irrefutable proof anyway, so let's use this time to come up with a plan. Just make sure Martin doesn't leak this or we are both compromised." Kateryna nodded. She knew exactly what Mick meant: the sharing of this type of information through informal channels, although common, was right on the edge ethically. It wouldn't be hard for someone to misinterpret or paint a different picture of everyone's motivation – especially in light of the forged email to Internet Security World. "Kat, thanks a bunch for letting me know!"

"My pleasure, Mick." Kateryna smiled weakly back at him. Mick couldn't resist smiling back which made her smile grow.

"OK, OK, I need to get back to work..." he replied.

Mick finished up with Kat and slumped in his chair. He needed to clear his head and figure out what to do.

He could release the details of his own mail server compromise to F.T.L. However, the linkage was not quite strong enough – the best information and data he had on Zed.Kicker came from LeydenTech, which he couldn't release without approval.

The whole situation suffered from non-transitivity, Mick decided. The 'Carbon' compromise was strongly coupled to LeydenTech's. And LeydenTech's was strongly coupled to the mail server discovered by F.T.L. Putting all three together made a very strong case for a new and dangerous set of programs. However, he could not strongly couple the 'Carbon' and F.T.L. compromises, without LeydenTech's. This meant only one thing: he had to have a discussion with Vince, and share a few more details and see if he would agree to release some details of their attack. It was a conversation he did not look forward to.

He spoke to Lars a few hours later.

"So, it is definitely rewriting the firmware," Lars began. He looked tired, as if he had stayed up all night, which he had. "I observed it on my slow clocked machine. I've figured out a way to restore the system, and I've brought mine back up."

"That's good. Did you share the info?"

"Didn't have to… a guy named Jasinski beat me to it. His solution was a little longer than mine, and not as elegant, but it will do the job."

"Sorry about that," Mick replied.

"I'm not worried. I think I may try to get to know him – he must be pretty good to have figured it out so quickly. There is a patch uploaded too, so this one is all over, bar the shouting."

"What do you think about the attack?"

"I'm still getting my thoughts together, but I think this is a watershed. The level of sophistication needed to launch this attack is quite staggering. Yet, the resulting attack was quite simple to find and clean. It kind of gives me a bad feeling..." his voice trailed off.

"What do you mean?" Mick asked.

"Well, to me, this feels like a test run – an experiment. The attacker wanted to try it out to see how it would work and what defenses would be used against it, but the rest was just for show. I know, it doesn't make any sense."

"Oh, no. It makes sense, unfortunately. I can't explain, but let me just say that I'm not surprised."

"But you can't say more than those maddeningly cryptic words?"

"Right. Sorry."

"No problems. I understand. I'm going to get some sleep now," he replied with a big yawn. "Sorry this attack ruined your Halloween plans."

"Yeah, I don't take many days off, so it is kind of a bummer."

Actually, Mick wasn't feeling sorry about it. He was energized with thoughts about the series of zero day attacks and Zed.Kicker. He knew there were hundreds of new attacks launched over the Internet each year, but to have three in a row that were linked, and seemed to target different types of servers, applications, and users. He knew something was afoot.

"Talk to you soon." Lars ended the conversation.

The next day, Mick cleared his calendar. His new book outline and industry analysis paper would have to wait. Today, he was determined to discover the steganography in the spam emails. He had a large dataset of spam messages. He first sorted out the ones that went between the computers he knew to be infected; if there were any P2P control messages, they would be there. The rest of the data might also contain messages, but he figured he had a higher probability of discovering them in the smaller set.

He then analyzed the different kinds of messages, sorted them first by subject, then by sender, then by date, but couldn't draw any new conclusions. Starting to run out of things to try, he just started reading the emails. He was amazed at the variety, the emotion, and the brazenness of some. He imagined himself a spammer (presumably in some anti-universe where he had turned his computer skills to evil) and tried to look at them as samples, as bait, and as marketing exercises. He got nowhere.

He was about to quit and go out for coffee when he realized he had been ignoring the attachments – the message bodies in the spam mails. He stripped them out and fed them through his scanning software. Not surprisingly, he found viruses, Trojans, key loggers, and various spyware and malware - quite a collection of digital nasties. Then, he found some that appeared not to be infected. Some looked like random binary data – perhaps these were attempts at malware that failed, and as a result didn't execute correctly. He loaded them on his quarantine computer, a sacrificial one he often exposed to various viruses in order to observe; they didn't appear to do anything. A couple were image files, and they didn't do anything either. He was about to move on when the thought bounced in his mind.

The image files don't do anything!

Why would a spammer include an image file if it wasn't either malware or an image related to the spam topic?

Mick turned his attention to the image files that would not open. He did some research on the JPG image format, then began going through the binary information in the files. He quickly discovered that the files were too big for the image sizes they were supposed to contain. Sure enough, in the middle of each JPG file was a block of data that was clearly not image data, but something else. He took out this data block and stored it in a different file. He analyzed it and found that it had all the properties of an encrypted file. He had broken the steganography and found the hidden message in the spam!

Gotcha!

He wrote a short script to do automatically what he had just done manually in his editor – split each non-working image file into two parts: the image file and the hidden message. The script ran, and Mick had a pile of information. He felt triumph at his success! He glanced at the JPG photographs. Now they had their secret payload removed, they were viewable. They were manipulated photographs of celebrities.

He almost called Gunter, but realized he shouldn't

share the results. Besides, Gunter would only ask what the messages were, and he didn't know that – yet! Dinner had passed him by, but his stomach growls became too loud to disregard, so he decided to cook up some noodles while he replayed the morning's discoveries again in his head.

Mick tried to decrypt the messages using some basic crypto analysis software he had, but failed to make any headway. He decided to contact his friend Mathison who had helped him in the past with similar problems. To talk to Mathison, he had to run some special encryption software that was even stronger than what he used daily, as Mathison was even more security conscious than Mick. Soon he was in a video call, looking at Mathison's unshaven face and rumpled clothes.

"Botnet control messages, eh? Sounds pretty cool... Any idea how big this botnet might be?" Mathison asked. Mick had been asking himself the same question lately.

"No, not yet. But I may know soon... Do you need to know?" he asked.

"Well, a large botnet will only use key management and distribution schemes that scale well, whereas a small bot could be more flexible."

"I'm assuming it is very large until I know otherwise," Mick replied. "And Math, take care of yourself, OK?" The last time they had worked together Mathison had ended up in the hospital, but continued to work on the project, breaking the encryption just before he was discharged.

"Sure, sure. I'll get to work, then," Mathison replied, saluting as he cut his video.

"OK, then," Mick replied to a blank screen.

Now that he knew how to identify the spam emails containing the secret messages, he wanted to see where else these messages might show up on the Internet. He shared the information with Kateryna, and she passed it along to her company's anti-spam group. She was nervous about getting in deeper with this unofficial information exchange, but apparently her curiosity got the better of her judgment.

Mick took a break from work during the afternoon for a short ride. He took the tunnel across to Jersey and went south on the Parkway. He exited in the pine barrens and rode a series of winding, sandy trails on his Scrambler, his first ride on it since its repair in Albuquerque and return shipment. It looked and felt great, and he enjoyed the autumn sunshine. Mick was surprised to discover when he returned home that four hours had passed. He felt refreshed, and ready for anything.

"Hey Mick, nice to see you again," Kateryna began as they started a secure video session later that evening. It was a planned call to touch base on the botnet investigation. She smiled at him, and he couldn't help but notice her casual attire. He hadn't seen her in sportswear before, and it distracted him.

"Likewise, Kat. How are things with you?" he asked.

Is she using this spambot investigation as an excuse to stay in touch with me? Or am I?

But her next comment completely derailed his thoughts.

"Mick, you won't believe what we found! Well, not me, our anti-spam guys. That spam signature you gave me... it's ALL OVER THE INTERNET!" she practically shouted. Mick was speechless. "They are still putting together the numbers, but it looks like 9% of all the spam they are seeing on the Internet has the same signature as your botnet messages." 'Signature' referred to the characteristics of the spam messages containing the corrupt JPG images Mick had shared with her. Mick knew the statistics on the amazing amount of spam on the Internet – over 8Ø% of all emails sent are spam – to have a significant percentage was astounding.

"You kid, right?" Mick finally got out.

"Kid? Oh, you mean joke? No, I don't kid!" she replied. "Are you certain that this represents botnet traffic?"

"No, you know I'm not, but I'm fairly sure. I have a crypto friend - I mean, I have a friend who is a crypto expert working on the actual messages themselves. Will your guys have an estimate of the number of spam sources meeting this signature soon?"

"Yes, by the end of today they'll have a first order estimate, and a better one in a few days. And, we still need that permission from your client for the rest..." she began.

"I know. I know. I'm working on it," he replied, stretching the truth a bit. He had been *thinking* about talking to Vince but had not actually started the conversation with him.

"OK. Mick, if this is a botnet, it is the biggest one I've ever heard of."

"Yes, by an order or magnitude or two," he agreed, meaning a factor of ten or a hundred.

"And Mick... be careful. Botnets these days are usually run by organized crime. One this big could really do a lot of damage to the Internet. If you are thinking of tracking and taking down this botnet, they won't like it very much at all."

"Don't worry, Kat," he replied.

After they signed off, Mick stood up, stretched, and realized that this was exactly what he was thinking. He knew he was the perfect person for this job. He was thinking of how he could track, infiltrate, and ultimately destroy this botnet. And he wasn't thinking about the cost.

CHAPTER 13.

*From the **Security and Other Lies** Blog:*

I read that a website had a 'Denial of Services Attack' launched against it. What is that, and how can I protect myself against it? LOLraptors

A Denial of Service or DOS attack occurs when an attacker directs lots of traffic (messages) towards a particular site or computer. Sometimes, a DOS attack can look a lot like a big surge in activity, such as when an otherwise obscure website suddenly becomes wildly popular, for example if it is Slashdotted (i.e. mentioned on slashdot.org – you do read Slashdot every day, don't you??). This phenomenon also occurs in telecommunications in the case of radio contests or TV voting.

The goal of a DOS attack can be to overwhelm an Internet connection, making it impossible for messages to be delivered over that connection. Or, it can be to overload the processor on a computer, making it run slowly or crash. Another example is to target something called an Internet name server, also known as a DNS server. A DNS name server helps you find sites and people on the Internet by resolving a human-friendly domain name (such as amazon.com) to a numerical IP Address (such as 69.195.97.72) that is routable on the Internet. If a name server can be overloaded using a DOS attack, a whole set of sites can be made unreachable. For example, if you can crash the name server for the 'yahoo.com' domain, then all web pages or email addresses associated with 'yahoo.com' become unavailable.

Essentially any type of packet flood is a type of DOS attack. Protecting yourself and your site from DOS is difficult to do, but basically involves filtering or blocking the traffic flood as close to the source of the flood as you can.

Detecting a DOS attack can be quite difficult, especially if it is a Distributed Denial of Service or DDOS attack. In this case, a bunch of different computers work together to generate the flooding traffic. For example, a botnet, an organized network of compromised PCs or computers, can be used to launch DDOS attacks by having all the hosts send a small amount of flooding traffic. Since each host does not send a huge volume, the attack often goes undetected until all the traffic converges at the target, making the attack difficult to block or defend against. DDOS can also be launched using cooperative computers, in a voluntary botnet, such as those organized by hacktivists both for and against Wikileaks.

There are some colourful names for different types of DOS attacks such as 'Smurf attacks', 'SYN floods', or 'Ping of Death'. Regardless, all DOS attacks use the same principles and can have the same disastrous results.

-> Your question not answered this week? Argue for your vote on the Shameless Plugging area of our discussion forum.

CHAPTER 14.

Mick O'Malley – *adores his sister.* *(4 comments)*

Halfway between Logan Airport and Lewis Wharf, Mick watched Boston Harbor stream past. Mick enjoyed the sea air as the water taxi bounced over the light chop. His sister's apartment's close proximity to the water allowed him the option of a water route, and, a check of the traffic confirmed his choice.

Disembarking, Mick walked the dozen blocks from the dock to the apartment. The day was beautiful, and the sun was making its way down between the houses tall. Mick enjoyed the atmosphere of the city. He was looking forward immensely to seeing Jocelyn, and, of course, Sam. Since his sister and niece wouldn't be home yet, he went in a nearby Irish pub. Strangely, it seemed to be filled with a convention of Pilgrim re-enactors. Thinking of Akihabara, he decided this must be cosplay, or costume play, Massachusetts style. When ordering, he quizzed the waitress, a Russian judging by her accent.

"Is your bar always filled with Puritans, or do other Dissenters have their days as well?" he enquired. She smiled back at him.

"When I came in today, it was already like this... Someone said there is something on the web that told them to come here dressed like this," she replied, sweeping her arm across the room.

He considered searching for the web page.

Could it be some kind of themed geocaching?

He decided against looking it up, thinking that if he didn't occasionally rein in his curiosity on the web, he could become a slave to it.

A few hours later, he showed up at the apartment. Jocelyn, her husband Joe, and Sam shared the entire top floor of the four-story building – quite a large space for Back Bay Boston.

Jocelyn gave him a big hug as he walked through the door, saying that it had been way too long since she had seen him. He refrained from mentioning that she only saw him when he visited Boston, and that her making a trip to Manhattan could reduce this interval considerably.

He had missed her as well. Jocelyn worked part time at a public library a few blocks away, mainly while Sam was at school. They caught up over a cup of coffee until Sam burst through the door, kicking off her shoes, dropping her coat, and shedding her book bag in a single fluid movement.

"Uncle Alec!" she shouted with a big grin on her face. Her hug was short as she grabbed his hand and pulled him up out of his chair and towards her part of the apartment. There were few walls in the space, but her corner was clearly identifiable by the artwork on the walls and colorful books on the shelves. "Let's do Origami!" she exclaimed, sitting down and pulling out colorful squares of paper. Fortunately, he had anticipated this and had learned a few new patterns in Nihon. They passed quite a few hours happily with one project naturally and seamlessly leading to the next.

Joe arrived home when it got dark, shaking Mick's hand firmly. Joe was a photojournalist for the Globe and had a weather-beaten air he had no doubt perfected on trips to Iraq, Afghanistan, and Palestine. Mick could see why Jocelyn would be attracted to him, but he couldn't really see how she could be married to him – they seemed too different. He suspected that Kateryna would probably enjoy talking with him about photography.

Later, he helped put Sam to bed. She asked for a story, and again he was prepared. He told a story from Tokyo about the Forty Seven Ronin, samurai left without a master after the murder of their warlord. They spent years plotting and planning revenge on a rival warlord responsible for the murder. When they accomplished this, they all committed ritual suicide together, known as Seppuku in Nihon. Mick hoped his sister wasn't listening in, or he would get it later, but Sam loved it, and wanted to talk about honor and self-sacrifice and why people do the things they do. Eventually, she went quiet and he managed to slip out as she drifted off into sleep.

At the kitchen table, Jocelyn looked tired, so he declined her offer of coffee, suspecting she was just doing it out of politeness. Mick hoped perhaps there'd be a chance to talk tomorrow. He shared a few choice observations about the evening with his social network, then retired without even checking mail.

The next morning, over breakfast, Mick was grilled.

"So, explain to me again what a 'buffer overflow attack' is?" Sam led off the questioning.

"Have you been trying to read Uncle Alec's dissertation again?" Jocelyn inquired from behind the sink.

"Yes, but I still don't get it," she pouted.

"That's OK… it is a little theoretical," Mick began.

146

Seeing that Jocelyn was about to interrupt, he continued. "I don't mind, really, sis. Let me try an analogy..." he began. He enjoyed the challenge of trying to explain complicated technical topics to his youngest admirer.

A few minutes later, Jocelyn had a look on her face that suggested that perhaps she just had a glimpse into her brother's world for the first time... Sam seemed satisfied for the moment, too.

"OK, I'm off to school. Bye Uncle Alec!" Sam said running out the door, waving to her uncle, kissing her mother, and dashing out of sight.

Joe joined them for breakfast a few minutes later, so Mick couldn't bring up his topic with Jocelyn. Joe continued the grilling where Sam had left off.

"Alec," he began, "What if someone invented an unbreakable encryption algorithm! Could you imagine what would happen?"

"Actually, there already is an unbreakable encryption algorithm, and governments of the world have been using it for decades now. It is known as a 'one time pad'!" Mick replied, having been asked this question before, probably as a result of a popular, but inaccurate fictional thriller on the topic.

"Oh, I see. Hmm. I had another question," he continued. "So you are the security guru and so you make us use all these weird programs to email you and call you and everything, right? You're big on security – I get that. But do you have triple deadbolts on your doors? Do you drive an armored car? It seems like you aren't consistent."

Mick nodded and leaned back in his chair. Joe had a good point.

"Well, I do keep my door locked at my apartment, I don't actually own a car; car sharing works quite well for me. But if I did, it wouldn't be an armored car. I don't go overboard on my physical security, and I don't think I go overboard on my Internet security, even if it perhaps appears that way. Here's the big difference: if criminals want to break into my house, they have to travel to my apartment, drive or walk down my street, break a window or door, right? If they want to steal something, they have to carry it out under their arm or throw it in their vehicle.

"Now compare this to my electronic possessions. If cyber criminals want to break into my computer and steal or delete my information, they can do it from anywhere in the world if I am connected to the Internet. They can sit in complete anonymity in any part of the globe and launch attacks on my computer. Consider the risk to them. Which is more risky, having to be present on my street, or typing in commands over the Internet?

"Think about tapping my communication. Before the Internet, to tap my phone, they would have to attach alligator clips to the phone wires in the wiring closet in my building, or climb a telephone pole on my street, or break into the local telephone company central office building where the wires that go into the mainframe computer (known as a telephone switch) are located. All of these involve a lot of risk; the wiretappers could easily get caught. Now with Internet phone calls, they can potentially listen in using a piece of software installed remotely on my computer or server. The software can then record all my calls and email the recordings to someone on the other side of the globe. The attackers never have to leave their house or have any physical connection to monitor me.

"And that's not considering the automation possible, that a single piece of software can search the Internet looking for any particular type of communication. So maybe they aren't targeting me personally, they are just recording calls, then doing automatic speech recognition to look for spoken digits that might be a bank account, credit card, or pin number, for example.

"Just as communication becomes very easy with the

Internet, attacking and monitoring someone becomes easy as well, and requires adequate security to protect against it.

Joe nodded slightly. "But isn't it just about who you trust? You don't trust anyone, and it forces you do all this?" he countered.

"Joe, the great thing about the Internet is that you don't have to trust anyone. Just by using proper security techniques, you can verify everything and everyone. Of course, this does all fall down if someone steals your secret keys or hijacks your personal accounts by learning your passwords."

"Yeah, I kind of get it. But don't you get tired of it all? Don't you feel like a spy or something? And, what do your girlfriends think?" Joe had hit close to home with this question. Sometimes, it did grate on Mick, but he just couldn't ignore it and pretend to be oblivious. Perhaps this was one reason why he had felt so comfortable with Kateryna: there was no need to explain this whole side of his life as she already got it.

Joe seemed to realize how much time he was wasting discussing such trivial topics, and packed up his things and got ready to set off.

"Oh, Alec, you said you'd tell me the address of that website that lets photographers securely upload their images for archiving."

"Sure, here it is," Mick replied, writing it down on a piece of paper.

"Why do you do that? Why do you put a slash through a zero?" he asked.

"To distinguish a zero from the letter 'O', of course," he replied, surprised it needed an explanation. Most programmers did this out of habit, as confusion between a Ø and an O could easily cause a password to fail, or code to not compile.

When Joe left, Mick finally had his sister to himself.

"So, Jocelyn, come have a *cuppa* with me," he called

out to her, offering a cup of coffee. She smiled and sat down in the chair next to him and took the cup.

"So, what's on your mind?" she asked.

"What makes you think something's on my mind?" he replied.

"I knew as soon as you walked through the door. What is it? Or should I say, who is she?" she asked. Mick smiled back at her. His emotional encryption was obviously just a two-time pad to her – encryption that was easily broken. He briefly wondered if this was obvious to others besides her.

"OK, yes, there is someone. Her name is Kateryna, but we're just friends..." Jocelyn smiled. "And she's married." The smile melted away. "I know, I know. We met a few weeks ago in Hiroshima, and then again in Seattle – I had no idea she was married." Mick held up his hand as Jocelyn looked about to interrupt. "We've been working on a few work projects together. Then last week in Vegas she tells me she is married. I just don't know what I'm doing, or even what I want..."

"Oh, no!" she began. Mick shrugged.

"I should be angry with her, but I'm not. I should stop thinking about her, but I can't. What's the matter with me?" Mick asked.

"You know the answer..." Jocelyn replied, and Mick nodded. "Any kids?" Mick shook his head.

"No. Her husband is a Romanian immigrant as well."

"Oh, Alec, please be careful. I know you can take care of yourself, but I think you've fallen for this woman," she began. "Does anyone know?" she asked.

"No one besides you, I think. Although maybe Liz has guessed."

"Sure, makes sense. You still need to sort things out with her, too, you know! So, brother, you obviously want to talk about Kateryna, so tell me about her." Jocelyn replied leaning back in her chair.

Mick gave a little grin in spite of himself and began to tell the story of how they met in Nihon and their adventures in Seattle and Vegas.

Thank goodness for sisters!

Nearly an hour later, Jocelyn indicated she had to head out to the library.

"Alec, I'd love to chat longer, but I have to get to the library early to check out the new RFID system," she said, referring to a Radio Frequency Identification system.

"Cool! So all the books have a little RFID tag in them? I'll bet it makes re-shelving and inventory a breeze," he replied.

"You're not kidding! We now have an automated system that sorts the returned books and tells us exactly where to put them back on the shelves. And inventory used to take days with the library closed. Now we just walk up and down the shelves with a reader, and it tells us which books are in the wrong place. It is just great!"

"OK, no problems. I have plenty to amuse myself here," he replied.

Mick thought it fitting that Jocelyn worked in a library. As children, they went together to the library nearly every day, and sometimes he couldn't get her to leave. She was one of the few people he knew who read more books than himself.

Mick relaxed when she left, replaying the conversation in his head. Jocelyn was right – he mainly just wanted to talk about Kateryna to someone. But he did plan on taking her advice seriously, and to not get more involved with Kateryna.

After the conversation about RFID tags, Mick did a little research about RFID trackers in clothing.

His next order of business was to have the conversation with Vince about releasing the details of the attack. He suspected the conversation would not go well, and he was right.

"Mick, you know I can't do that. You agreed when we started that none of the data or results could be shared or publicized," Vince began after Mick made his request.

"I know, but you must understand. Your attack is not an isolated incident. In fact, I don't even think it was directed at you in particular. I think that this attack and the other attacks are some kind of trial run: a series of tests to see how well it works and see what kind of responses the security community will generate. Something really big is happening out there." Mick could tell he was not making any progress with Vince, and decided to play all his cards. "There's more. I didn't tell you, but while I was in New Mexico, I was followed and threatened by a couple of guys. I'm fairly sure they were involved in organized crime. They linked your spambot compromise with last month's web server compromise. They are from the same place, the same source." Mick could tell he made an impact with this.

"Why didn't you tell me? Did you report this to the authorities? We need to increase security on our premises."

"Well, you should do what you think best, but I think the threats were directed against me, personally, rather than at LeydenTech. I've been involved in investigating and fighting these attacks – all of them, one way or another. I might be the only person who can put all the pieces together. And –" he continued but Vince interrupted.

"You need to talk to someone in the government. I have a friend in Homeland Security. We were at Harvard together. You should talk to him, and maybe he can do something."

"Can I mention your attack?"

"Yes, if I can be on the call," Vince replied. "And you need to give me all the details of your encounter."

"Sure, I'll mail you all I know." Talking to the

Department of Homeland Security didn't make Mick feel comfortable, but it felt like the right thing to do, to tell someone in the government. Surely the National Cyber Security Division would be interested in hearing about the attack?

Vince agreed to set up the call and get back to him.

Mick caught up with Lars that afternoon on a secure voice call. He filled him in on the latest on the botnet, but decided to leave out the part involving Homeland Security. At the end of the call, Lars went back to his second favorite topic.

"Hey Mick, I read a great article in the Times about the use of Helvetica in the New York subway system! It is such a great font! I wish we used it in Helsinki," commented Lars.

"What font do they use there?" Mick asked, then realized his mistake. "No, don't tell me. Save it for next time we are together. I should run now." He signed off a few minutes later.

The next day, Mick was on the Acela Express train halfway between Boston and Washington, D.C. With the Shinkansen experience fresh in his mind, this was hardly high speed rail, but it wasn't bad by American standards. It had been decided that a face-to-face meeting with Homeland Security was more appropriate than a call, even a secure one. Whom he was meeting was a bit vague... he was supposed to wait at a street corner near the Lincoln Memorial. Mick joked to Jocelyn that he was going to meet 'Deep Throat.' He planned to be back in Boston the next day for one more day before flying home to New York.

Mick alighted the train at Union station and set off walking towards the Mall, enjoying the cool November air. He checked into his hotel after making a brief stop at another hotel. He had plenty of time, so he wandered around a little, enjoying the sights. He idly recalled having been here for inaugurations, festivals, and demonstrations.

Mick waited, standing at the specified corner. He passed the time people watching. Mick was always amazed at how much he could deduce with a little observation. Besides the ubiquitous Korean and other tourists, there were lots of Americans from all over the country, judging by their accents. Despite the cold, the crowds were pretty big.

A black van pulled to a stop in front of Mick. The front window went down and a voice called out to him by name. Mick walked towards the van; the side door opened. He leaned over to look, and he was pulled inside, the door closing behind him. Before his eyes could adjust to the gloom, he felt his hands being restrained and a hood pulled over his head.

"Don't be alarmed, we are taking you to our office."

A loud hissing noise filled his ears, and he realized they had turned on a white noise source to cover any road noises. He gave up struggling and instead tried to keep his senses sharp.

Serves me right for getting into bed with the government...

CHAPTER 15.

Mick O'Malley – *"Distrust and caution are the parents of security"– Ben Franklin. (13 comments)*

After an indeterminate amount of time, the van stopped and the noise ceased. Mick was lifted to his feet, and he moved his legs, trying to get out the pins and needles. He was frog-marched down a corridor then pushed down onto a chair, and the hood was removed. He blinked in the light, looking around. A man removed the plastic restraints from Mick's wrists, and he rubbed them.

"My apologies for the 'cloak and dagger', Mr. O'Malley, or should I say, Mr. Robertson?" began a tall, thin man sitting across the table. When Mick made no reply, he continued. "We appreciate your cooperation in this matter. You have some information about the recent zero day attacks that we need. First of all, tell us how you became involved in this."

"I came to D.C. to share what I know with Homeland Security, but I didn't expect this treatment. However, I will answer your questions anyway. May I know your name?" Mick paused but received no reply. "Can I have a glass of water?" After another pause, a bottle of water appeared on the table. Mick took a sip, then began telling his story.

He explained how he had foiled the web server zero day in Hiroshima and had monitored the mail server zero day. He described the results of the LeydenTech investigation, and the threat from Pavel Michalovic and company. He explained his hypothesis of the Zed.Kicker botnet using spambots to hide P2P control messages.

"And tell me about your personal server compromises."

"Well, my personal web server was compromised by the 'Carbon' attack, but my mail server was not hit as I suspect that the attack –"

"I don't mean those. I mean your Zed dot Kicker compromise."

"I'm afraid I don't know what you are talking about." On the long ride, Mick had thought hard what information he was willing to reveal and what he was not willing to reveal. He had decided to not discuss his personal server compromise, as he was unwilling to share these logs with the government. His server logs contained all kinds of information about the location, type, and software running on his servers. Also, there was still the matter of the unexplained private key theft.

"You know exactly what I'm talking about. I understand one of your personal servers was compromised and your private keys stolen. We already have all the logs from LeydenTech, but we need your logs as well." There was a long pause.

"Sorry, I've told you everything I know. If you have all the LeydenTech info, then you know as much as I do. You really need to get on top of this botnet... I think it is the biggest and most powerful by a few orders of magnitude. The new codebase is extremely sophisticated and who knows what they might target next. Don't you have your own server logs to examine?" he asked, knowing the answer already.

"As you are no doubt aware, all our information technology has been outsourced to UBK. They have shared their logs, but they aren't as useful as they could be, as their servers were hit hard and most logs were erased."

"Why don't you just ask for their source code? You could then do your own analysis." There was a pause before the answer.

"We have. They have refused, citing the confidentiality clauses in our contract." Mick couldn't suppress a smile.

"Oh that's right, closed source... intellectual property... Bad luck about that. You really should only do business with companies that implement security best practices."

"This is now a matter of national security. An inter-department task force has been set up. I have been authorized to offer you a role in this investigation. Here are the terms and conditions." He paused and passed a thick sheaf of paper across the table. Mick didn't look down.

"Sorry, I don't do government work. I would like to go now, unless I am under arrest?"

"I don't think you understand the seriousness of this situation... or of your own situation –" Mick let his anger show.

"*I* don't understand? *I* don't understand? Industry and government alike have been ignoring the threat to the Internet from botnets for years now! Even small botnets can cause big disruptions. This botnet... this one is not like any I've ever seen. It is made up of perhaps millions of zombie computers, all over the world: ordinary computers on people's desks, in their living rooms, perhaps even in your office! Have you kept up to date with your software updates? From what I can tell, this botnet is just warming up; we have not yet seen its full power, but I am certain we soon will! And as for my 'own situation', I am just a private citizen doing my job. What right do you have to drag me here to Ft. Meade and treat me like a criminal? May I remind you that this is America, and I have rights."

The man stood up and walked out of the room. For the first time, Mick saw another person seated in the back of the room. The man wore a military uniform.

"Who are you?" Mick asked, but had no time for a reaction or reply when the hood was put back over his head, and he was bundled away.

The General got up and walked to a nearby conference room to discuss the interview he had witnessed with a team.

"Since he won't cooperate, go through his intercepts," demanded the General. "I want to see transcripts of all his calls, mails, and messages. Also –" The other man interrupted him.

"Sir, he uses ZRTP encryption for all his calls, and strong encryption on all his messaging. We know who he communicates with, but we haven't been able to break any yet..." He looked at the General who appeared to be thinking hard.

"What about his computers – his servers?"

"He was only carrying a mobile, which had no data on it."

"He wasn't carrying a computer? That is strange," the General commented.

"We think he keeps most of his data on offshore servers. We've located some, but they are well protected and in countries where we have little intelligence cooperation."

"Damn! Well, he doesn't have everything offshore, does he? I want some leverage on this guy! I want 24-hour surveillance on him. I am authorizing non-traditional means to get around this guy's paranoia. Dismissed!"

As the room cleared, the General fought back his anger. He glanced down at an intelligence report that he had just received. Based on this information, he had a choice to make: to do nothing and let things take its course, or to intervene. He had been considering intervening, but now...

Who the hell does this Mick O'Malley think he is?

Mick rolled to a stop on the sidewalk, after being dumped from the van. With his hands freed, he pulled the hood off his head but was not able to read the license plate of the van as it sped away.

Not that it would be any help. Who would I go to, the police?

Mick got up and dusted off his clothes. He pulled out his mobile and fired up the GPS. He was on a side street in D.C., not too far from his hotel.

The whole situation seemed quite surreal. He had made major progress with the botnet, and now he was being threatened by his own government... Fortunately, all his critical data was stored on his Internet servers, which were safe... for now. He thought about the questions he had been asked. The government seemed preoccupied with its own security, provided by UBK these days. He recalled how many government sites had been taken down in the web server zero day.

Could the attacks be aimed at the government, with others just being collateral damage?

It was an intriguing premise. UBK could make for a convenient target: centralized, probably using similar software and hardware everywhere to keep costs down. If true, this would just be the cyber analog of the classic organized crime protection racket. But this didn't quite make sense to Mick: extortion would be much more effective against private companies, especially shady ones on the edge of the law, than against a government or a government contractor. It just didn't ring true with what he knew of cybercrime businesses.

Down the street, he stopped to examine his mobile. It had been taken from him when he got in the van and returned just before being dropped off. He checked the location log and found that it was blank for the entire time of the meeting. The mobile was on, but it had no location or other wireless contact during the period. Most likely it was put inside a Faraday cage. And most likely it now had a bug installed in it. He gave a wistful smile as he removed a small chip from it – the SIM card – then threw the mobile into a dumpster. He would have to buy a new one tomorrow, and download and compile the operating system.

He stopped at another hotel a few blocks from his hotel. He gave the bellhop a claim ticket and five dollars. The bellhop returned a moment later with the computer bag Mick had left earlier that morning. He smiled to himself as he walked out.

Safe from prying eyes…

Back in his hotel room, he paced back and forth, his body still coursing with adrenaline. Mick wanted to tell someone, but was reluctant to involve anyone else. He checked his mail, and found a contract termination notice from Vince – it seemed his LeydenTech work was over. He wondered what other surprises were waiting for him.

Maybe I should have played along instead of refusing outright? Too late now…

He decided to stick to his plans, and headed to the Smithsonian to try to clear his mind. Mick had visited the Air & Space Museum many times in the past but never the Steven F. Udvar-Hazy Center. It was literally a whole new museum, located near Dulles airport. For Mick, the highlight was seeing Enola Gay, the actual B-29 that dropped the atomic bomb on Hiroshima. He read the plaque that merely outlined the history of the plane. Mick recalled the controversy that erupted when the bomber was first shown in the museum, with a description of the atomic bomb detonation and resulting casualties. The current lack of context seemed a shame to Mick. Despite its propellers, Mick thought it looked modern, sleek, and even menacing. He had seen pictures of it in the museum in Hiroshima, including grainy color movies. He felt he had somehow connected the dots, having been to Hiroshima, stood under the hypocenter, and now was looking at the actual bomber which was overhead that fateful day.

Gradually, Mick started to feel almost normal again.

He spent a few hours in his hotel in Washington catching up with his social network. Lars was fairly quiet these days, no doubt busy studying the latest attack. Gunter was traveling again in Europe, and enjoying the variety of the food. Kateryna was planning some sightseeing in Europe before next month's security conference in London and was looking for suggestions. Mick shared his favorite spots, from the standing stones in Cornwall to the moors in the Lake District.

Finally, Mick was able to concentrate again. There was much work to be done on the botnet, but he no longer felt the weight of being the only one who knew the relationships between the zero day attacks. He had done his duty, even if he had antagonized the government. Tomorrow morning he would ride the train back to Boston, and enjoy one more day with Sam before heading home to Manhattan.

CHAPTER 16.

*From the **Security and Other Lies** Blog:*

What is a digital certificate? What does it mean when my browser gives me an error message about a certificate? Should I just click OK? wateraptor

A digital certificate is a document that a computer can use to prove the identity of another computer or user. For example, a digital certificate can be used to secure a web banking session. When I type in https://bigbank.com into my browser, my browser gets a certificate from the web server. If the certificate says that Big Bank, Inc. operates a web server called bigbank.com, then my web browser will display a padlock or otherwise indicate that this is an authenticated and secure web session.

Now, this might not seem all that secure. Fortunately, a certificate is not like a diploma displayed on a wall (or those tremendously important elevator certificates) – these documents can be easily stolen or duplicated by a bad guy. Instead, certificates are only issued and signed by a few companies - so called Certificate Authorities. Your browser can tell if a certificate is valid or not based on whether the digital signature on the certificate itself is valid. Secondly, no one else can use the certificate beside the owner, because in order to use it, you need to know the secret private key associated with it. Therefore, even if a bad guy copies your bank's certificate, he can't successfully use it, because your web browser will require him to prove that he knows the bank's private key, which he does not.

Now let's talk about those certificate errors that generate pop ups that almost all of us (myself definitely not included!) just click OK to. This can happen for a number of reasons. If the certificate is issued by a Certificate Authority that the web browser doesn't recognize, it will generate an error. This is not too common, but does happen.

Another case could be that the address you typed into the browser doesn't match the address in the certificate. For example, if I type in bigbank.com into my browser, but the certificate obtained by my browser says the server it is talking to is Spammers R Us, Inc. running the spam.spam.spam.wonderfulspam.com web server, then my web browser will pop up one of those warning messages to say that something is wrong. Now, usually, the error is more subtle than this. For example, the Big Bank, Inc. certificate might say bigbankinc.com instead of bigbank.com, or the certificate might have expired last week.

When I get one of these errors, I *never* click OK. Instead, I copy the information and send a nastygram to the CIO or CTO of the company, explaining to them that they are in violation of their fiduciary requirement for security and hence liable to attacks, lawsuits, and all kinds of bad press. But, that is just me. YMMV. Hope this helps, wateraptor.

-> Your question not answered this week? Argue
for your vote on the Shameless Plugging area of
our discussion forum.

CHAPTER 17.

Mick O'Malley – *can't stand governments, all governments. (4 comments)*

Mick's train ride back to Boston was uneventful. His walk from the train station to Jocelyn's apartment was a different story.

As he walked down Charles Street, there were quite a few other pedestrians out and about in the afternoon sunshine. On an impulse he stopped in a corner shop to buy some flowers for his sister. As he exited the store with a bouquet of yellow tulips, he noticed a man standing on the other side of the street; the man looked vaguely familiar. Mick realized he had seen him waiting outside the train station a few minutes earlier. Mick continued walking down the street, his mind racing.

That man is following me!

Mick became more aware of his surroundings, noting every person around. As he stopped at a crosswalk, he could no longer see the man, but he noticed a woman walking ahead who he had previously seen hailing a cab.

Is she following me?

He decided to find out.

When the light changed, he didn't walk, pretending to look at his mobile. An empty taxi cab approach the intersection and started to turn in front of him. He stepped out into the street, stopping the cab suddenly. Mick opened the door and jumped inside the cab.

"Drive!" he shouted. Looking out the back window, he saw the woman talk to someone in a car who began following the taxi.

"Where to buddy?" the driver asked. Mick gave his sister's address, and was dropped outside a few short minutes later. He walked in the door and up the stairs, still slightly in a daze. His life had just changed dramatically in the past twenty-four hours.

I'm under surveillance now.

He stopped on the stairs to compose himself. He had no intention of telling his sister about his encounter with the government – he didn't want her to worry. Besides, he still had a naïve hope that things would settle down and his life could go back to normal.

Sam was finishing her homework with help from his sister when he entered the apartment. Sam bounded over a few minutes later, and he was able to put the recent events completely out of his thoughts.

That evening, the two of them continued reading *The Two Towers*. They discussed it afterwards as Sam lay sleepily in her bed.

"I can't believe the Black Gate is closed," she said sleepily. "They traveled so long and hard to get there, deep into Mordor, and now they can't get in!"

"I know it looks bad, but I have faith in the hobbits," he replied.

"But they must feel so disappointed! I guess fighting evil is difficult. I wonder how they do it..."

"I know," he replied, not thinking about the book. Sam drifted off to sleep a few minutes later.

Later, just before he fell asleep, Mick wondered how things had come to this. He now was almost afraid to communicate with his friends – he didn't want to drag anyone else into his mess. Being tailed, presumably by the government, would complicate things for him. He was annoyed at himself for the afternoon's theatrics. With a bit of thought he probably could have confirmed the tail without them knowing. Now they knew that he was aware of being followed. He realized, however, that one of the goals of the surveillance was probably to unnerve him.

The next day Mick left for the train station, heading to Logan for his flight back to New York. He had a short wait in the First Class check-in line.

"Checking in for the 11:10 to JFK," he said, handing over his drivers license to the woman behind the counter. She typed for a moment.

"What is your date of birth?" she asked. He told her. "What is your middle name?" she asked.

"I don't have a middle name." he replied. She looked up at him, surprised. "It's just Mick O'Malley. Here's my passport, if you want to see that," he continued, handing it over to her. She looked down and continued typing and paging through screens. She picked up the phone and pressed a button.

"Yes, yes... OK," she said hanging up the phone. "Mr. O'Malley, if you could step over here. My supervisor needs to talk to you."

"What is this in reference to?" Mick asked, looking at the time.

"In just a moment my supervisor will explain. If you could wait right here, thank you." She motioned for the next person in line to come to the counter. She did not return his driver's license or passport.

Three minutes later, the supervisor came over.

"Mr. O'Malley? I'm Jay Bishop. I apologize for the

delay. I just need you to come to my office so I can ask you a few questions." The supervisor picked up a printout and what he presumed was his driver's license and passport.

"OK," Mick replied, trying hard not to become annoyed. He had lots of experience with officialdom, and knew that showing anger or annoyance only made these situations much, much worse. He patiently followed the supervisor past the ticket counter and up the stairs to a small office. The supervisor motioned for Mick to sit down.

"So, Mr. O'Malley, you do not have a middle name?" he asked.

"No."

"And is this your correct address?" he asked, holding up the drivers license.

"Yes."

"And your date of birth?"

"Is correct on both the passport and drivers license, yes." he replied. "Can you please tell me what this is about?"

"Well, Mr. O'Malley, your name is on the Transportation Safety Administration No-Fly list, so I'm afraid you won't be able to check in for your flight today."

"What? That's ridiculous? I am a frequent flier! I fly all over the world! How could I be on the TSA list? There must be a mistake..." A burning feeling spread through his body as he made the connection with the events of the previous day.

This is no random bureaucratic snafu – this is another message to me!

A uniformed police officer entered the room, startling Mick.

"Don't be concerned. We just need to ask you some questions..." Bishop began as the policeman sat down and pulled out a notebook.

Three hours later, Mick left the office after answering a bunch of questions about his recent travels and history. He also made them telephone a higher-level supervisor and spoke to the supervisor himself. The responses were the same each time: he can go to the Transportation Security Agency website and file a Department of Homeland Security Traveler Redress Inquiry form. He was told they would review the case and give him an answer in a reasonable timeframe. There was no way he was going to board a plane today. He was just happy to not be detained further.

Mick needed to decide on a course of action. He considered going back to Jocelyn's, but again decided against it. He needed to get back to Manhattan. Looking for a change from the train, Mick jumped on a bus and was at a car rental counter a few minutes later, arranging a one-way rental. According to his GPS, it was just over 4ØØ km or about four hours of driving at this hour. At the rental counter, he had another unpleasant surprise.

"Mr. O'Malley, I'm afraid your credit card was declined. I'm required to keep the card – my apologies." He rarely used credit cards due to privacy concerns about credit card companies collecting databases of purchasing habits and data. Renting a car was one of the few cases when Mick needed to use a credit card instead of the prepaid debit cards that he mostly used. He tried to think the last time he used this card. He decided it had been a while.

This is very odd...

He took the train instead.

Back in Manhattan, he filed the TSA online paperwork, although he did not expect it would do any good. He wondered how he would do business if he couldn't fly.

Next, he checked his U.S. bank accounts, and confirmed his worst fears. His accounts were frozen! This explained the declined credit card at the rental counter.

For now, he had no access to his money. No one at the bank would talk to him about it or tell him what he could do to regain access to his money, but he presumed it was done using anti-money laundering laws. He decided not to check his foreign accounts – they were only for emergencies, and he still had plenty of cash and a couple of debit cards – enough for the moment.

The government was definitely putting the pressure on him. He wondered exactly which branch of government they were, if they had National Security Agency connections, and if his guess about Ft. Meade in Maryland, just outside of D.C. was accurate.

Mick decided to tell no one – no one except Kateryna, with whom he had planned a video call that evening.

"Mick, you look terrible!" was how she started the call, looking at his high definition image in alarm.

"Thanks, and so do you!" he joked weakly, even though she looked fantastic, as always. "I was denied boarding on my flight back to New York, so I had to take the train. Apparently, I'm on the No-Fly list."

"No way! You're kidding me right? You are pulling on my leg or something? This is crazy!" she began.

"I am totally serious, Kat. No joking. I am persona non grata at airports until I get this cleared up... I am so mad, I don't know what to do."

"Mick, I am so sorry! I wish I could help in some way. I presume you've called your contacts and spoken to everyone you could."

"Yes, I did that. No one can help me, and I don't have any friends in Homeland Security, unfortunately."

"Me neither. Wow. This is hard to comprehend. Do we live in such a society now?" asked Kateryna.

"Kat, please keep quiet about this No-Fly list thing. I really hope to have it sorted out soon, and I don't want to lose any consulting jobs as a result."

"Of course, Mick! You know you can trust me..."

"Don't worry – I'll sort it all out," he managed a grin.

"I know you will," she replied. They signed off shortly. He had decided not to tell Kateryna about his bank accounts as it would have required explaining his 'interview' with the government. Mick was also now operating on the assumption that his apartment was bugged. With his use of encryption for all his communication, it was the only way for the government to listen in to his conversations.

After a fitful night's sleep, Mick decided to take the morning off and do something fun. The engine in one of his bikes needed new rings, which fit between the piston and the cylinder walls. When the rings no longer provide a tight seal, the engine has low compression and runs poorly. Mick had been saving the job for a day when he was in the right mood, and that day was today.

Mick wheeled the 1978 Ducati 9ØØss on to the work stand, and raised it about a half meter off the ground, putting the engine at a comfortable level for working. He removed the fairing and windshield, the gas tank, and the seat. He disconnected the exhaust pipes.

Mick pulled up a stool and set to work on one of the cylinders. He removed the valve cover and paused to admire the pair of desmodromic valves, used to regulate the flow of the fuel into the engine and the exhaust gases out of the engine. Mick even got out his camera and a flash unit and took a few pictures, admiring the unique desmo valves, the ultimate in Italian engineering in high revving racing engines.

Mick continued removing components until he had one piston exposed. He was getting ready to remove the old rings and install the new ones when he suddenly realized he wasn't into the job anymore. Mick put down the tools and went back to his apartment, frustrated.

Mick checked his messages and found a PGP encrypted

mail from Mathison waiting for him. His pulse raced with anticipation as he opened it. He let out a shout after reading the first few lines – Mathison had done it! He had broken the encryption and included the keys for a few of the messages. Mathison had not read any of the messages, respecting Mick's privacy, and also not wanting to get involved. Mick read Mathison's summary of how he had broken the encryption:

```
...  I noticed a pattern where there would be an
initial exchange of three messages, which would
then be followed by a number of messages in one
direction, then a number in the other direction.
I suspected the first few messages might be a
key negotiation.  I analyzed them and determined
that it was a simple 512 bit Diffie-Hellman
exchange - hardly strong at all, but enough to
keep most people out.  I used the BoltCutter
distributed network to break a few messages for
you.  I've given you off-peak access to the
network, so if you script it carefully, you
should be able to break about three messages per
day.  Good luck with whatever the hell this is!

Cheers,

Math
```

Now that he had a way to break the botnet encryption, Mick planned to learn all about the operation of the botnet, and in particular, the hostnames and addresses of the control servers, or boot servers. This might ultimately lead to a way to disrupt or destroy the botnet.

One step at a time.

Mick set to work.

Breaking encrypted messages, or reading them without knowing the secret key, takes a lot of computation on a powerful computer, and each set of messages exchanged within the botnet network used a different key. Mathison used a distributed computer network for this work, which combined the computational power of thousands of computers, effectively turning them into a supercomputer. His offer for Mick to use the BoltCutter computer network for a few minutes each night was incredibly generous one. Such computational power was available to a very few, and almost no one unaffiliated with a government or large corporation. However, he would only be able to decrypt about three messages per day with the off-peak access, so the analysis of the botnet control messages would take time. However, he had confidence he could figure it all out.

Mick was still going through the messages when he received an anonymous message which read:

```
Mick O'Malley,

I have heard that you are working on the
Zed.Kicker botnet.  I also happen to know that
you are good at what you do, but that won't be
enough.  You need my help and I am willing to
give it, but I'll only communicate in person.
Let's just say I have *personal* experience with
Zed.Kicker.  To get you started, here's a link
you might find useful:

    http://svn.softsource.org/p2pmsg

I'll be at the EuroSecurity conference next
month - I presume you'll be there too?  I'll
introduce myself and share the information I
have.

Good luck!  You're going to need it!

Turing
```

```
------BEGIN PGP SIGNATURE-----
3wCcTs5TyFY1OKRAVs/s3VRT3mltmp
FFX+qhy/v9iQPDsPWKVWndBr7lseGH
T046PMOPcqbs12nViuhjL2ICgDsoHu
o82uuLrwCz5N2oq1hENnh783VB7kEw
qYD8H5KEdNyFyVeBoSig9L4zz7TTQn
------END PGP SIGNATURE-------
```

Mick couldn't believe his luck: both good and bad. He was being followed by the government, who had frozen all his assets and put his name on the No-Fly list. And on the same day he was able to look at actual decrypts of the Zed.Kicker network, he was contacted by an insider, someone who could be key to him bringing down this network. But to meet up in London! Not likely for him.

Mick liked the alias of his correspondent; obviously it was a reference to Alan Turing, the British code breaker and computer pioneer. He followed the link which led to an apparently abandoned open source project on peer-to-peer message routing. He noticed Turing had checked in lots of code on the project – very interesting...

He analyzed the P2PMSG source code, and excitedly set to work reading the decrypted messages. He quickly figured out the syntax or structure of the messages, a simple TLV, short for "Tag Length Value" encoding. With further analysis, he confirmed the messages were indeed botnet control messages, used to coordinate the activity of the individual computers. And as he suspected, the botnet was very, very large. One of the messages seemed to contain an order of magnitude estimate for the size of the peer-to-peer botnet network, which he deduced was a power of 2. In this case, it was 2 to the power of 24 or over sixteen million hosts! Mick took a deep breath, realizing this was the biggest botnet ever documented on the Internet! It was no longer surprising to Mick that these messages accounted for such a large percentage of spam traffic.

Unable to focus on anything else, Mick went back to the garage to the motorcycle. He hated leaving a job undone, and needed some time to think. Mick needed a plan, and a good one. By the time he was torquing up the last few bolts the cylinder head, he had a plan. He had decided to tell no one. It would mean some lying to his family, friends, and even Kateryna, but he was determined.

The next day, Mick made his preparations.

He got out a prepaid mobile phone with a data plan that he had purchased with cash and activated a few months ago. He removed the SIM card and noted the serial number of the phone. He then removed the existing SIM card in his mobile, reprogrammed the serial number to match to the other phone, then put in the new SIM card. He carefully destroyed the other phone to be sure that the serial number could not be retrieved from it. Anyone trying to track his phone would be out of luck now!

He wondered whether he was going rogue, or just being overly careful...

As darkness fell, Mick packed a few things in a backpack and rechecked the 9ØØss. He had run the engine on the dyno the previous day to ensure the rings were properly seated. He made a voice call to his sister and talked for quite a while. He told her he would be busy on a new project for the next few weeks. He ended by saying he was going to bed. Instead, he dressed warmly and went out to his workshop. With the lights out, he opened the door silently, wheeled the 9ØØss outside, and put on his helmet. Closing the door and locking it behind him, he looked out into the drizzling skies, which glowed brightly in the city lights. The wet streets would make this a little more difficult, but he would manage.

Mick fired up the engine and roared off down the street. In his mirrors he saw a dark sedan start up and pull out behind him. He accelerated up to fourth gear, running two stop signs before turning right and heading uptown. The sound of squealing tires told him his pursuers were not far behind.

A car pulled out from a parking space in front of him, forcing Mick to swerve the Ducati, but he kept upright. A garbage truck ahead was blocking the road as it was loaded. As he approached, he spotted a side street and turned left sharply down what turned out to be an alleyway. Ahead he saw a stack of wooden pallets that had collapsed blocking the alley. He made a split second decision not to stop, but instead picked a spot where the pallets were piled in a rough ramp. As he approached, he lifted the front wheel off the ground in a wheelie, and braced for impact. His front wheel cleared the pile but his rear wheel made contact, throwing the bike into the air. He absorbed most of the impact with his knees, and pulled up on the handlebars to keep the front wheel up. He landed on his rear wheel and stuck the landing. He slowed to a stop just in time to see the following car plow into the pallets and come to a halt. Mick smiled, then took off again, spinning the rear wheel on the wet pavement.

Mick took an unusual route to the Lincoln tunnel, keeping his speed down to avoid attracting attention. But once he entered the tunnel towards New Jersey, he let loose the ninety-degree L-twin engine and opened the throttle, mostly riding along the line dividing the two lanes as he passed cars left and right. He prayed he would make it out before the far end could be closed. He approached the motorcycle's top speed of 204 km/h as he exited the tunnel, the engine screaming just below the redline. He could see police moving into position, but he was already past!

Making a sharp left turn, he was soon on the back streets of Hoboken. He pulled up outside his storage unit, unlocked the padlock, and rolled the bike inside.

Glancing up and down the street, he closed the door and set to work. First, he removed the gas tank and the side pods. From another bike won in a recent auction still in a shipping crate, he removed the same components and put them on the 9ØØss. The silver paint scheme was not as nice as the original bright red, but that was, after all, the idea. The replacement parts mounted with just a few minor modifications. He transferred the fuel from the old tank to the new. The final step was transferring the

Arizona license plate from the other bike.

Next was a short walk to a nearby outdoor outfitter to buy a complete set of warm clothes. Back at the storage unit, Mick took off all his clothes and put on the new outfit. While the risk from RFID trackers in the clothing was minimal, Mick wasn't willing to leave anything to chance. He strapped two heavy panniers to the bike, put on the backpack, and set off riding south.

I've definitely gone rogue...

PART II.

CHAPTER 18.

Board Members:

I understand from your reports that the plan is moving forward. I have a few issues that I will address. I expect immediate action on these items.

Timeline. We will need to move up our timeline since UBK has involved the U.S. Government. Our insiders inform us that an inter-department task force has been created to deal with the threats. I need a review of possible scenarios with potential outcomes by next week's meeting.

P2PMSG. Not unexpectedly, Turing has shut down the P2PMSG open source project when the reason for our interest in it was discovered. My opinion is that Turing does not represent a significant threat. We have made many changes to the source code, and it is protected by layers of encryption, and hidden under volumes of spam email.

O'Malley. It appears that he continues to investigate. In fact, our attempts to marginalize him may have motivated him further.

In addition, we have word of a meeting between him and the U.S. Government. It is possible that he is now working for them. It is unlikely that he poses an immediate threat to our operation, but he is dangerous because he seems very adept at putting together the pieces of the puzzle. It is a priority to find him and take him out.

In summary, we need to continue to execute.

The Chairman.

CHAPTER 19.

Mick O'Malley – *loves fresh fish.* *(∅ comments)*

Halfway between Charleston and Antigua, Mick took a break from coding and stretched his arms and legs. He glanced down at his GPS, noting the speed with satisfaction – 11.6 knots – pretty good considering the light breeze. Mick made an exception in this case for archaic units, as knots, or nautical miles per hour, are used the world over for water speed.

It was a clear and sunny day on the Atlantic Ocean. The catamaran, a twin-hulled, single-masted yacht, was making excellent progress sailing to London, England.

Mick had told everyone that he wasn't attending the EuroSecurity conference, saying he was just too busy. Only Kateryna knew the real reason he had cancelled. Mick was worried that Turing might hear that he wasn't coming and give up on making contact, but he tried not to think about that, and instead chose to believe that Turing would still expect Mick to show up somehow. He looked forward to a surprise appearance at the conference, and no one would be more surprised than Kateryna.

Four days had passed since he first read the mails from Mathison and Turing. Two of those days had been on land, while the other two had been spent at sea.

Mick's ride from New Jersey to Charleston, South Carolina was a little cold, but acceptable. On the first night of the ride, he had called his Australian friend Ian Brown from a payphone and explained his plan. Ian was happy to help out, and began immediately prepping his catamaran named 'Gypsy Moth' for the voyage. When he showed up at Ian's door on the second day, Ian was almost ready to set sail.

"G'day, Mick!" Ian said as he opened the door.

"G'day, Ian! Ready to go?" Mick asked.

"If you've got it?" Ian asked, rubbing a thumb and forefinger together. Mick threw a duffle bag at Ian, who grabbed it and peered inside. Seeing the cash, Ian grinned back at him. Mick knew Ian wasn't doing it for the money; Ian would have helped Mick without it, but provisioning for a three week trip (and the return) would cost quite a bit of money. Mick had other reserves, but for now he was just going through his emergency cash.

Less than an hour after parking the Ducati, Mick stepped onto the Zodiac dinghy that took him from the shore to the moored Gypsy Moth. Before darkness fell that day, they were sailing out of Charleston Harbor into the Atlantic. Ian's Brazilian girlfriend Mariana was also crewing on the trip. She was an amazing brunette with piercing brown eyes. Not to be mistaken for arm candy, Mariana was an accomplished sailor in her own right.

The first two days sailing had been very nice, with the weather getting warmer each day as they tracked south. On the first day they hit the Gulf Stream, and the water warmed up considerably. Although the northern route was shorter, this time of year the southern route was more comfortable, and allowed them a stop on the way.

By the fourth day, Mick had slipped into a routine. Lying in his bunk with his computer open, he could hear Ian moving around above decks, probably adjusting the trim of a sail. Ian was an ocean yacht racer at heart, and a charter captain to pay the bills. Even though they weren't in a terrible rush, Ian couldn't help himself making little adjustments and honing their speed.

Mick checked mail again, getting decent broadband speed from Ian's satellite Internet antenna mounted on the deck. The usage charges would be pretty high, but well worth it. Mick wasn't concerned about having his Internet traffic tracked because he was using Ian's account, and all his traffic was encrypted and relayed through a P2P anonymization network then to his own Internet servers. No one monitoring his traffic or his servers would notice anything different in his traffic patterns. A bigger challenge would be spending nearly three weeks at sea without sharing any of the fun with anyone. He had decided to tell no one of the unusual travel arrangements until he was safely in London.

There was a conversation Mick knew he needed to have. He had been delaying it but decided to get it over with. He poked his head out the hatch.

"Ian, I'm going to be on a video call, so don't do anything loud, OK?" he called out. Ian, a knife between his teeth, gave him a thumbs-up as he worked on the starboard safety rail. He looked at him quizzically.

Some kind of pirate homage?

He ducked below decks, set up a background, and fired up the video software. A moment later he was looking at Kateryna in her office in San Francisco.

"Hey Kat, how's things?" he asked.

"I'm good, Mick... So what's the news? I haven't had any mail from you these past few days," she started.

"Well, that's what I wanted to talk to you about, actually," he began, not quite knowing how to begin. "I'm getting a little nervous about all our emails – don't get me wrong, I enjoy writing them and even more reading them from you. But I'm worried that someone else could read them, or even just notice the frequency of our mails, and draw conclusions. I'm sure you don't want to deal with any of that aggravation."

"I understand," she interrupted. Mick noticed her body language shifting subtly. "I admit I've been thinking along the same lines myself. You are right. We should stop exchanging them. But we can still keep videoing and calling, right?"

"Of course!"

"OK, then. This is fine. So I guess you aren't going to make it to London."

"No," he lied. "Not this year."

"When are you going to get your flying problems sorted out?" she asked.

"Don't worry, I'm working hard on it," he replied, grinning. She gave him a killer smile that instantly made him feel better.

"Good. I'll be arriving in England the week before the conference starts. I'm also considering a trip to the continent the week after the conference. It has been many years since I've been back to the old country or even Eastern Europe."

"That sounds great," he replied, feeling relieved. He hoped she wasn't sensing that he was hiding things from her. "Oh, I forgot to tell you, I have a new consulting job that is keeping me really busy," he lied.

"With JCN? Gunter asked me to convince you to take it but I told him you were a big boy and could make up your own mind," she replied.

"No, a different one... lots of work, at least for a couple of weeks. And, I need to run now, actually."

"OK, sounds good! Hey, I'm glad we had this conversation, Mick. Thanks for bringing it up."

"No problems," he replied and they signed off.

Three days later, they were joined by dolphins. Mick took pictures, wondering when he would get to share them with his friends. They swam alongside and in front of the hulls for hours, occasionally leaping out of the water. They seemed to live only for fun, and Mick envied them. They swam so close to the hulls that they must occasionally touch, Mick thought. He wished he could dive in and swim with them, but he knew he wouldn't be able to keep up. He watched the dolphins the entire two hours they swam with Gypsy Moth, as they might be their only company on the long trip.

Mick kept active on his social networks, but avoided saying very much about himself. He read about Lars' annoyance with a broken link on the website of the "Journal of Irreproducible Results," and about Liz's dilemma with an old friend from high school who, having reconnected with her on a social network, wouldn't leave her alone.

During the voyage, Mick and Ian had developed a kind of end-of-evening ritual in which they would jokingly discuss Mick's predicament.

"So tell me again why the bloody hell you can't fly to London on an aeroplane like a normal bastard?" Ian asked one evening.

"I told you, I'm on the No-Fly list – you know, the one filled with terrorists and eight-year-old cub scouts?" he responded.

"So which are you, then?" was the response.

"Neither, I'm just a nobody who must have pissed off someone."

"And why is it so bloody important you get there? There's a sheila involved, right?" Ian said, using Australian slang for a woman.

"I told you, I've been set up. The botnet that I'm fighting –"

"Yeah, right. Whatever floats your boat… I'm going to bed – 'night!" Ian replied as he headed below decks.

"Very funny," Mick called out.

Mick heard a bang and a swear word as Ian hit his head on the bulkhead.

It was Mick's turn on watch so he stayed up on deck. When he wasn't scanning the horizon, checking their course, or monitoring instruments and radar, he was looking up at the night sky. He looked up star charts and identified the constellations and planets. He reacquainted himself with Ian's sextant and used it to take bearings and readings. He even did the math to see how accurate it was, compared to the GPS, and found his sights were fairly accurate. In short, he distracted himself and made the most of this unique opportunity. He also thought a lot about Kateryna. Now that he didn't get a mail from her every day, he found himself thinking about her more. He wondered what she was doing, whom she was with, and what she was thinking and feeling. He estimated it was still over ten days until she would leave for Europe. He debated sending her a mail, but decided against it.

He enjoyed the sensation of seeing the horizon in every direction – nothing but water and sky. Out in the middle of the ocean, it was not hard to understand why sailors believed in the edge of the world, where the maps ended, often labeled 'here be dragons.'

Five days later, they hit the first 'weather' of the trip. The wind had been building to twenty knots, and the seas increased to about two meters in height. Fortunately, the wind direction was from the north, giving them a nice broad reach on their southeasterly course, the fastest and most stable point of sail. His GPS indicated they were making almost 18 knots as they cut through the waves.

He mused about the origin of the knot as speed over the water. Back in the early days of sailing ships, speed was measured using a wooden board, known as a 'log' that was thrown overboard with an attached rope. As the ship sailed away from the log in the water, the rope was payed out. The rope had knots tied in it at regular intervals. By counting the number of knots that went past in a set amount of time determined by an hourglass, the ship's speed over the water, in 'knots' was determined. This information was taken regularly and recorded in a book that became known as the 'log book'. The term also found its way into computer jargon. A computer generates 'log' entries every time a user does something or runs a program. To use a computer, a user 'logs in' in, which involves being authenticated by the computer, gaining access to the computer.

In the rough seas, Mick gave up doing any work and stayed above decks; he felt it was better to get a bit wet than get seasick. Mick had avoided any seasickness so far, helped greatly by the gradual buildup of wind and waves. He was almost fully adjusted to life at sea. He knew he would experience the reverse when back on dry land: a feeling of queasiness due to the lack of the wavelike motion of the sea that would take a few days to overcome.

Mick hoped to eventually be able to infiltrate the botnet, to read and understand messages sent in it, and even be able to send his own messages. But first, he had to fully understand the messages. With his daily decrypted messages, he was building quite a dataset of the operation of the botnet. Using the P2PMSG source code provided by Turing, Mick was able to interpret the botnet messages. He was even able to turn one of his servers into a member of the botnet. But, he was very careful not to tip off the owners that their botnet was being infiltrated.

Mick cranked the handle on the winch – the 'coffee grinder' Ian called it even though it was actually a modern self-tailing winch. Mick made a slight adjustment to the jib – the forward sail – for the umpteenth time today. The wind had picked up even more. With enough wind, a smaller catamaran such as a Hobie would start to fly one hull – leaning or heeling over until it lifted out of the water. An ocean-going cat such as Gypsy Moth would not do this, but instead would start to bury the leeward (side away from the wind) hull in the water. When this happens, the sailors have to either reef the sail (reduce the sail area to depower the boat) or change course so the wind isn't blowing so hard on the sail. So far, they had not needed to do either.

A few days later, after the weather had passed, the crew of Gypsy Moth sat around the cockpit enjoying the warmth of the morning sun on their skin. They were now far enough south that they all wore shorts. Mariana wore a bikini top. Mick suspected that Ian had told her that he was a Yank/Pom (Aussie slang for an American/Englishman) prude, or some such, and she should refrain from going topless on deck. Mick greatly appreciated this.

"Mick," Mariana began, taking a sip of her latte, made with Ian's excellent espresso machine in the galley. The stored coffee reserves below decks were quite impressive as well, and Mick enjoyed the aroma. "You've obviously done some cruising before. What have you sailed, and where?"

"Well, besides a few months with Ian in the Whitsundays a few years back," Mick began, referring to a series of tropical islands off the coast of Queensland in Australia. "I've chartered yachts in Puerto Rico and sailed from Helsinki to Stockholm, once. I've also done my share of dinghy sailing – my favorite are eighteen foot skiffs. There's nothing better than racing them on Sydney Harbor!"

"Very nice! The Atlantic is nice, but there's nothing

like the Pacific. I wanted to thank you for financing our little autumn getaway. I had been itching to go offshore but hadn't been able to break Ian away from his little yacht building project," she replied, reaching out with her foot to tap Ian.

"You are most welcome. You have no idea how important this trip is for me – I owe you one. But Ian, you haven't told me about this project," Mick replied.

"Ah, well, it is a twenty meter long trimaran, built using composites, and designed to fly a hull!" Ian began. Cruising trimarans keep all three of their hulls in the water, but performance ones are designed to heel over a little so that one hull (or even two) lift out of the water, for less drag and faster speeds.

"What a beauty!"

"I know. But I've just started construction. It will probably not be until late summer or autumn next year before she is ready to launch. I've been working on her a lot, but I did need the break. And this trip will be nice, even though I have to put up with having your sorry arse aboard!"

"Ian! That is no way to talk to your friend!" Mariana replied, scolding him. Mick and Ian just laughed.

"Mariana is a smart girl, but she has difficulty understanding the Aussie sense of humor," Ian said to Mick. He turned to Mariana. "Mick is a mate, not just a friend – there's a big difference. And, I've told you before, dearest, the more I like someone, the more I hang shit on them."

"Yes, yes... whatever," Mariana replied, looking bored.

"Don't give me that look!" Ian replied, sliding over and putting his arms around her slight frame as he pulled her into his lap. She giggled back at him.

Mick knew how this would end, so he finished his espresso, excused himself and went forward on the port hull. Ian and Mariana's berth was astern in the other hull, so they'd have plenty of privacy. He clipped his safety harness on the rail, and slung one leg over each side of the bow, feeling the occasional spray on his bare legs, and tried not to think of Kateryna.

The next day, being Wednesday, it was time to change all his passwords. Mick thought for a few minutes then typed:

```
R3adyAboutHardalee@sea
```

It was Mick's turn to cook the day's meals, and he was feeling hungry for some fresh fish. He opened the fishing locker in the port hull and got out the tackle. A few minutes later, he had two lines trailing in the water behind them. He didn't have long to wait until he had a decent sized fish hooked. It took him more than fifteen minutes to land the fish; it fought all the way to the boat. Hooking it with the gaff pole, he lifted the tuna into the cockpit and readied the line for another cast. Once he had two fish, about three kilograms all together, he stowed the lines away. He cleaned the fish, cut six large steaks and headed to the galley. He slowly grilled them over the gas with a little lemon juice and basil. The dinner was a great success, and Ian and Mariana toasted his culinary prowess.

Mick posted to his friends about the meal, even including a picture of his plate. Of course, his friends had little idea of how fresh the fish really was.

A few days later, Mick sent his first message to be inserted into the P2P botnet communications network. The next morning, Mick examined some decrypted responses from the botnet and was pleased to identify a reply to his message. The message he sent was nothing more than a glorified "Hello World!" program, designed to generate a simple response from another computer in the botnet. If he got an error or no response, it would have suggested he didn't fully understand the way the botnet communicated. Fortunately, he did get a response from another computer, confirming he was on the right track.

The information he had gleaned from the link Turing had provided him had proved to be invaluable. It proved that the Zed.Kicker botnet was definitely using the P2P communication and messaging software developed by Turing. Being able to send a message into the botnet didn't mean he could control the botnet. He still needed to do a lot more work before he could pretend to be a botnet controller and issue commands to the botnet. But at least now he could read and understand the commands and knew how to create them. He began to document the differences between Turing's open source code and the actual Zed.Kicker code.

The following day, Mick looked over the latest deciphered botnet control traffic. Although he was sure he had deciphered it correctly, he couldn't understand what it meant. He saw a list: "biz coop aero" with a date and time, the next day at ØØØØZ, which meant midnight Zulu time or GMT – Greenwich Mean Time. Mick recognized the three words in the list as Internet Top Level Domains (TLDs). For example, company.biz domain name could be registered by a business and used for its web address or email addresses. The other two were also TLDs, but they weren't in common use. The aero TLD was used for the aviation industry and coop was used for cooperatives. Mick couldn't think of any companies that used these domains off the top of his head but with a little searching, he found a few.

He also received a fraction: 1/1Ø24. He could not figure out what this fraction meant or represented. As Gypsy Moth progressed eastwards, his current time zone was getting closer to GMT or Zulu time, so midnight in England was now evening for him. He arranged for Ian to take his watch that night so he could be online at that time to see what would happen.

At exactly ØØØØZ, Mick monitored the botnet traffic but didn't see anything unusual – a steady stream of spam was moving, but otherwise nothing. Then he sent a message to one of the .biz domains he had looked up the previous day – there was no response. He tried another – the same. He tried his list of .coop and .aero domains and found them all unresponsive. He knew exactly what this meant: the botnet must be targeting the domain name servers for these TLDs with a flood of traffic to take them out – a classic denial of service or DOS attack. He performed a DNS trace using a utility called 'dig' and confirmed it: there was no response to either the .biz, .aero, or .coop domain servers.

Mariana poked her head inside Mick's cabin as he was looking over the traces.

"Hullo there!" she called out. "Ian says you are all excited about something!"

"Yep, I'm analyzing a denial of service attack on the Internet by the botnet I've been tracking," he began, and seeing little comprehension on her face, he continued. "You know the Internet addresses we use all the time, like amazon dot com or google dot com? Well, they are called 'domains' and there is a bunch of computers, called domain name servers that help computers on the Internet find the services associated with these domains: for example, how to find the web server of that domain, or how to deliver an email message to that domain. The botnet is flooding some of those key domain name servers with too many fake requests, making them crash and go offline. So right now, you can't send mail or get to the website of company dot biz or airline dot aero or apartments dot coop. In short, part of the Internet is broken, which is a very serious thing." He searched her face to see if this helped.

"You are an intense guy!" was her only reply, as she

shook her head and resumed her duties above decks.

Mick now understood the fraction; it was the fraction of the hosts in the botnet that participated in the distributed denial of service (DDOS) attack. In this case, only .1% of the Zed.Kicker botnet was needed to completely crash these top level domains! This was one powerful botnet!

He did some quick web searches and couldn't find any confirmation that this was occurring. He attributed it to the fact that these domains were little used. If this had happened to com, for example, in which every website or email that ended in .com would suddenly stop working, the reaction would be a lot bigger. Mick realized that this attack, like the others over the past few weeks, was just a dry run: an experiment, a test. A successful test, he noted. He quickly wrote a script that polled the name servers at five second intervals to note the exact time when the outage would end. He didn't have long to wait – at about Ø1ØØZ, the outage suddenly was over. Mick found the control messages just prior to this time and sent them out to be decrypted. He hoped they might have some information about the source, the place from which the botnet instructions were originating.

One thing kept bothering Mick: the count of zombie computers in the botnet. Now that he was reading botnet messages, he realized that there was a discrepancy. About 15% of the computers did not seem to be sending messages, even though they were part of the botnet. He still could not rule out that this was a mistake on his part, or perhaps a bug in the botnet software. He had a feeling, however, that it meant something. What, he didn't know.

In the morning, he did find discussion on the Internet about the outage. He also came across some interesting speculation on a web wiki about Zed.Kicker for the first time as well, although it was mistakenly classified as a worm rather than a botnet. However, the news failed to make the mainstream media or even the corporate press.

No one seemed to know what had happened. Most people just assumed it was a screw-up by the operator, under the incorrect assumption that the three top level domains were all operated by the same company. It seemed, once again, only Mick knew the truth.

The last few hundred nautical miles were spent working northward towards the Canary Islands where Ian planned to stop over and re-provision. Mick was feeling impatient about arriving in England; he felt he was fast running out of time.

The wind had shifted to the northeast, which forced them to tack, or zigzag their way along. It slowed their effective speed towards the port, since they couldn't sail directly towards it. But, it also meant a fun maneuver that involved everyone aboard.

When it was time to tack, Ian would get everyone up on deck, even if it meant waking from sleep. Ian took the helm, steering the catamaran. Mick worked the winch to pull the jib, the sail in front of the mast, from one side to the other. The mainsail, supported on its bottom edge by a horizontal pole, known as the boom would also swing to the other side during the tack.

Mariana watched all the ropes, called 'lines', to make sure they all flowed freely. When everyone was in position, Ian called out "Ready about!" As he steered the bow of the catamaran into the wind, he called out "Hard alee!" which was meant he was turning the wheel so that the helm was hard to the leeward side of the yacht, which turns it towards the wind. As the jib started luffing or flapping in the wind, Mariana released the line on one side and Mick winched it over the other side. As the bow crossed in front of the wind, the wind caught on the other side of the main sail, moving the boom across. The flogging jib caught the wind on the other side, and Ian straightened the helm. He had steered the yacht through about 9Ø degrees of course change, completing the tack.

They did this about every four hours, or six times per day for the last three days of the voyage to the Canaries. By the second day, Ian let Mick or Mariana take the helm except at night when he did it himself. Mick could feel his muscles toning up, and his appetite increasing.

On the nineteenth day of the voyage, Mick sighted land; they made for the port of Tenerife. As they approached the harbor, Ian fired up the inboard diesel engines, and they motored in. They found a dock and came ashore, heading for the customs office.

Being on dry land felt very strange to Mick: the ground felt very hard and unforgiving. When he stood still, it seemed the horizon moved and swayed slightly. He knew this would wear off in a day or two if he stayed on dry land, but he hoped to only spend a minimum of time there and get back to Gypsy Moth. The London conference was only two weeks away, so they didn't have much time to waste. They still had over 15ØØ nautical miles to go.

Mick was slightly nervous when he handed over his British passport to the customs official, but, as expected, they did not have a computer in the office, and it was stamped with only a cursory inspection.

They next walked down to the market and stocked up on fresh supplies, especially fruit, vegetables, and coffee. They arranged for a pile of food to be delivered to their dock later in the day. They changed some U.S. dollars into British pounds and Euros. Mick also purchased a couple of prepaid mobile phones with data plans.

Mick was glad to be back on Gypsy Moth a few hours later. As his body had adjusted to the constant motion of the boat on the water, Mick had felt a little ill back on dry land. His worst moment of 'land-sickness' came when he used the bathroom in a shop. Inside the stall, the walls seemed to move and sway and he was almost sick. Being back on the ship made him feel comfortable and relaxed.

Ian and Mariana wanted to go out for the evening and Mick was perfectly happy to stay aboard and keep watch.

Mick took the opportunity to connect to a wireless network accessible from the harbor, enjoying the faster speed and lower latency Internet connection than the satellite link he had been using.

The next afternoon, they cast off and sailed right out of the harbor without running the diesels.

That evening, Mick watched as Mariana worked away in the galley with some kind of vegetable in a small circular bowl and what looked like a long stick. She noticed his quizzical looks.

"Ever had chimarrao before?" she asked. When he shook his head, she explained. "It is a traditional Brazilian hot drink made with yerba – kind of like tea."

"Interesting," Mick replied, and continued watching. Once it was prepared, Mariana put the long stick inside the bowl, which turned out to be a type of straw. The three of them sat around the cockpit. Mariana took a sip, then continued to drink until she apparently finished. She smiled at Mick as she refilled the bowl with hot water and stirred for a few moments.

"Now your turn... Drink all of it," she instructed. Mick drank, and was amazed at the taste – kind of like a cross between coffee and tea.

"That was really different!" he said, and continued drinking until he had emptied the bowl. "Does it have caffeine?" he asked.

"I don't know," Mariana replied. "Probably." She refilled a third time and Ian drank.

They each had a few more, as they watched the sun set over the water.

The weather turned colder and the seas heavier as they headed north towards England. They were crossing very busy international shipping routes, so someone always had to be on the lookout for other vessels. The new AIS or Automatic Identification System software Mick had purchased and installed on Ian's computer was really showing its value now. The screen now showed the position, name, course, and speed of all the other yachts and ships in the vicinity, so they could make early course corrections to avoid collisions or close encounters. The small AIS radio receiver supplied this information via a USB port.

One day, Mick saw another sail on the horizon but he couldn't identify the yacht or hail them on VHF radio, and they didn't have AIS. On the next night watch, Mick saw a supertanker off to port, named 'Mariposa'. He estimated its length as over 300m from the onboard radar. Since its cruising speed was only a little faster than Gypsy Moth's, according to the AIS, and they were headed in the same direction, Mick watched it most of the night.

Even with the higher seas, the catamaran still cut nicely through the waves. Everyone was back to wearing foul weather gear above decks such as waterproof jackets and pants with fleece underneath. Mick was sure that Mariana wished they had stayed and explored the Canary Islands, or somewhere else warm, instead of heading north into winter, but she didn't complain. He needed to come up with a good way to thank them both. He hoped, perhaps, that the two of them could take their time on the way home, presuming that he was able to find another way home. Actually, he hadn't been thinking very much beyond making it to London, meeting his mysterious contact Turing, and attempting to shut down the botnet. This wasn't the first time he had been so single minded, he knew, but it was perhaps the riskiest.

As they approached the coast of England a few days later, Mick got ready. He packed up his luggage into a single roller bag, which he gave to Ian for delivery to London. He packed a few things into a small water-proof backpack. He put on a thick wet suit, mask, snorkel, and fins. He hugged Mariana goodbye and shook hands with Ian, thanking him again for all his help. Then, when they were less than two kilometers off the coast, Mick strapped on his bag and jumped overboard into the icy black water. He treaded water for a few minutes as he watched Gypsy Moth sail away towards Plymouth where they would put in a few hours later. He set off swimming towards the shore.

CHAPTER 1A.

From the Security Wiki

Zed.Kicker (worm)

Jump to: navigation, search

Zed.Kicker is a newly discovered worm that is spread from an infected web server to another web server using HTTPS transport. It is effective against version 2.0 and earlier of Apache. It was first identified in October when it was used in the 'Carbon is Poison' exploit that affected a significant percentage of websites [1]. In addition, it is known to install a spambot which sends out a significant volume of spam emails.

The worm reportedly uses a TLS connection over port 443, although this has not been confirmed

An unknown number of web servers are still

compromised. The number is estimated to be in the tens of thousands [2].

The source and origin of the worm has not yet been determined, although there has been widespread speculation about linkages to eco-terror organizations due to the environmentalist message posted on the web page.

CHAPTER 1B.

To the members of the Joint Anti-Botnet
Information Taskforce:

Perhaps my previous memos have not been clear.
I will be perfectly blunt in this one to ensure
there is no confusion.

We believe that O'Malley knows more about the
botnet than he has been willing to share. As a
result, finding and apprehending him is a top
priority. The grand jury subpoena issued for
him to testify next week should give us the
necessary grounds for this, as he is unlikely to
show up.

In preparation for this, I want a list of all
his known family members, associates,
residences, hangouts, etc. I want a complete
list of all his bank accounts, debit and credit
cards. He will eventually run out of cash and
this will be an opportunity to locate him.

He also may have additional identities besides
the two of which we are aware. He could be
using another identity or Internet alias right
now without us knowing. We need Langley's help

on this.

Do we know if he has left the country? We must reach out to Canada and Mexico, as that would be the easiest way for him to flee. We should notify MI5 and G2 as well.

I want our best code breakers on his communication intercepts. First priority will be his written communication, followed by his VoIP communication. Get help from the NSA as needed.

We should be able to track his mobile communications. We should also analyze traffic into and out of his servers.

Finally, I want us to review those contingency plans for keeping basic government functions up and running if Zed.Kicker is unleashed, based on what we know about the botnet.

Additionally we may need to break out non-traditional communication methods that do not rely on the Internet infrastructure.

General

CHAPTER 1C.

Mick O'Malley *– knows life isn't always smooth sailing.*
(2 comments)

Mick took a break from swimming after about a half hour, and to confirm his course, pulled out a waterproof GPS that Ian had loaned him. The stars no longer seemed so bright, and he could see the glow of civilization in the distance. He was on track.

Another half hour of swimming, and Mick picked a landing spot, a dark area that seemed to have fewer rocks and breakers. He knew the most dangerous part of the swim would be next. He reached down as he swam with his hands to feel for the bottom. When he touched the bottom with his fingertips, Mick put his feet down and pushed off towards the shore. A moment later he was on dry land. He looked back and was convinced that this little sandy area was the best place to come ashore – on either side were rocks and a little further on was a sheer cliff.

Mick found a place behind some bushes out of the wind. He stripped off the wetsuit, dried off quickly, and dressed in his clothes from the backpack. He dug a hole in the dirt and buried all the swimming gear in a plastic bag, noting the coordinates in the GPS. Mick got out his wallet and passport and put them in his coat.

He had chosen to swim ashore to avoid having his passport stamped and scanned, just in case his name was on some kind of international terrorist watch list. Mick carried only his British passport. As he was still a British subject, he felt like he hadn't actually done anything wrong. He was legally entitled to be here, even if he had sidestepped the official procedures Ian and Mariana would be going through. He set off walking towards Penzance, wondering if he might meet some pirates, thinking of the Gilbert and Sullivan opera. He walked rapidly and started to warm up, despite the chill of his damp hair.

It was a frosty morning, and Mick saw the sun rise over the fields as he hiked towards town. He came over the crest of a hill and Penzance opened up below him. He recalled a long weekend getaway in Penzance with his parents many years ago; the happy memories warmed him up even more.

Mick didn't need the GPS to find the main street in town.

As Mick walked through the streets, he soaked up the English cityscape: the shops, the buses, the smaller cars zipping along on the "wrong" side of the road to his Americanized eyes. There were also lots of motorbikes, scooters, and taxis. Feeling a little cold, he stopped at a small shop and bought a warmer hat and gloves. In another shop, he bought two prepaid mobiles with data plans. He activated the phones then removed their SIM cards. He added them to his small collection – about two dozen all together. He put the SIM card in his mobile, reprogrammed it, and was online again. He planned to switch SIMs every day or so to make his wireless Internet access more difficult to trace.

Mick took a moment to send a mail to Ian saying "The eagle has landed," their non-original phrase to indicate he had made it safely ashore, along with the coordinates of the buried wetsuit and gear.

At a bookshop, he flipped through various motorcycle, racing, and sailing magazines. He was killing time before he caught his train to London, and he needed to get his 'land legs' back.

Stopping at a café, he sat at a table by the window and sipped tea. He never drank tea in America – it just wasn't safe. Here, however, he knew it would taste just like his mother made it: hot, strong, with lots of milk – not weak, strange colored or tasting, or with lemon!

He continued walking down to the waterfront. There were some other visitors and couples strolling, as well as some Korean tourists. He saw various working vessels and ships moored there, and a couple of pleasure boats as well. Mick wondered how Ian and Mariana were doing in Plymouth, just a few kilometers up the coast. They were hopefully moored and through all their customs paperwork. Perhaps they were planning for a night out at a pub. He already missed being aboard Gypsy Moth with his shipmates, but didn't dare visit them; they had done him a huge favor by bringing him here, and he didn't want to risk getting them into trouble.

Sitting in a nearly deserted park, he decided to finally contact Kateryna. He knew from her social network that she was traveling in Northumbria in Northern England.

"Mick! How are you?" she asked, her face filling his mobile screen. The quality was obviously inferior to their usual desktop video setup, but it wasn't bad. As his video was also lower quality, Kateryna knew right away he was traveling as well. "Or should I say, where are you?" she added.

"Would you believe Penzance?" he replied. The quizzical look on her face made him continue. "In

Cornwall… England?"

"No, really? How did you? Really?" was all she could reply, making him laugh.

"Yes, really! I'll be in London tonight. I'll see you at the conference!"

"OK, so forget the conference, congrats on getting your No-Fly problem sorted!"

"Actually, I haven't… I didn't fly. Would you believe, I sailed? I set out twenty-eight days ago from Charleston on my friend's cruising catamaran, and voila! Here I am," he explained, enjoying himself. Kateryna was speechless. After a short pause, he continued, "So how do you like the North? Did you visit Lindisfarne yet? It is well worth a visit!"

"Ah, I like it a lot… you sailed? You sailed the Atlantic Ocean to get here? Just for the EuroSecurity conference? You truly *are* crazy! Did you have any problems with customs and immigration?" she asked.

"Let's just say it went swimmingly. And yes, I came here for the conference, but also I'm meeting someone here about my latest project… I'll explain when I see you in person."

"Wow – that is amazing! I can't believe I'll be seeing you tomorrow night, Mick." Mick hoped the flush he felt going through his body at her mention of his name didn't show over the video. He reminded himself that he was still upset with her over her deception.

"Me, neither. Well, I'll let you get back to your holiday. By the way, don't tell anyone else – I want to surprise everyone!"

"Of course! Liz was just telling me the other day how much she was going to miss you at this conference… Everyone has been talking about you. It seems you are some kind of fixture… or mascot."

"Thanks… I think?" Mick replied. "Until Sunday, then!"

That afternoon he walked to the Penzance train station and caught a First Great Western train to London. He found the trip was very civilized and comfortable. The English countryside felt very familiar to him, but he knew London would feel almost like home. He wondered if perhaps later in the week he would have a chance to visit some cousins and family friends.

Mick knew from his social network where Lars was staying and which pub he was frequenting tonight. Alighting at Paddington Station, he transferred to the Tube, the unofficial name for London's underground railway. After studying the map for a minute, he noticed the font and made a mental note to ask Lars about it. He rode to Piccadilly station, where he emerged into the crowded streets for the short walk to where Lars was hanging out.

He noticed a large percentage of the traffic was cabs. The congestion tax that had to be paid to drive a car into central London seemed to be having the desired effect of reducing traffic. He surprised Lars who was leaning on the bar with his elbow.

"Bloody hell, I can't believe you are here!" was his greeting from Lars.

"Yeah, great to see you, as well!" he replied. "Hey, I don't have a room to stay in. Can I camp out in yours?"

"Sure, Mick! You are lucky my room got upgraded to a suite with two beds in it or you'd be on the floor..."

"And you think you got that complementary upgrade by chance?" Mick asked, grinning at Lars. "I upgraded your reservation for you..."

"No way! You are too much, Mick!" Lars replied, shaking his head. "So what's up? I thought you weren't coming?"

"I'll explain as we walk," he promised, but he only told Lars half the story. He left out his 'interview' with the government, his financial difficulties, and Turing. He would have like to tell Lars, but he didn't want to involve him in any further.

At the hotel, he asked Lars to check with reception to see if anything had arrived. Lars returned with a bag and a puzzled look. Mick was pleased to have his luggage, which had been sent on by Ian. Up in the room, he was excited to retrieve his computer, which had nothing on it besides the operating system. He had performed a disk wipe on the solid state storage before he packed it on Gypsy Moth. He knew that a disk wipe was much more secure than reformatting, as it writes new data to every storage location, multiple times, making recovery of information virtually impossible. Just deleting files on a disk does nothing more than removing a pointer from the disk directory index – all the information is still on the disk, and can be retrieved by a data recovery expert. Mick was not willing to risk his private information falling into the wrong hands.

He established a secure connection to his servers on the Internet and restored all the files and folders on his computer from a disk image backup. Less than an hour later, he was up and running again. He looked over the latest decrypts from the botnet.

Mick checked in with his social network, giving what he hoped was a final less-than-truthful posting. He learned Liz was flying an ever-so-long Dallas-Heathrow non-stop flight. Kateryna was still traveling south on the train towards London. There were no recent postings from Gunter.

Lars had already picked up his conference registration badge, so Mick was able to make a reasonable facsimile that would give him access to most conference venues without having to register, or pay. It felt wrong, but he couldn't take the risk.

The next day, Mick took it easy and fully adjusted to

life on land. He had a nice video call with Sam. Instead of reading, she asked Mick for stories about England and London, and about their relatives. By the end of the conversation, she had moved England up two places on her list.

The fun Mick had in the evening surprising everyone at the pre-conference social event almost made all his No-Fly difficulties worth it. Liz had screamed and then hugged him. Kateryna did a good job of acting surprised to see him. He felt a little like the prodigal son. Even his nemesis Miles came over to talk and was strangely pleasant. All the while, Mick kept a lookout for Turing, hoping that he hadn't heard that Mick wasn't coming. Of course, with all the attention Mick was getting, he couldn't really tell if anyone in particular were watching him, as nearly everyone was, just out of curiosity.

It's a shame I can't present on my current project – that would generate some buzz! Hopefully, after it is all over, I'll be able to share the work. Or not.

Although he really wanted to get back to his decrypts, Mick agreed to go to a pub with a group including Lars. They set off walking down Oxford Street until they found a street with a sufficient density of pubs to commence their crawl. Mick had yet to detect any signs of surveillance, which either meant there was none, or it was being done very professionally. He knew it was risky being in public, and that eventually the U.S. Government would learn he was here. However, right now making contact with Turing was more important. And for that to happen, he needed to be seen to be at the conference. For a few minutes, he reflected on his electronic trail since departing Manhattan; he could not find any obvious mistakes that would make it easy to track him. This thought reminded him to switch SIM cards in his mobile again.

Mick mused that there were few places as good as London for a pub crawl, although perhaps Melbourne,

Australia was close. Mick bought his 'shout' or his round of drinks early, thus allowing him the freedom to leave when he wished. To leave a pub before taking his turn of buying drinks for the whole group was an unforgivable breech of etiquette that Mick couldn't possibly commit. A little later when he told Lars he was retiring early, Lars followed him out of the pub and into the street to talk.

"Stay a while longer, Mick. There's a lot I want to tell you..." Lars began.

"Yeah, like what?" Mick replied.

"Well, for one thing, I've been trying to track down Jasinski – you know, the one that helped figured out the mail server zero day we worked on? Well, this guy must be a Halloween ghost or something. I haven't been able to find out anything about him or find anyone who knows about him. You and I know that someone with his skills doesn't just come out of nowhere. I'm puzzled, but I'm going to keep searching."

"That's interesting, Lars. Keep me posted on what you find out."

"Will do, mate," Lars replied.

"I really do need to turn in," Mick replied.

"OK. Well, I'd better get back to my drink! Have a good evening – I'll try not to wake you when I return!" Lars saluted, turned, and held open the door for a group of chattering young women who were entering the pub. He winked at Mick, and then followed them in.

Mick enjoyed the walk back to his hotel. London really felt right to him. Despite living in the greatest city in the world, he could still miss London at times like this.

The next day, there was the usual slew of industry announcements, gossip, and rumors making the rounds at the conference. Unlike Hiroshima, Seattle, or Vegas, this conference had an exhibition floor where various vendors and companies showed off their latest hardware and software products. Mick did a quick tour through to see whether there was anything new or exciting, or any good giveaways. He avoided the booths that were scanning barcodes; his barcode looked legit but would never validate. Besides, he got enough spam. At the very least, the show floor was usually good for a laugh, to see what the clueless marketing types had come up with to hock their wares.

He spotted Lars across the hall and waved. Lars was hanging out at a booth that, coincidentally, had the most attractive women handing out literature.

He was heading out of the hall when he was surprised by Miles.

"Mick – got a second?" Miles began.

"Sure, what's up?" he asked warily.

"Umm… let's talk in the speaker's lounge," Miles suggested, and they walked through the crowds, sitting down at a table in a small room.

"Take a look at this," Miles said, handing his mobile to Mick. Mick quickly read from the screen:

```
...  Because of this appalling state of affairs,
I am forced to take action.  In three days I
will demonstrate a series of zero day attacks
against  a  variety  of  open  source  Internet
applications.    Some    may    think    this
irresponsible, but perhaps this will finally get
the community to wake up and take action!

Mick O'Malley
```

He looked up at Miles in confusion and anger. Mile's software showed that the digital signature validated – according to the crypto, this was an authenticated email message sent by Mick!

"Did you –" he began.

"Definitely not!" Miles interrupted. "I received it this morning as an attachment from an anonymizer service. I think whoever sent this wants me to distribute it for them."

"And are you?"

"No, of course not. I know you didn't write this! I knew you didn't write the *ISW* mail either, but that one was mostly harmless. This... this mail could get you a trip to Scotland Yard!" Miles explained. Mick nodded, somewhat surprised by Miles' admission. Mick always assumed their antagonism was personal, but apparently, not this personal. "Do you have any idea who is doing this to you? Or why?"

"Well, I have some clues... it relates to a contract I took on a while back."

Another private key compromise! Unbelievable!

"Mick, there's more," Miles began, pausing for a moment.

"More?" he asked.

"Take a look at the forwarding mail... the full set of headers," he paused while Mick examined the mail that had forwarded the forged note. It took him a moment, but he saw what Miles had seen.

"What the hell!" he cursed, louder than he intended. He immediately stood up as others turned to look at him.

"I know," Miles began. "I'm really sorry, Mick. Don't worry, I'm not going to do anything with this mail except archive it..." Miles was still talking as Mick left the room and sprinted down the hall. He stopped at the technical support desk for the conference. There was no one getting helped, so he was able to talk straight away to the young woman with bobbed dark hair.

"May I borrow a small flathead and a Philips screwdriver, please?" he asked, catching his breath.

"Sure, love. Here you go," she said pulling two tools out of a case.

He threw his computer on the table, flipped it over, grabbed a tool, and set to work removing the tiny screws on the case. He held his palm against the end of the driver and rapidly spun it around with the fingers and thumb of his other hand in a rapid motion, as if he were a mechanic in a Formula 1 pit stop. With all the screws out, he slid the other screwdriver between the join in the case and pried it open. In another moment, he had the keyboard disconnected from the motherboard – the main circuit board of the computer. He swore again, this time under his breath, staring at a tiny, evil-looking circuit board that was crimped onto the keyboard connector – a hardware keylogger. He ripped it off, dislodging the keyboard cable. Glancing up at the girl, he slipped it in his pocket. He removed the motherboard, extracted the sold state drive, then smashed the motherboard across his knee, bending and splintering it.

The woman stepped back, aghast.

He composed himself, then asked "Do you have a rubbish bin handy?" She lifted a trash can up from behind the counter, and he dropped the pieces into it, holding onto the case and the screen.

"Sorry about that," he replied. "I just really hated that computer!" he explained, then turned and walked away.

Having removed the keylogging circuit, Mick knew that his computer was most likely secure again, but he just didn't want to take a chance his firmware or other chips had been tampered with. Plus, it had felt good to take out his anger.

Who put the keylogger on my computer? And when?

Whoever put it there knew everything he had typed: all his carefully chosen passwords, every mail, and every line of code he had written! This must have been how they stole his private key. The thought of it made him crazy with anger again.

Mick now needed a new computer. Buying an off-the-shelf computer in a shop was obviously out – how could he be sure it didn't also have a keylogger or other malware built into it? Mick located a few computer parts stores on his mobile. He ignored the closest and most obvious shop and instead chose one a little further out.

Is my paranoia getting the best of me?

He plotted a route there on the Tube and set out.

Mick arrived nearly an hour later and set about building a new computer from scratch. He had kept the screen and his old case. The case was a one-off custom CNC case he designed himself last year, and was machined from a block of aluminum.

First, he selected a motherboard. He chose the fastest processor ignoring the usual speed/battery life tradeoff. He selected RAM (Random Access Memory) and a flash drive – no hard drive needed. The video card was the hardest choice. He studied the specs for a few minutes before selecting one that seemed to have the right resolution for his screen. A keyboard (sans keylogger!) completed his new computer. He skipped the battery isle. Mick pushed the now full cart to the checkout.

"Someone's getting a *fab* new computer!" the checkout guy said, wowed by the set of components chosen by Mick. Mick didn't really hear him as he handed over some pound notes. Mick asked whether he could use a work bench for an hour. The clerk nodded, and after completing the sale, took Mick to the back.

Mick unpacked the components. He attached an anti-static guard to his wrist to ensure no static electricity buildup that could damage the sensitive electronic components. He worked quickly and completed the build in about half an hour. When he turned around, he was surprised to see a small crowd of employees on their lunch break watching him work. They scattered quickly.

With everything assembled, he retrieved what he had been using as a bookmark from his copy of *The Innocents Abroad*, bent out the connectors on the top, and connected it into the wiring harness of the motherboard. He grinned.

No computer has a better battery life than this one – thanks Vince!

Thinking of Vince brought to mind his difficulties with the U.S. Government, and the fact that at some point he needed to sort them out. He resolved to do so, but later.

He powered up the computer and verified that the BIOS (Basic Input/Output System) functioned properly by running some tests and utilities. The rest of the install he would have to do on the network, so he packed up and took the Tube back to the hotel. With the new computer on his knee, he marveled at the weight of the unit, and did a mental calculation of how much lighter it would be in a titanium case... and how much more expensive.

Back at the hotel, he met up with Lars who loaned him a memory stick with a secure kernel and operating system, which he proceeded to install. Then, he connected to the network, downloaded the source code of his favorite applications, compiled and linked them, generating the binary files. He then connected to his server and downloaded his disk image.

Mick was back in business again.

First, he changed all his passwords and generated new keys, revoking all the old ones. He was starting to feel better. He made a mental note to find out what Miles most enjoyed in eating/drinking/collecting and give Miles an abundance of it. He really owed him – Miles, of all people!

CHAPTER 1D.

From IRC Channel #314 for SecAdminAnonymous:

...

Anonymous_1:   anyone clued in on last week's DNS outage?

Anonymous_6:   what outage??

Anonymous_1:   .coop and .aero were down for 43 mins...

Anonymous_5:   they weren't, just some domains... not that anyone cares!

Anonymous_1:   incorrect. See the logs at http://root-logs.cfm.c2b/cgibin

Anonymous_6:   WTF! how did this stay out of the blogs?

Anonymous_1:   no idea

Anonymous_9:   heard it was a pretty sophisticated ddos on them

Anonymous_42: might just be a server outage

Anonymous_9:   there's all kinds of crap

              happening these days that no one
              seems to notice

Anonymous_19: one word for you zed.kicker

Anonymous_9: never heard of them

Anonymous_19: you will. remember the carbon web
              server Ø-day?

Anonymous_1: of course. everyone got hit on
              that one

Anonymous_19: that was zed.kicker, too

Anonymous_1: who is it? how do you know?

Anonymous_19: i've seen the source code... it
              is good stuff. someone with a
              clue

Anonymous_6: probably usgov

Anonymous_19: or .cn

Anonymous_1: either way its bad. can you share
              the source?

Anonymous_19: no don't have it anymore will try
              to share if I can

Anonymous_1: cool... keep us posted

...

CHAPTER 1E.

Mick O'Malley – *knows how the emperor with no clothes felt. (7 comments)*

The next morning found Mick sitting in a conference session, sipping his espresso (not bad), and still trying to come to grips with the fact that someone had installed a keylogger on his computer. As soon as he saw Kateryna, he wanted to tell her everything that had happened.

They left the conference and set off walking towards St. James Park as Mick told her about the keylogger. Kateryna was both amazed and concerned, especially about the implication that someone had physical access to Mick's computer to install the bug.

"How did you find the keylogger? How long had it been there? Who put it there?" she began excitedly.

"Well, the mail Miles showed me was generated with a particular well-known piece of malware of Russian origin that is typically associated with both hardware and software keyloggers. I was fairly confident that I didn't have a software keylogger... I mean, I'm not such an idiot that I could have a rootkit on my computer, so that meant a hardware keylogger. As for how long it had been there, I have no idea. I've certainly had strange things happen to me ever since I was in Los Alamos and Vegas... I guess whoever is trying to discredit me and disrupt my work put it on there. Think about all these things: the forged email to *ISW*, the threat in Los Alamos, the No-Fly list. Which were done by Zed dot Kicker and which were done by the government? And, who even knows I am working on this project?" Mick paused.

"I know, it is incredible..." she replied, and they were silent for a few blocks.

"The mention of three days in the forged email suggests that is the date they are working towards. If I had to guess, I'd say the full force of the botnet will be unleashed in all the ways they've been testing it: against web servers, mail servers, and DNS servers in the ultimate zero day!"

"You could be right," Kateryna replied.

"I know I am. I need a break... something to give me an edge against this botnet... and soon," he replied, and drifted off into his own thoughts.

By the time Mick and Kateryna reached the park, their conversation, influenced by their surroundings, had moved on to other topics.

"Walking around London and England makes me think of Jane Austen – Pride and Prejudice is my favorite novel of all time," Kateryna replied.

"I know how you feel. Myself, London makes me think of Sherlock Holmes," Mick replied. "You can't beat Victorian times. By the way, are you familiar with 'steampunk'?"

"No, what's that?" Kateryna asked. Mick raised his eyebrows.

"Well, let me tell you about it!" Mick replied, then launched into an explanation.

As the afternoon passed, they sat down on a bench in a

part of the garden with a nice view of the lake. Kateryna took out a water bottle, twisted it open and took a sip. She raised the bottle and looked at him, asking a question without words. He nodded. She took another sip then passed it to him. He put it to his lips and felt a thrill of intimacy, putting his lips where hers had just been.

Sitting in the afternoon sun, they watched some equestrian riders go by in the park as the clouds moved across the sky. They returned to the conference later, and Mick felt the stress of the situation had drained out of him.

That evening, Mick was tired, but still couldn't sleep. He was feeling keyed up over the logger. In his mind, he kept going over all the places his computer had been, looking for where an attacker might have had access to it to install the keylogger. He couldn't come up with any instances that he had left his computer alone with a stranger.

He was interrupted in his musings by a knock at the door. He knew Lars wouldn't knock. Mick jumped out of bed and looked out through peephole, but didn't see anything or anyone. He noticed a piece of paper on the floor that must have been pushed under the door. On it was printed:

```
Alec, be at these coordinates at 2am.   Turing
```

Finally, Turing had made contact! He was impressed both by Turing's knowledge of his Alec Robertson identity, and that he was staying in Lars' room. Mick wondered what else Turing knew about him...

He examined the printout carefully and realized it was printed using a dot matrix printer – how quaint!

Mick put the coordinates into GPS and got a location in the East End of London. He checked the time and decided he had plenty of time if he left right away. He set off on the Tube, bringing his computer, determined to never let it out of his sight again. Ever.

Arriving at the building located at the specified coordinates at slightly before the hour, Mick walked up to the door and knocked. A young man with multiple piercings and a Mohawk answered the door.

"Hello, there. I'm Mick... I was told to come here?" he asked. The man nodded and stepped aside. Mick stepped inside and walked down a long, dark hallway. As he progressed, the music got louder, until he could barely hear himself think. He turned a corner and noticed a small room to the one side. In the room there were a dozen or so people, all younger than him. A single bare bulb hanging from the ceiling provided illumination. The walls had peeling paint, and the unpleasant smell of stale beer and cigarette smoke permeated the room. Mick realized he was probably in a squat: an abandoned, illegally occupied building. On a table in the center of the room was a single computer. A young woman stood with her back to Mick, then turned around. She was dressed in punk style, with platform combat boots, fishnet stockings, miniskirt, and a ripped tank top. Her hair was short, spiky, and pink.

"Mick!" she called out to him, and he stopped walking.

"Yes?" She motioned for him to come in, which he did, glancing around the room at others. "Turing?" he asked.

"You got my message?" she asked, smiling at him. He tried to place her accent, but couldn't get further than Eastern European. Perhaps, as she said more, he could figure out more. He nodded and walked into the room.

"So, the famous Mick O'Malley thinks he can take down Zed dot Kicker?" she asked. The others smirked and made barely audible comments in the background.

"I plan to, yes. I've already broken the encryption and figured out the P2P routing protocol – by the way, thanks for the link! But I haven't been able to disrupt the botnet controllers. Can you help?"

"Perhaps. Are you sure you want to do this? You have no idea who you are up against. You are being targeted now, but if you take this further, you'll have more to worry about than just the criminals."

"I am sure," he replied. "And if these guys thought that threatening me and getting me into trouble would dissuade me, they couldn't be more wrong. I will get this damn botnet!"

"I believe you just might," she replied, slowly walking around him, looking him up and down. "I have information that you will find very useful: the location of the criminals running the botnet, and something that could help you take control of the botnet. It is all on this computer," she said, pointing at the machine in the middle of the room. Mick looked at her, waiting for more. She pointed again, and Mick walked over and sat down. He hit the enter key and the screen turned on, displaying a login prompt:

```
login: |
```

Someone in the back spoke up.

"Doesn't he know how to hack a computer?" he sneered.

"Oh, I think he does," replied Turing. "He's so good at what he does, that he must have once been on the other side of the fence. He must have been one of us. If he can remember *who* he was back then, he'll succeed."

"Is this some kind of a test?" Mick asked, making note of her emphasis.

"If you want to think of it that way, yes. I am risking my life sharing this with you. I'm only willing to do so if you are in fact good enough to use it." She paused and leaned over him almost whispering. "So, go get it!"

Mick glanced around the room, then focused on the job at hand. He did enjoy a challenge after all, although it had been quite a while since he had broken into a computer like this. Turing was right – he had once been a hacker, and as a teenager had hung around with a crowd like this, and used to enjoy showing off. But that was a long time ago.

First, he had to determine which operating system was in use – this only took a second. It turned out to be a popular closed source operating system, but the usual graphical user interface had been disabled, only allowing typing, a so-called command line interface. This eliminated a number of easier ways to get into the system, but not all of them.

The first step was to gain access to the system. He would need to login with system administrator rights, also known as 'root' or 'super user', to the computer to find the information he needed. He tried some common tricks but they all failed. He tried a number of common usernames and passwords but none worked. Then he thought about what Turing had said about him remembering who he was. He looked quizzically at her, then typed:

```
login: eireforce1
password: **************
```

After a pause, the screen showed a command prompt, indicating that he had successfully logged in:

```
$ |
```

A murmur spread around the room.

"Very good!" Turing said. "Next..."

"I have no idea how you learned my hacker alias from all those years ago, or my favorite password back then..." Mick said, truly mystified. Turing just shrugged, and he focused back on the job at hand.

Mick now was logged in and had command line or 'shell' access to the computer. He still needed to get 'root' access. He tried a number of approaches but they all were patched. An idea came to him as to how he could break into the system. It was a risky approach, but he suspected he needed to take a chance in order to succeed.

Mick set about writing a script. Most of the script implemented a simple approach that he was fairly certain would fail, but he planned to hide a few lines of his real attack inside the script. The botnet steganography had given him the idea!

Mick could see Turing looking over his shoulder and watching as he typed. As he entered the critical lines, he turned, caught her eye, and winked at her. Then he quickly scrolled the lines off the screen before she glanced back. If nothing else, he would definitely get style points for this exploit, if it worked!

He finished up and got ready to execute the script.

"Ready?" Mick asked, looking around the room. He hit enter, not looking at the screen. He saw the others staring at the screen, then heard their laughter. He turned to look and saw a series of error messages scroll off the screen. The computer beeped, then restarted, going through its booting up processes: loading the BIOS, loading the OS kernel. He swore loudly and profusely, as Turing walked up to him.

"Don't take it so hard, Mick. Not many could break into this computer. I'm certain none of these clowns could – they definitely aren't in your league." She looked disappointed, but at the same time seemed to be enjoying the feeling of superiority. The computer finished rebooting and was back to the login prompt.

```
login: |
```

"I don't believe this computer even has any other accounts," Mick snapped. "That's the only possible reason I can't break into it."

"Au contraire!" Turing replied. "Watch..." she said, turning to the computer and proceeded to login as the 'root' user:

```
login: root
password: **********
```

She turned back to Mick and smiled sweetly at him, but was surprised at his expression, which had instantly changed from bewildered to smug. "Oh SHIT! You DIDN'T!" she shouted, turning back to the computer. She stared at the screen, which read:

```
Thank   you   for   the   root   password   to   this
computer, Jasinski!
Transferring files: 100% complete.

$ |
```

The others looked on in disbelief. One of the thickest, perhaps a boyfriend of a female hacker, asked another what had just happened.

"The tosser wrote a script that made it look like the computer crashed and rebooted – it hadn't! It was still running his script, waiting for her to enter the root password so it could login and copy all the files! He didn't even hack the computer – he just used social engineering!" a kid explained.

Mick was already thinking how he would tell the story to Kateryna. During the conversation, he had figured out that Turing was most likely the mysterious Jasinski that had helped foil the Halloween attack. No wonder Lars had been unsuccessful in trying to find 'him'! Turing recovered quickly.

"Very impressive, Mick, I must say. And yes, I am also known as Jasinski... although you have done me no favors by telling everyone here," she replied irritably as she glanced around the room. "I was worried that no one would figure out that mail server attack, although it seems your friend Lars had it covered, no doubt with help from you." She paused and became very serious. "I know how to cover my tracks – something you will need to be good at from now on... But you are quite good at this little game, I must say," she said. Mick gave a little bow. "I am as good as my word, Mick. You have the promised information. One file contains an address. If you want to catch those running Zed dot Kicker, you need to be there, very soon. And you will also find an X.509 certificate. That certificate is a Certificate Authority for Zed dot Kicker. You will be able to issue a new control certificate and revoke existing certificates using it. In short, you can now use it to control the botnet."

"You have a CA certificate for the botnet?" Mick asked, incredulous. "How?"

"They helped out on my P2P open source project, but then I learned what kind of a-holes they were. They generated a cert for me to test a new feature. I told them I revoked it when my testing was complete, but I didn't... I don't think they have any clue it exists. I'm through with them now, and if you want to destroy their botnet, that's fine by me."

"Thanks for all your help, Jasinski," Mick began. "I appreciate it. And thanks for the challenge... I enjoyed it. Well, I'm off, then," he said, heading towards the door. She followed him.

"Wait! How did you break the botnet encryption? And how did you even find the botnet messages?"

"You wrote the code, didn't you? Can't you guess?" he replied, surprised.

"Not that part – someone else wrote the crypto," she replied.

"I see. Who?"

"Dunno. I never met the guy." She put her arm out to the corridor wall, blocking his path and leaned close to him. "Mick, why not stay a while? You interest me, and I plan to disappear in the morning and be untraceable by anyone until all this blows over," she said, leaning toward him.

Mick did admit that he was intrigued by her, and wondered how she had discovered so much information about his past. And, he did find her attractive. But his thoughts were already going back to Kateryna.

"Sorry, must go... Lots to do, you know, botnets to take over, et cetera, et cetera..." he explained, lifting her arm out of the way. She frowned. "Cheers everyone!" he called to the room, then turned and walked away.

He felt her angry eyes on his back, but kept walking out the building.

Back at the hotel, Mick examined the transferred files. The location Jasinski provided was:

```
203 Knyazhyi Zaton St
Osokorky
```

He looked up the city and swore when he saw the location.

How the hell can I get to Ukraine?

He knew he could not risk traveling using his British passport or he might find himself detained. He paced the room, back and forth, thinking, but nothing came to him. Lars still wasn't back, and he was beginning to wonder if perhaps he had made other arrangements. Mick sent a message to Kateryna saying they needed to talk, and was surprised by an immediate reply.

What is she doing awake at this hour?

Mick invited her up to the room, and she accepted.

As Mick let Kateryna in a few moments later, he smelled her perfume as she walked by, and began to doubt whether this was such a good idea. He turned on a pseudo white noise generator on his computer in case someone was listening in.

"So, what's up?" she asked, sitting down on the window ledge, swinging her legs and glancing out at the view of the London streets. She was wearing jeans and a knit sweater.

"You won't believe what I did tonight..." he began, and told her the story. At the end, she was almost on the floor laughing.

"I can't believe she fell for that! That's the oldest trick!"

"Yep, perhaps too old for someone as young as her... plus she was so sure that I'd fail that it didn't take much to convince her."

"So what information did you get?" she asked. Mick took a deep breath.

"Kat, I need to go to Ukraine," he began. Her jaw dropped. "I have the address where the botnet developers and controllers are located. It's in Kiev. I need to get there in the next few days to try to stop them from launching their big attack."

"You want to go to Ukraine, and do what?"

"I need to shutdown this botnet and find the people responsible for it, and I think I'm the only one who can do it."

"So let's say I buy this, which I don't by the way, how are you going to get there?"

"I don't know, I guess I could sail to Sevastopol on the Black Sea."

"That's not going to work. It would take way too long."

"I know, I know."

"The train is the best way to get there, at least for someone who can't fly."

"I agree, but there are lots of borders between here and there. I don't think my odds of making it there are very good, especially if more forged email threats come out," he replied, referring to the fake email Miles had refused to distribute.

They sat in silence for more than a few minutes. Finally, Kateryna spoke.

"I have a thought," she began.

"What?"

"When I arrived here, I discovered my husband's passport in a side pocket of my carry on bag. I think he left it there from his last trip to Canada," she paused to get his reaction, and got none. "So, perhaps you are unaware that your face is somewhat similar to his? You are a little taller, but not too much and he wears glasses, but..."

"Kat, are you suggesting... are you suggesting that I travel using your husband's passport?"

"I'm not suggesting you travel alone. We would travel together. I'm sure it would work... we'd just need to add some highlights to your hair, and get some glasses to match..."

"No way – thanks, but no. There's no way I'm getting you involved in this. Anyway, that is really breaking the law. Up 'til now, I've just bent the law a little. Thank you for suggesting it, but I'll need to find another way."

"Such as?" she said, putting her hands on her hips.

"I don't know. I'll think of something. Maybe I could get a fake passport or something."

"And that's not illegal? And besides, you know they do automatic facial recognition at British airports, so regardless of what your passport says, you'll be picked up."

"True."

"Well then," she said, getting off the window sill. She walked over to Mick, standing right in front of him. She touched his arm, imploring him. "Mick, why are you so opposed to this plan? Is it because of breaking the law, or... is it because of me?" Mick didn't answer. He studied her face, bathed in the lamplight, trying to read her thoughts.

"Um... it is a little of both," he replied carefully. "Traveling under someone else's passport is wrong. And traveling as... as your husband, also feels wrong."

"Mick, I don't think you are being truthful. I don't think it will feel wrong for us to travel together... I'm far more worried about how *right* it might feel..."

"Yeah, that too..." Mick muttered in reply.

"I think we can deal with that – we're both grownups. It would be silly to let that stand in the way of you doing what you need to do," she replied.

"Perhaps," he replied. Mick wondered how much more of this conversation he could stand. He thought hard about how he could bring this uncomfortable situation to a close. It occurred to him that Lars might get the wrong idea if he returned at this moment.

"You didn't say what this Ms. Jasinski was like?" Kateryna asked. Mick shook his head, holding back a smile. "What?" Kateryna said, starting to smile as well. "Never mind. Look, Mick, it's your decision. I'll slide the passport under your door later on so you can see for yourself. After my presentation tomorrow morning, my schedule is free. I really want to do this. I want to see this through with you. But it's your call," she said, turning away from him and heading to the door. Mick was still staring into space as she stepped out into the hallway and pulled the door shut behind her.

Mick was still wide awake when he heard the passport slide under the hotel room door. Picking it up, he looked it over; he had to agree that there was a resemblance. He held up the passport to the mirror and looked at it and his reflection, trying to mimic the same bored look as Kateryna's husband, Milos, in the photo. He just could not make up his mind on his course of action.

With the late hour and the time difference, it was a good time for a video call with Sam. He smiled seeing her tousled hair and sleepy look.

"Are we going to finish the book tonight?" he asked.

"Definitely!" she replied, opening up the book to the last chapter. When they were finished, they talked for a few more minutes. "I know Frodo is going to succeed, but it is hard to see it right now with him captured by Orcs," she commented.

"I agree. Sometimes you just have to have faith that things will work out, even when things look black," Mick replied, putting away his well-worn copy of the book.

"I hate cliffhangers, too. Will we start *The Return of the King* next week?" she asked hopefully.

"We'll see," Mick replied. "I might be a bit busy. You know how unreliable we grownups are..."

"I know! Well, I can wait a little while for you, but if you wait too long, I'll just have to start it on my own."

"Understood. I really want to read with you, Sam, but you have my permission to go ahead without me if I can't for some reason."

"OK. You look beat! What time is it there?" Sam commented.

"Really, really late. I need to hit the hay. Hope to talk again soon..."

"Me too, Uncle Alec. Good night!" she replied, signing off.

Sometime during the conversation, Mick had made up his mind, and quickly fell asleep.

That night, Mick dreamed that he was lost in a strange city. He wandered the streets without being able to read any of the signs. No one could understand a word he said, nor could he understand their language. After a while, he started to notice that there were many ladders against buildings. In desperation, he climbed a ladder, and was amazed to find a whole other level of the city. He was about to start exploring this city, this new world as well, when his alarm went off.

CHAPTER 1F.

*From the **Security and Other Lies** Blog:*

No Q&A this week.

Instead, I want to thank everyone who has participated in this blog over the years. It has been a lot of fun, and you have asked good questions. And I've especially enjoyed the Raptor aliases you have created. It just shows how something can quickly become a tradition online, and how culture can be created. Or, maybe it shows how much you like dinosaurs!

This might very well be my last posting. No, I'm not dying! I'm just moving on to other things. I have dedicated my life to Internet security, but now I think things may be changing.

Now, this might not be the end of this blog, however. I've just reset my admin account to a password that does not meet my usual standards, i.e. it does not have enough randomness or entropy. As a result, a clever or determined person might be able to break the password and take over this account. If you do so, I'd just ask of you two things:

Ø. Keep the archive - there is lots of good
information and good questions and comments over
the past 4 years.

1. Keep the spirit of this blog alive, to help
Internet users have better security.

So that's it. Good luck to everyone!

I'll check in from time to time if I have a
chance.

Cheers everyone!

CHAPTER 2Ø.

Mick O'Malley – *knows that when you start a journey, you don't always know where you will end up. (14 comments)*

Less than halfway between London and Paris, the view out the window disappeared, and the GPS stopped working. The Channel Tunnel was an amazing piece of engineering, and Mick eagerly anticipated the experience of riding through it. He glanced over at Kateryna, his 'wife' for the duration of this trip, and felt a twinge of nervousness.

They had left late that afternoon from St. Pancras station in London and boarded the Eurostar high speed train to Paris. Kateryna's presentation that morning went well, or so she had said. Mick had avoided it and he told others that a short-notice business meeting meant he had to leave the conference early.

Kateryna shopped for glasses, and found a pair that was close enough to her husband's. Mick had shopped for clothes.

They checked out of the hotel separately and made the short walk to the station at different times. Mick wore a hat to cover his dyed hair, and was relieved not to meet up with anyone he knew on the way.

When they met up at the station, Kateryna had laughed at Mick.

"What?" he asked, a little annoyed.

"Nothing..." she replied, regaining her composure. "It's just, I've never seen you wear such clothes before."

"Are they that awful?" he asked.

"No, not bad at all. Just... different," she replied, looking him up and down for a moment.

"It's the cravat, right? I'm going to take it off."

"No, leave it. It looks fine. It's sharp actually. I'm sorry – I will behave myself for now on, *Milos*," she replied.

Kateryna purchased the tickets for herself and her 'husband' for the first two legs of their trip.

The GPS had shown the train was fast, but not as fast as the Shinkansen – they had only touched 25Ø km/h so far. Probably they would go faster on the other side of the English Channel. With nothing to see out the window, they conversed.

"It is a shame we won't really have any time in France," Kateryna commented.

"I know. I love Paris. And, I always find Parisians friendly."

"Me, too. But perhaps that is because I always mangle their language," she added.

"The rudest display I ever experienced was when I was in a group with a French speaker, but he was French Canadian. The waiter was incredibly rude, but the food was great, still."

"We can still get some coffee, though, before we catch our connection," Kateryna replied. "Do you have any pictures or stories from your transatlantic crossing?"

"Of course! I've got them right here," he replied,

pulling up the pictures. He told stories about his adventures with Ian and Mariana.

"Ah ha! Your 'fresh' fish dinner! I just figured that out! And your 'life isn't all smooth sailing' post! You think you're so clever, don't you?" Kateryna chided him.

"Only sometimes," was his reply.

The train arrived on time at Gare du Nord station, with a top speed of 285 km/h recorded on GPS. Mick wished he could share the trip with his friends, but knew this was yet another experience he would not be able to share with anyone. Except, of course, with Kateryna, who seemed much more relaxed than he did. He suspected she had not noticed *wagon-lits* printed on their ticket for the next leg. He had looked it up and confirmed that their ticket was for a sleeping car on their Paris to Berlin overnight trip.

Mick enjoyed the short walk with Kateryna from Gare du Nord to Gare de l'Est station where they were to catch the Perseus train to Berlin. They stopped at a café and lingered longer than they needed to drink their coffee. Paris, even this far from the Seine and the tourist hotspots, still had a unique feel and flair to it.

At Gare de l'Est, Mick let Kateryna check them in so he could watch her reaction to the traveling arrangements. He caught a slight look of astonishment as the lady behind the counter explained their accommodations, but Kateryna quickly recovered. Mick wondered if she were covering it up for the benefit of others, or for his benefit. He couldn't resist a small smile afterwards when she glanced at his face.

"You knew!" she whispered, punching him in the arm. Mick shrugged, rubbing his arm. "You should have told me... I was surprised back there and had a hard time covering it up... Ah, I see... that was the point, wasn't it?"

"We shouldn't fight in public," Mick replied.

"Yes, we should – French couples often argue in public

and think it strange if others don't," Kateryna countered.

"I have no idea what you are talking about... *Allez!*" he said to her, grabbing the passports and tickets from her hand and heading towards the platform.

As darkness fell, their train pulled out of the station, heading north by northeast. Mick mused that the compartment was larger than some hotels in Nihon he had stayed in. Of course, he had been alone then. They ate simple baguettes for dinner. Mick walked down to the dining car and brought back decaf espressos.

They sipped the coffee as Kateryna read her book and Mick worked on his newly built computer. He was very happy with its performance. He had yet to charge the LeydenTech battery, and it was showing no signs of discharge.

They were due to arrive in Berlin at around eight the next morning.

How long are we going to stay up?

"Shall we turn in?" Kateryna finally asked, closing her book.

"OK," Mick replied, shutting down his computer for the night.

Mick opened up the bed; it folded down over where they had been sitting, taking up nearly all the space in the compartment. Kateryna rummaged in her bag, then took out a few clothes and things and slipped into the tiny bathroom. Mick took advantage of the situation and quickly changed himself, putting on his tracksuit pants and a black long-sleeved shirt. Kateryna came out a moment later. Mick glanced in her direction, and was relieved to discover she was also in a tracksuit – in white and day glow green.

Expecting lingerie? I'm such an idiot!

He went into the bathroom to wash up. When Mick came out, Kateryna had already climbed up in the bed and was lying on her back under the covers, with her mobile

ALAN B. JOHNSTON

reader in hand.

Mick took a deep breath and climbed up carrying his book. He slid under the covers and started to read his novel.

"What are you reading?" she asked, closing her book.

"Still *The Innocents Abroad*," he replied. "And you?"

"Still *Anna Karenina*," she replied, imitating him. They were silent for a long moment. "Mick, are you satisfied with your life?" she asked, looking at him.

"I will be, once this botnet is offline," he replied. She glared at him, so he tried again. "I think I'm pretty satisfied and happy, yes. Although sometimes I admit my life is a little solitary. I mean, I have lots of friends, and I share all kinds of things and adventures with them, but I also don't share a whole side of myself with them, if you know what I mean."

"I think I do. I've spent the last few years concentrating on my career. But work isn't everything, is it?" said Kateryna.

"No, it isn't. And we have a strange life, don't we? We travel the world; we don't even live in the same country as most of our friends. The work we do is self-motivated and self-directed, instead of being given to us by a boss. We have such a different outlook on the Internet and the online world that everyone navigates every day, taking it for granted. We see and participate in the daily battles and skirmishes that go on between developers and service providers and the bad guys."

"This whole Zed dot Kicker thing – it is kind of surreal, isn't it?" she added.

"It is. And who can we talk to and tell about it? Who can really understand us and what motivates us?" Mick replied.

"Well, for me, it has been such a pleasure working with you on it, so exciting and exhilarating. And to be able to share the experience with you..." she paused.

"I know. It has been unique."

"So Mick, I'm really sorry about what happened before. I should have told you right away, and not let you make incorrect assumptions..." she began.

"You are correct."

"I'm truly sorry. I just had no idea things would go the way they did. You have probably figured out by now that I'm attracted to you, Mick. I love spending time with you, and talking to you about everything and anything. When we aren't together, I have these imaginary little conversations with you in my head – I know it's silly. I haven't felt like this since I was a teenager." She had been speaking quickly but now paused. Mick was silent for a moment.

"You know that I'm attracted to you, too, Kat. But you are married!" Mick exclaimed. Kateryna took a deep breath.

"Milos has been a good husband to me. But, to tell the truth, I really can't stand him these days. I knew when we married that he had quite traditional views about the role of women, and a blunt way of expressing them. I guess I thought it didn't really matter, and that I could put up with it. I think it really makes him angry that my career has gone a little better than his over the years, and I actually make more money than he does. And he makes a lot of comments about my priorities. Anyway, I just don't know how much more I can put up with it... and it has seemed more difficult to put up with since I met you.

"And these days, I find myself thinking a lot about you, Mick. I know you are consumed by this botnet and all the attacks, but I just wanted you to know that I am here, and I want to help you in any way you might need it." Kateryna had been staring at the ceiling the whole time she spoke. Now, she rolled over onto her side, facing Mick. He shifted to his side, facing her as well.

"Kat, thanks for sharing that with me. I don't want you

to take this the wrong way," he began carefully. "I just want you to know how much I appreciate everything you've done for me, and how much I appreciate your help. But..." he paused.

"OK, you don't need to say anymore, Mick, please," she interrupted, rolling over to face the cabin wall.

Mick thought about trying to restart the conversation, but couldn't find the right words. He was still thinking hard about everything when he heard the sound of her sleeping.

He closed his eyes and eventually drifted off to sleep as well, as their train wound its way through the European countryside.

Early the next morning, they were all packed and ready to disembark by the time the train slowed coming into Berlin Hauptbahnhof station. Trains to Kiev only departed in the evening, so they had nearly eight hours to kill before then. As Mick had never visited Berlin on his previous trips to Germany, he was looking forward to exploring.

They had a light breakfast of coffee and croissants before leaving their bags in a locker at the hotel and setting out. With his previous trips to Hiroshima and Los Alamos, World War II was still on Mick's mind. He knew that it was the German atomic program that led to the creation of the Manhattan Project, and ultimately, the detonation over Hiroshima. Of course, history showed that the Germans were never close to building any kind of bomb, and were more interested in finding a power source for their submarines – a precursor to today's nuclear powered submarines that can stay underwater for six months or more.

They strolled along Unter den Liden, under the Linden trees along the most famous and beautiful street in Berlin and enjoyed the afternoon sun, although there was a slight chill in the air. They eventually stopped at a café to rest.

Mick's new shoes still needed to be broken in, but he didn't complain to Kateryna. He had also stopped wearing the eyeglasses except when they went through customs and immigration, as they gave him a headache.

"About last night," Mick began, breaking the silence on the topic. "I just wanted you to know –"

"Mick, you don't need to explain," she interrupted him.

"Yes, I do, Kat," he interrupted her, pausing to collect his thoughts. "I think about you every hour of every day. For those three weeks while I was at sea when we didn't mail or video, probably more often." He looked up and could see that he had her attention. "I just don't know what to do. You have a husband, and I have... I don't know... motorcycles?" She smiled weakly at him.

"I've been thinking about you a lot, too," she responded. She reached over and took his hand. Mick liked how it felt. "This is just a crazy situation we are in. And all the secrecy and excitement of this adventure just seems to magnify it."

"I know. I think we should just take it very slowly – get through this and not do something stupid we might regret later." Mick squeezed her hand, and she smiled again.

"You are right, of course. Perhaps it will fade once this trip is over. I don't know what I was thinking last night..." then she changed the subject. "So, are you all set to take down this botnet?" Mick leaned back in his chair. It took him a moment to shift gears in his mind.

"Well, I can't take it down, but I think I can paralyze it – by making it so that the botnet can't initiate an attack. Jasinski gave me a root certificate for the botnet with revocation privileges. Now that I have figured out the encryption and the format of the botnet control messages, I can use this to effectively lock out the criminals so that I'm the only person who can give the botnet commands. But the criminals will know about it as soon as I execute the script, and I think they will know it was me."

"Or Jasinski."

"Or Jasinski – good point! I think I understand why she planned to disappear."

They enjoyed the rest of the afternoon together exploring Berlin, but they were both distracted. By the middle of the afternoon they were back at the station getting ready to board their train to Ukraine. Mick read a mail from Sam.

```
Cheerio Uncle Alec,

I am glad you are having fun in merry old
England.  I read that the London Science Museum
has a working version of Babbage's Analytical
Engine!  If you haven't seen it, you must!  Do
you think they'd let you write a program for it?
Could you write a buffer overflow attack for it?

When are you visiting Boston again?

Take care, my favorite (and only, LOL) uncle,

Sam
```

```
------BEGIN PGP SIGNATURE-----
xa+LGuDQ/BRnUJVHpC0qb4YFZyIoaA
cBhA/JJ62Kkyu7pwAnR95Vlr6ydU4T
tGXa7k51KrJAg4uQJDACfcMgSOZAwA
Ta6fWb7VNS4S19Em00AnjDYOr+50Gt
juBdmpNCMw2GFqE+4KHqFcXqy4H82a
------END PGP SIGNATURE-------
```

He smiled and fired off a reply as they waited to board.

Their train, known as the Kashtan, departed Berlin as the sun set. They had another sleeper car, but this time Mick didn't feel as nervous as he had the previous night. He wondered how they could go through such an awkward situation, and so quickly get past it. Their 'relationship' certainly was nothing like anything he had ever experienced before. And he didn't know where he was going... besides Kiev.

Skipping coffee, Mick and Kateryna enjoyed a packed dinner of schnitzel. Mick finished up his script; he was ready to disrupt the botnet tomorrow once they arrived in Kiev and staked out the Zed.Kicker headquarters. Just before bed, they discussed several scenarios for the next day. This way they could react quickly without lots of discussion. Of course, there were too many unknowns to really plan properly.

As he fell asleep, Mick felt both sorry he had involved Kateryna, and thankful for her steadiness and contributions to the effort.

Mick awoke first, slowly regaining consciousness. For a minute he did not know where he was, then he remembered. He felt Kateryna snuggled up against his back as he lay on his side, and he tensed up. Then he realized that she (or perhaps he) had probably initiated the 'spooning' while asleep. He stayed in that position for a few minutes, feeling her breathing and her warmth against him. As the train shook slightly rounding a bend, Kateryna stirred, and Mick took the opportunity to slide away from her. She made a noise and rolled over in the other direction. He sighed silently in relief, then began to focus on the day ahead.

After customs and immigration in Kiev, they would get a hotel and a rental and find the Zed.Kicker location. He pulled up a map on the GPS, noticing Chernobyl, about 200km north of Kiev near the border with Belarus. He recalled the nuclear power plant accident there in 1986 and the bravery of the firefighters who prevented a meltdown and brought the fire under control despite knowing that they were receiving a lethal dose of radiation. Mick wondered if the radioactive cloud that drifted across Europe afterwards and circled the globe were at all similar to the 'black rain' that fell on Hiroshima after the A-bomb.

He knew he probably wouldn't have a chance to visit, and wondered whether there was anything to see on a tour.

Mick was up and about before Kateryna stirred. He again dressed in the strange – for him – clothes. He found them unsettling. Mick thought he didn't care much about clothes, but he was beginning to realize that perhaps he did care.

Are my clothes my armor against the world, another layer of security? Or is my life cosplay?

He wondered if he could get used to wearing clothes besides his 'uniform' in the future.

When Kateryna awoke, she sat up on her elbows and smiled up at him – her dark hair disheveled. Looking at her, Mick realized he didn't seem to tire of spending time with this amazing woman.

As they reached the border with Ukraine, the train stopped and reversed direction, heading into a literal sidetrack. Kateryna looked out the window, alarmed.

"Don't worry: we are just shunting so the train's wheels can be changed – the countries of the former Soviet Union do not use the standard rail gauge of 1.435m used throughout Europe, but instead use 1.524m." Kateryna looked surprised. "I remember my cousins in Australia saying how in the old days, train travelers between Sydney and Melbourne had to change trains at the border town of Albury, as the states of Victoria and New South Wales used different rail widths," he explained. He was about to pontificate about the value of standards when he noticed that Kateryna was already back reading her book.

Mick had been ignoring most of his mail since leaving London, but he couldn't ignore one from Liz. It had a Subject: I know you are with Kat. He opened it, feeling nervous:

```
Mick,

I hope you can forgive me for writing, but I
couldn't sit here and say nothing.  I knew the
```

second time I saw the two of you together that
something was going to happen between you. I
also knew it didn't happen in Vegas, but it was
obvious to me the day before you left London
that you were planning something, and when you
both inexplicably disappeared, well... Don't
worry, I don't think anyone else knows your
little secret, but that's because they are blind
to these things.

I don't want to interfere, but I will anyway. I
am just so worried about you – I know you don't
have casual affairs, and I can't for the life of
me figure out what Kat is up to, running off
with you like this. I am presuming that it was
her idea and you are just going along with it to
see where it leads. Please, please be careful.

Do you really know what she is after? Do we
really know her that well? I don't mean to
slight you at all – you are an intriguing,
attractive guy, but...

OK, I will stop here. I hope we can still be
friends after this is over – your friendship has
always meant a lot to me, Mick, and I would be
very, very sorry to lose it. I just want you to
know that you have friends who care about you
and will do anything for you.

I also won't expect to hear back from you,
wherever you are... Just take care, Mick...
See you again soon.

Yours,

Liz

------BEGIN PGP SIGNATURE-----
oUtea4F0An2eK54x56aOO2jUKPClcR
etHYjjRa61fFxgCfeCH/W0/Fljeh6Z
8VKQsypbimU2UAniOnZDWZkLSJnZqG
iD7AAMFMwrfACgkQP7jp0uceFkR+EQ
CaAjpyN5Fwx8CtCyQt87sQYh3cK6QA
-------END PGP SIGNATURE------

    He read and re-read the message a few times, not quite
knowing what to make of it. He couldn't recall Liz ever

writing such a note. He resolved to tell Kateryna about the mail, but later.

Had Liz sent a similar note to Kat as well?

He looked at her as she sat across the compartment from him as she read. His thoughts were interrupted by their arrival into Kiev.

They cleared customs and immigration without any problems, although Mick got an elbow in the ribs from Kateryna when she caught him staring at the customs officers. They were not your usual government bureaucrats; they were all young women, and their uniforms consisted of extremely short, tight skirts and stiletto heels.

At the instant when one of the blonde women stamped both passports, Mick wondered how Kateryna was going to explain the stamps to her husband. Mick noted that their passports had been scanned this time – the first time since leaving England. If any governments or agents were tracking them, they would know where they were now. Both he and Kateryna had been ignoring their social network since they left London. Liz's note had reminded him how much discussion and speculation might be now starting about each of them, or worse, about the both of them.

They found a small hotel a short walk from the station that was cheap but clean, and Mick had a good wireless signal there after replacing SIM cards yet again. At the hotel, he registered them as Mr. and Mrs. Petrescu while Kateryna looked on. Mick's signature on the register was a very good facsimile of Milos Petrescu's. He had thought it would be difficult for him to assume this new identity, but it wasn't. In a way, didn't he do something similar every day of his life?

While Kateryna showered, Mick set out to rent a vehicle. He returned just over an hour later, finding parking on the street nearby. Mick then showered quickly and was ready for the day.

Mick got out one of Kateryna's digital cameras and verified its impressive digital zoom. He cut a small, unobtrusive hole in the side of a small backpack he had bought so the camera could film without being taken out of the bag.

Leading Kateryna to their rental, Mick walked down the stairs carrying his computer and the camera bag. Out on the street and down a block, he stopped to get the key out of his pocket.

"So, where is it? The Škoda?" Kateryna asked looking for the vehicle. Mick was impressed by her knowledge of car makes – the little car in front of them was a Škoda, manufactured in the Czech republic, but it had taken more than a glance for him to confirm this fact.

"No, that's not it," he replied, trying not to smile.

"Which one then?" she asked looking around at other cars nearby. "Wait, it isn't... you DIDN'T!" she replied, looking closer.

"Yep. You don't really mind, do you? It was a great deal and –" he began, now smiling.

"You rented a motorbike instead of a car? Are you insane?"

"Yes and no – there are lots of bikes here – you must have noticed, so we won't stand out. And the weather is going to be fine the next few days – no rain... or snow."

"Can't you focus on the job at hand? How are we going to navigate? How will we talk?" she replied, getting more annoyed with each passing moment. "This isn't one of your brightest ideas!"

"Look, Kat. It will be fine. My mobile will speak the directions to me, and I have a backup earpiece for my mobile that you can wear in your helmet so we can talk," he explained. Kateryna's annoyance abated, or perhaps she decided that to continue their argument in English here on the street wasn't such a good idea.

Fine – give me my helmet," she replied, holding out her hand. Mick grinned triumphantly, but then wondered if he might pay for this later.

"Here's a key for you – in case you need to get something out of the panniers," he said, handing her a key. She took it in silence.

Mick opened up the pannier bags on the back of the bike and got out the full-face helmets he had rented along with the bike. It was a blue late model Honda CBR 125 – quite a bit smaller than his usual sport bike, but perfectly adequate. He just hoped Ukrainian weather predictions were accurate...

Navigating through the streets was not difficult, and Mick felt quite comfortable on the bike. At first, having Kateryna's arms around his waist and her legs up against his was distracting, but it quickly felt normal. She also seemed at ease, leaned with him in corners, and was otherwise a model pillion passenger. He wondered if perhaps she had done this before.

Mick stopped a few blocks from the address Jasinski had provided, just close enough to see the main entrance of the building and the two floors of windowed offices. There weren't any parking places, but he didn't need one for the bike – he rode up on the sidewalk and parked next to two other motorcycles. Switching off the engine, Mick sent Kateryna to go for a walk up the street and reconnoiter. He got out the camera bag and turned on the camera, setting it for maximum zoom. With the bag resting casually on the seat of the motorbike, he filmed the street and the front of the building while he pretended to talk on his mobile.

Kateryna reported back a few minutes later.

"Inside the building, I saw a receptionist and a security guard, judging by his physique. I could see a few workers in the offices upstairs, but most offices look empty.

Here's what the sign out front says," she paused and showed him a word she had copied on a piece of paper. 'Облако 8++' means 'Cloud 8++' in Russian which is kind of funny, given that their P2P software is a type of a 'cloud computing' application... and, of course, eight plus plus means eight incremented by one, or nine!"

"You know Russian?" he asked her in surprise.

"Yes – I studied it in school back in Romania."

"Don't people speak Ukrainian here in Ukraine?" Mick asked.

"Yes, but lots speak Russian as well. Business, especially software development, uses almost exclusively Russian. Anyway, there is a small loading dock in the rear of the building, but I'd say it isn't used much. Besides the street parking, there seems to be a small garage on the other side. There's also a coffee shop one block up."

"Good work, Kat! This will work nicely. I'm going to ride past, park, and set up in the coffee shop. You should do a long block and meet me there in a few minutes," he replied. She nodded and began walking in the opposite direction.

Mick slid his helmet back on and pushed the start button on the handlebars. The CBR came to life. He walked it down to the road, then set off, cruising slowly past the office. There was nothing special about this office, except that the programmers working there had created the world's largest and most dangerous botnet – with some help from Jasinski, and perhaps someone else, he amended.

Mick parked on the sidewalk again, locked up the helmets, took out his computer and set off for the coffee shop. He was amazed at how similar it felt to other coffee houses he had visited all over the world. While the homogenization of the world through multinational brands and chains was well documented and lamented, this was the other side of the same coin. He ordered lattes and took a seat at a table by the window where he could see all the comings and goings from the building.

Mick got out the camera bag, placing it on the table next to his computer. He checked the viewfinder to verify that he had a clear view of the front of the building and started recording. Kateryna arrived a few minutes later. Her face was slightly flushed from the exercise, or perhaps the excitement. Mick passed her latte over to her as she checked the camera, satisfied with the view.

"Ready to do this?" Mick asked her, showing her the script to generate the botnet messages that would take control of the network.

"Make it so!" she replied, a slight smile in the corner of her mouth.

"Aye, Captain," he replied in a terrible Scottish accent, and executed the script.

"How long until you know if it worked?" she asked after a moment's pause.

"Not long. I'll ping three hosts in the botnet, and see if they respond, or if they are off in la-la land," Mick replied, drumming his fingers on the table. Kateryna put her hand on top of his to stop the tapping. They sat that way for an indeterminate period of time, before a message from the script made Mick jump.

"Wow! Already? I thought it would take a little longer for the messages to propagate, but I guess not. We are in business," he said, glancing around the coffee shop to see if anyone were taking an interest in them, but the few other customers seemed engrossed in their own conversations. "Now, we wait," he said.

"Now, we wait," echoed Kateryna, sitting back in her chair.

After about an hour and a half, they left the coffee shop, moving a few buildings down the street to a small restaurant for lunch. Sitting at their table on the street, they saw a car arrive.

It was a large, black car, which pulled up outside the building. It had barely stopped moving when a suited man got out and strode into the building. The driver then got out of the car and started smoking a cigarette. Mick immediately recognized him as one of the men who chased him in New Mexico.

Hello, Pavel Michalovic!

Mick saw him again in the corner office a moment later, having an animated conversation with two others. They left a moment later, and all appeared to be making phone calls. Mick thought wistfully of alligator clips. He took this activity in the management ranks to be a further indication that the plan was working.

Kateryna uploaded the video clips from her camera to Mick's server and extracted freeze frames that showed their faces. She worked on the digital images for a few minutes to make them sharper and cleaner.

Let's see if any of the programmers show up.

Another hour passed, and there were two more arrivals – programmers by the look of them – regardless of nationality, Mick could identify his own kind. Mick watched them enter the building and go upstairs for a series of conversations. The more he watched, the more convinced he became that he was watching a corporation in action: this was a textbook case of an 'escalation' of an outage impacting important customers.

Kateryna uploaded all the video files, adding the faces to Mick's 'rogues gallery' of Zed.Kicker, which they now knew was the botnet created by the Cloud 8++ Corporation.

Mick checked for activity in the botnet. Now that he had control of the botnet, he was able to send and receive botnet control messages without worrying about drawing attention to his activities. He saw a few new commands being sent, probably originating from the office in front of him. These commands failed, giving Mick a feeling of satisfaction.

The next part of the plan was the part that Kateryna liked the least, and argued against on the train the previous night. However, Mick was not deterred; he needed more information about the creators of the botnet, and he hoped the GPS trackers and bugs would produce exactly that. Unless all the members of Zed.Kicker were caught, they could simply create another botnet.

He said goodbye to Kateryna, leaving his computer and camera with her, setting off in the opposite direction of the building, intending to come around the back entrance. He forced himself not to look over his shoulder as he turned the corner.

Mick never saw the elbow that connected with his face as he walked past the alleyway.

CHAPTER 21.

*The account of **Mick O'Malley** has been closed.*

Mick felt the world spinning, first rapidly, then more slowly. He saw only blackness, felt nothing but pain. Then, he saw some light, gradually getting brighter. The pain became focused on his head, hands, and feet. With difficulty, he opened his eyes, and things began to take shape. He tasted his own blood.

Mick's brain began to function, and he realized he was tied to a chair in a room with a single high window and a door. He could see and feel the duct tape holding his wrists and ankles to the chair, and the dried blood staining his shirt – likely his own. He wiggled his fingers and toes, and decided that perhaps nothing was broken. Then he breathed, and changed his mind. The pain that shot through his chest suggested he might have a broken rib or two. His mind raced.

He could not believe how his life had been turned upside down by the investigation.

Where am I?

He knew the reason he was still alive was because he

was the only one who could control the botnet.

Mick heard footsteps outside the door, and the sound of a deadbolt retracting. He steeled himself.

"Why the hell did you do this?" came from a familiar voice from a familiar silhouette in the doorframe.

"Gunter?" Mick mumbled, astonished. The door closed and a light flared. Gunter sat down in a chair and glared at him.

"We tried to be subtle! They wanted to kill you as soon as they learned you were starting to make connections between the attacks, but I convinced them to threaten you instead," he began. When Mick didn't respond, he continued. "In New Mexico? Remember?" Mick felt the blood burn throughout his body. "Then I tried to get fancy, putting that keylogger on your machine in Vegas, tracking your progress and stealing your private key. Then you show up in London – how the hell did you get there? Did you travel in Kat's bloody suitcase? Getting someone's name on the No-Fly list usually dampens their travel plans... as does freezing their assets."

Mick was confused: Cloud 8++ got his name put on the No-Fly list? Gunter continued. "Don't look so surprised! It is quite easy to do with some planted chatter by people who know their communication is being monitored by the NSA. I told them there was no way you were working for the Americans... Are you freelancing or something?" Mick couldn't recall Gunter being this angry.

"You are involved with Cloud 8 plus plus! You wrote Zed dot Kicker? Why?" Mick asked in shock.

"Why not? They paid well. All my hopes for a comfortable retirement went down with the market these past few years. Stupid governments – trusting idiots like UBK for their security! UBK only knows how to secure its own bank account... My botnet is overkill for their pathetic network. I didn't need that open source crap code! I could have written the whole thing in one day!

But why are you here? What possessed you to take all these risks, just to take over some botnet?"

"I had to stop the zero day!"

"You did: the web server attack, the mail server attack," Gunter replied, puzzled.

"I mean the big one – I saw the mail forwarded to Miles. It said in three days the ultimate zero day would be launched. I had to stop it!" Now Gunter looked surprised.

"What? I don't know anything about that. They are still doing tests and trials. I don't think these guys are even in charge anymore," he said, motioning out the door. "Someone else is calling the shots." He paused for a moment, thinking, then continued. "Did Turing ever contact you? When you removed the keylogger I lost my little window into your world." Mick didn't answer. "And why did you have to involve Kat? I liked her." At this, Mick pushed off with his feet – he had been gradually working them loose. His chair jumped in the air, and he tipped over in the direction of Gunter. Gunter jumped up, swore, and then started to laugh. "Yeah, I get it. You've been getting to know her, I'm sure. And I always thought you had principles, Mick... We actually don't have her yet, but we will, don't worry! I'm not supposed to tell you that, but what the hell! Listen, Mick, you and I can still get out of this all right. I have a way out of here. I just need to know I can still trust you. We could –"

Just then, the door burst open and another man came in and said something to Gunter that Mick didn't understand. They both left the room without saying anything more, bolting the door, leaving Mick lying on the floor.

Why did Gunter say there was no big zero day planned? Could it have been a fabrication to set a trap for me?

Mick awoke later to an odd sound that he could not immediately identify. It was a metallic sound, a sharp sound like metal pipes being struck with a hammer. He realized with a shock it was silenced gunshots. The door burst open and a man came running through. Another burst of silenced shots erupted, and the man fell to the ground next to Mick, dead, as a pink mist slowly settled. Two soldiers advanced through the door, fingers still on the triggers. A word from the other room made them relax, and they lowered their weapons. They exchanged a few words in what he presumed to be Russian. Mick then noticed that none of them were wearing any markings, ranks, or insignias. He began to wonder if this was an improvement.

They stood him up, cut the tape from his arms and legs, and led him out of the room. Mick caught sight of a few bodies slumped in the adjoining rooms. As they went down the stairs, he recognized it as the building that he and Kateryna had been staking out. They pushed him into in a Mercedes SUV parked in the loading dock and sped off.

The soldier next to him offered a cigarette, which he refused. His ribs hurt, and he wondered if he was going to be sick.

On the outskirts of Kiev, they bumped along an isolated farmer's field and stopped beside a stone building. Inside, the soldiers sprawled around the small house. One stood guard by a door. They gave him some bread and water which he hungrily ate. The officer in charge sat down and spoke to him in heavily accented, but understandable English.

"O'Malley, it is good to meet you. You are free of criminals. You have been liberated by a Spetsnaz commando brigade of the Russian Federation. You will be safe in Mother Russia in few hours when our transport plane lands. In gratitude, you will help us of course..." He leaned over and in a quiet voice added, "We both know what a special botnet this is, yes?" He raised his eyebrows

and grinned at Mick. "Now, relax!" He motioned Mick
towards another door. Mick opened it and sat down on the
bed. Exhausted, he had only one thought before passing
out again.

This is not good...

The next thing Mick felt was a slight tingling behind
his ear. He realized he had probably blacked out for a
while, and tried to come to his senses. The tingling
continued, but he was still confused. Then, with a flash of
cognizance that he could almost see, he whispered
"Answer!" Mick was amazed when his mobile phone
recognized his voice command through his implant and
answered the incoming call. "Hello?" he croaked, his
voice breaking.

"Alec?" said a familiar voice from the other side of the
world. "You sound strange..."

"Jocelyn?" he whispered.

"Why are you whispering? I'm sorry if this is a –" she
began, but he interrupted her.

"Jocelyn, I'm in trouble in Kiev, Ukraine. Call the
State Department. Tell them I'm being held by Russian
special forces. Mention the Zed dot Kicker botnet, Cloud
8 plus plus. Oh, and tell them my name is Mick
O'Malley..."

"Alec, have you been drinking?" she asked.

"I am deadly serious, Jocelyn," he whispered to his
sister. "Please do exactly as I say. Lives are at stake. And
tell them Kateryna Petrescu is in danger, too. Got it?
Repeat it back to me..."

"OK, OK. Kiev, State Department, Zed dot Kicker,
botnet, Cloud 8 plus plus, Kateryna, and you are Mick
O'Malley – why that name?"

"I'll explain later Jocelyn. Please don't delay!" he
hissed. He adopted a different tone of voice and said
"Share Location!"

"What did you say, Alec? I will do it right away... Love you!"

"You too..." Mick whispered. "Disconnect!"

He marveled that his Russian captors hadn't turned off his mobile. Perhaps they had been trying to break into it – good luck to them with that! He also realized it must be in the other room, as his implant had a limited working distance. With his mobile on silent, it would have given no indication of the phone call, besides activating his implant ringer. He hoped his location sharing with Jocelyn's phone had gone through. He felt some optimism, but would there be time? He drifted off again.

Images floated through Mick's concussed brain. He watched a raptor prowl around the room, looking for other, smaller dinosaurs to devour. He heard more voices, banging. He saw a man speaking to him, but he could not hear the words. Something that looked like an IV was connected to his arm. He hoped the raptor would leave him alone...

CHAPTER 22.

Mick awoke in a hospital. He had all kinds of wires and tubes in his body. He also noted hand and foot restraints, which alarmed him. He had no idea how much time had passed or where he was. A nurse walked by, noticed he was conscious, and hurried away. A moment later, another person, presumably a doctor, came to his bedside.

"Doctor O'Malley, I am Doctor Pushkar. I am very glad to see you are recovering well. First, I remove these," he said as he reached down and undid the restraints. "I give you apology, but you were confused when they brought you in here, something about a dinosaur – I don't know, but not surprising, considering what happened to you. I leave them on until you were fully conscious."

"Am I in Moscow?" he asked feebly.

"Moskva? Why would you think that? Ah, of course! You don't know.... Take it easy! I give you the good news that you are safe here in Ukraine and that you will be fine. Your nose and ribs will heal. We keep you overnight for observation, but you should be discharged tomorrow."

"My nose?" he asked, reaching up and touching it –

another mistake as pain shot through his head. "What day is it?"

"Wednesday," the doctor replied. Mick's first thought was that nearly two complete days had passed since his capture. His second thought was for Kateryna.

"Kateryna?" he asked and when he got a blank look from the doctor, he started to get up again.

"Hold on, Doctor O'Malley. Someone will be here momentarily to answer your questions – I don't know anything besides your condition," he apologized. "We did treat a few other injuries from the operation –" his explanation was interrupted by the entry into the room of a familiar looking man in uniform.

"You?" Mick sat up again, startled, and undeterred by the pain. He recalled the uniformed figure in the room from his government interview.

"Hello Mick. Glad to see you are recovering. Thank you, Doctor," he said to Pushkar and waited patiently for him to leave the room. "Good to finally meet you properly. You have led us on a quite a chase! You may not believe me, but our following you and restricting your travel was for your own protection. Our intelligence indicated that the Russians were looking for you," he paused. "We know about their close relationship with companies such as Cloud 8 plus plus, but their interest in this company is different. Do you have any ideas?" asked the General.

"No," Mick replied, not entirely truthfully.

"I guess you would like to know what happened?" the General continued. Mick nodded. "Well, the phone call from your sister eventually reached the right analysts who put the pieces together. We were able to locate your mobile and alert the Ukrainian government. Their military successfully executed the rescue operation. This will not be part of the official narrative, but you probably realize that you were being held by a Russian special forces group, a very senior group. You almost ended up in Russia! I hope you realize how lucky you are!"

"What about Kateryna? Petrescu?" he asked, not quite processing all the data.

"The Romanian? We don't know where she is. Her husband is on his way to Kiev, by the way." Mick winced in pain, but this time not from his injuries.

"Which reminds me, you have broken a few laws along the way, haven't you?" the General began, but Mick made no reply. "Oh, don't worry – I don't expect you will be prosecuted. Despite your recklessness, you have done an incredible job in taking control of this botnet." Mick looked at him wondering how he knew this fact. "We have our sources of information," he explained, not very helpfully, then continued. "We are looking forward to your help with this botnet. Our best guys couldn't even figure out how to monitor it, let alone hijack it the way you did! I'd trade an entire department for one person with your skills! So what exactly did you do to it?" he asked.

"Oh, nothing special. I revoked their control certificates so their commands would not be accepted by the botnet and put it into an inactive mode. I also ordered it to stop sending spam. There might actually be a noticeable drop in spam traffic right now as a result."

"Well, I have no idea what that means, but my guys will want to hear all about it and examine your script. Do you know where your computer is?"

"No, I don't," he replied, thinking of Kateryna. "Anyway, you don't need the script – the real work will be tracking down and cleaning all those infected computers, millions of them around the world. I still don't know how many of them were compromised in the first place. Without patching the machines and cleaning them, they could be herded into another botnet. I know Homeland Security has developed plans for how to deal with situations like this. This will be an excellent test of those plans."

"Of course, but –"

"I need to find Kateryna," Mick said.

"We will. By the way, how well do you really know her? Did you know she speaks Russian? Did you know she was a member of the Communist Party in Romania?"

"Are you trying to say she was somehow involved?" Mick began.

"I don't know. It is strange that she hasn't contacted us these past few days... I suspect that someone must have told the Russians that Cloud 8 plus plus was holding you. There's no way Cloud 8 plus plus would have told anyone until they had regained control of the botnet..."

"If you have an accusation to make about her, you should just make it!" Mick replied, starting to get angry.

"I only have questions... questions that must be answered. It was a shame about your friend Gunter Schafer, even if he was involved with the criminals."

"What?"

"I'm sorry – I guess you don't know. He was killed by the Russians, along with the rest of Cloud 8 plus plus in the building... The place was a bloody mess." Mick was speechless.

Gunter? Dead?

"Anyway, there's someone else who wants to see you, so I'll go for the moment. Mick wasn't listening as a smile spread across his face, hurting him in new ways.

"Jocelyn?"

"Alec!"

Mick hugged his sister as tightly as his broken ribs would allow as the General left the room.

"You look like heck, but you're safe!" She kissed the top of his head.

"Jocelyn – you did it! I can't believe you called when you did! You never call me! Why did you call?"

"Well," she began, a little embarrassed. "When I got

the call from your landlord, I wondered what was up and decided to call –"

"My landlord?"

"Yes, I guess with all your travels you got a bit slack with your finances. He said your rent auto payment failed, and when he checked with the bank, they said your account was overdrawn or something. Are your finances OK, Alec? I can help out if things are a bit tight for you..."

"Thanks, sis – I'm sure it is just a mistake – my finances are fine, don't worry," Mick replied, knowing that his finances were far from fine. "Anyway, you called the State Department?"

"Yes, right away. At first they were kind of short with me, and kept asking for the name of the person I wanted to talk to. But I just kept talking, and asking to speak to a supervisor. When I hung up, I didn't think the message got through to the right people. So..." she paused for dramatic effect. "I said to myself, what would Alec do? How would he share information with the government, when the government didn't seem to want to hear it..." she paused again, and Mick had an inkling where she was going with her story. "So I picked up the telephone – my landline – and started making phone calls. I called Joe and told him the whole story. I said all of the names and places you mentioned. Then I called a girlfriend and did the same."

"Jocelyn, you are brilliant!" Mick almost shouted.

"Am I?" she replied modestly. "I admit I was ecstatic when someone from the State Department was at the door an hour later with a plane ticket!" She beamed at her brother. "They didn't tell me about the rescue operation until we landed yesterday. By then it was all over and you were safe. I kept asking about Kat, but they said they didn't know anything... Is that true?" Mick nodded somberly. "What's happened to her?" she wondered.

"I don't know, Jocelyn, but I've got to find her!" Mick felt paralyzed with fear for a moment, but then shrugged it off. "I need you to help me get out of here as soon as possible. Something just isn't quite right." Jocelyn nodded and squeezed his hand.

"I'm sure it'll be OK. She is such a smart woman! Maybe she's just hiding out." Mick nodded. "And can I ask you a question?"

"Sure – anything."

"What is with this 'Mick O'Malley' name?" Mick looked into her eyes and saw his worlds colliding. He took a deep breath.

"It's my professional name. Six years ago when I became a citizen, I changed my name and I've been using that name ever since. I didn't tell you or anyone else in the family, because... because... well, I wanted to keep my family and professional lives separate. I didn't do it to hide things from you, or anyone. I don't know... looking back, it is hard for me to recall my exact decision process, but it seemed like the right thing. And it became a habit. You probably think I need a shrink or something..." he trailed off.

"'Or something', is right!" Jocelyn echoed, then started laughing.

"What?"

"You are still just my silly little brother," she hugged him again. "I don't understand, but I'm sure you didn't mean to hurt anyone by it, and you haven't hurt me. I'm just... well... surprised, that's all. I *would* say that you have an over active imagination, but hey, look where we are and what's just happened!" Mick hugged her back, and wondered how anyone got along in life without an understanding sister.

"Jocelyn, I need to get out of here. Now!"

"Now? OK, now I'm worried about your sanity. Let's talk again in the morning and plan what we will do next."

"OK, you are right," Mick replied, then he leaned over and whispered in her ear, "Jocelyn, I must leave right now. I'm still in danger here! And so is Kat! I need a computer and some clothes." Jocelyn looked at him in shock, then just nodded her head slightly, and left the room.

She returned a few minutes later with her computer. "Here are the pictures of Sam at her concert last week," she said, handing it to Mick. He gratefully took it, fired up a command line prompt and set to work.

It took a few minutes to figure out the hospital's network and server infrastructure, which was fairly well secured. He then moved on to the hospital's remote monitoring site and was able to confirm several commonly unpatched vulnerabilities. A moment later, he was in and able to control cameras, alarms, and the fire systems at the hospital.

Jocelyn returned fifteen minutes later with a canvas bag. Mick turned the computer to her, saying "Those were very nice pictures." She read on the screen:

```
Do you have my clothes?  My script will execute
in 2 minutes and we will need to leave quickly
via the far bank of elevators.
```

She nodded, and a moment later the monitoring system next to Mick's bed turned off with a click, and the camera shut off. Mick got out of bed, disconnecting his wires and monitors. He dressed as quickly as he could. Jocelyn supported him as he stood up. The pain wasn't too bad – he could walk. Mick paused for a moment until the fire alarm lights in the ceiling turned on, but no siren sounded.

They walked briskly down the hall. The staff were confused, not sure if it was a drill, a fire, or a malfunction. They walked quickly to the far bank of elevators and made it inside without attracting any attention. In the elevator, Mick leaned against the wall, trying to make things stop spinning.

They walked through the lobby to the outside, the cool air hitting his face. Mick knew he was being impulsive, but he also knew he had to get away. He didn't trust the General or the government, and no longer believed everything he had been told. During the conversation, he realized that the General was much more interested in Mick's script than in disabling the botnet. With the creators and developers of the botnet dead, Mick was the one person who was able to control the botnet. Mick could not in good conscience allow the government to take control of the botnet. Somewhere between Charleston and Kiev, he had realized that this botnet was effectively a weapon, and such a powerful weapon that no one, not even his own government, could be trusted with it.

Jocelyn and Mick boarded a bus as it pulled up and rode towards the center of Kiev. They alighted near the train station and set off walking. A squeal of tires made Mick look up to see a motorcycle come to a rapid halt beside them. He looked on in amazement as the rider lifted the visor.

"Get on the back, Mick!" Kateryna called to him, making him stare.

"Kat?"

"Don't just stand there. I saw you leave the hospital. They noticed your absence a few minutes later – I'm sure they are on their way here." Mick looked to his sister. She nodded.

"Go with her, Alec – I'll be fine."

"Jocelyn, I don't know when I'll see you again."

"I know that."

"Thank you for everything," he said, turning to her.

"Go... go!" she pleaded.

"Tell Sam... tell Sam..." he faltered. "Tell her: don't believe any FUD! She'll know what I mean," he said as he climbed on the back of the motorcycle and pulled on his helmet. Kateryna twisted the throttle and the CBR roared off down the street. Mick looked back and saw Jocelyn join a group of Korean tourists walking along the street.

Wonder what will happen to her... to all of us?

CHAPTER 23.

Kateryna rode for twenty minutes until they had left the city limits and driven for about 1Økm along a side road. She slowed down and pulled off to the side near a small grove of trees. Mick's knees were shaking, and his head swimming. He climbed off, removed his helmet, and sat down on the grass. He looked up as she pulled off her helmet and shook her hair free. Mick smiled to himself, recollecting a thought he had long ago in Hiroshima.

"Kat – what happened? I was so worried about you!" he began.

"You worried about me? I was worried about you! When you didn't return, I eventually took your computer and rode the motorbike back to our hotel, and checked us out – just as we agreed the night before. I *so* wanted to go and find you. Your face is a mess, by the way."

"I'm glad you followed the plan!" he said. "But where have you been? How did you find me?"

"Well, I found another hotel and hung out for a day, reading all the news stories I could find. That evening, I read about the raid and started checking local hospitals. I found a police presence at the hospital, and staked it out. I even managed to see you while you were sleeping, and that is when I overheard the discussion about your sister arriving. I just waited it out. I knew there was no way I could get you out alone. I thought maybe I could talk to Jocelyn but she was escorted everywhere. When I saw you coming out the door on your sister's arm, I couldn't believe my luck. I saw you get on the bus and followed you. But now, I want to hear your story."

"Wait – you never told me you could ride!"

"Oh, that. Well, I don't really, but my brothers taught me how to ride their dirt bikes. You should have seen how wobbly I was at first, although I like this bike now."

Mick told her what he had learned from Gunter, the General, and Jocelyn. By the time he was finished, Kateryna was quiet. She turned away.

"I can't believe it about Gunter!" she said, choking up.

"I know. He was like a different person..."

"And now he's dead?" Mick stood up, walked up behind her and slipped his arms around her. She leaned into him for a long moment, letting out a sigh. Mick relaxed for a moment, but Kateryna continued. "How are the Russians involved?"

"Well, there are close ties between botnet companies like Cloud 8 plus plus and Russian authorities as you know, but I haven't figured it all out yet. And how did they know I was being held? If they worked together, why did they kill the entire Cloud 8 plus plus team? It just doesn't make sense..." he trailed off into his thoughts. Then he recalled the discrepancy in the botnet node count – the computers that weren't sending any messages, seemingly just waiting for something.

There are sleeper zombies inside UBK, inside the U.S. Government network!

It made perfect sense now! There was no value in sleeper zombie computers to the Ukrainians: they couldn't participate in denial of service attacks, or send spam, or do anything that generated cash flow. But they could be invaluable for other purposes, especially to a foreign government. Kateryna interrupted his thoughts.

"Did you meet my husband?" she asked. He was speechless for a moment.

"Ah, no. How do you know he is here?"

"He left me a message. So are you going through with it?"

"Yes. Did you pick up the package?"

"Yep. I didn't open it – it is in the pannier – I followed your directions exactly and picked it up at the post office." She replied.

Mick took out the package. It was mailed by Ian from Plymouth to Kiev, and contained his last-resort fallback plan.

"Are you sure you want to do this?" she asked, referring to his plan that he confided to her on the train the previous night.

"What else can I do? I won't give control of the botnet to anyone. Everyone else associated with Zed dot Kicker is dead. Except for Jasinski, of course. I got away from the government once, well twice now, but that's not likely to happen again..."

"I guess. But can't someone recreate the botnet?"

"Maybe, eventually. I never did discover how they actually compromised some of the computers in the botnet, or how they stole my private key. But perhaps if security researchers can study this botnet, as an example of a new breed of sophisticated bots, new defenses can be developed."

Mick was starting to put all the pieces together in his mind. He had realized that the sleeper zombies were probably compromised using a different zero day – a silent exploit that no one had yet discovered. He was starting to realize that he might be able to find evidence of it on his server, if this exploit had been used to steal his private key while he was in New Mexico. While these sleeper zombies were part of the botnet, they only 'listened' to botnet commands through the spam that came their way – they did not send messages or actively participate in the network. Mick did not know what command would make them activate and reveal themselves.

"I see your angle." Kateryna smiled at him. "Would you be the one to leak this information to the community?"

"Perhaps. I can think of one or two ways to get people's attention without doing any real damage or harm."

"This may not work, you know."

"True, but I have to try."

"I wish I could come with you," Kateryna said, looking away, "but I just can't…"

"I know."

"But what about you? Are you just going to walk away from your whole life?"

"I already have – when I rode through the Lincoln Tunnel, I knew I most likely wasn't coming back. All my assets in the U.S. have been seized. Fortunately, I have enough currency moved offshore, so I won't be hurting for money."

"And, why did your sister call you 'Alec'? Is this another identity you have?"

"Yes, I was born Alec Robertson, but changed my name when I became a U.S. citizen. I know, it is strange…"

"Considering what we've just been through… not so much. Do you have any other identities?" she asked, and Mick shook his head and put a finger to his lips. "Oh, I see – that explains why you didn't want me to open the package unless I knew you weren't coming back," she concluded. "But, everyone will be on your trail! Even now I'm sure they are reviewing traffic cameras and will eventually track us here."

"I have an idea of how I can throw them off," he replied, looking out towards the setting sun.

"Will I see you again?" she asked. Mick had been asking himself the same question.

"I don't know. What are you going to say to your husband?" he asked.

"The truth, mostly... Don't worry about it, Mick."

"I'm really, really sorry I got you involved in all this..."

"Don't be – I have no regrets. You are one amazing guy, and I feel lucky to have had the chance to get to know you."

"Thanks, Kat. I feel the same. I wish I hadn't involved you in all this, but I don't know what I would have done without your help. But I still feel there is so much more I want to know about you," he began.

"Like what?"

"I don't know... do you have any tattoos?" he asked. Kateryna laughed in spite of herself.

"Some things are best left as mysteries!" she replied. Mick laughed, too, and they hugged one last time.

Mick waved goodbye to Kateryna as he rode off on the CBR. He felt a lump in his throat, but it was soon replaced by anticipation. Mick hoped her part in the plan would help her avoid trouble from the authorities. He still had twenty minutes until Kateryna would make her phone call to initiate the chain of events.

Mick had memorized the map from his computer showing a nearby section of freeway where it crossed the river. Before getting on the freeway, he rode along a dirt road that ran along the riverbank. He stopped and changed his clothes, putting some clothing and his computer in the canvas bag from the hospital. He carefully noted the location, riding towards the bridge. He paused surveying it, paying particular attention to the guardrail on the entrance curve.

This could work, but it will be risky!

He turned around and rode to the freeway. He parked the bike and pretended to check the engine.

How long will I have to wait?

He imagined the phone call he asked Kateryna to make to her husband. She would pretend to be upset, saying that she had tried to persuade him to give himself up, but they had argued, and Mick had ridden away on the motorcycle. She would tell which direction he went, saying she just didn't want him to get hurt.

In less than fifteen minutes, he got his answer. First, he noticed the flow of cars on the freeway stopped. In the eerie quiet, he got back on the bike and started it up. In his mirrors, he saw three vehicles in the distance approaching at high speed.

Time to go!

He took off, going through the gears. The vehicles were closing, as the CBR did not have the torque to leave them behind.

Come on! Stupid gutless 125!

He could see the bridge ahead, but the cars closed rapidly. He hoped that he would be able to make it.

As he approached the bridge, he steered out of his lane towards the small gap in the guardrail, standing on the foot pegs and crouching down. As the bike went airborne, he stood up on the pegs, lifting the front wheel.

He flew through the air for ten meters, preparing for the impact and the pain. He let go of the bike just before he hit the water; everything went dark.

CHAPTER 24.

To the Joint Anti-Botnet Information Taskforce:

While the first month of this taskforce has not covered itself with glory, I have no doubt that this team will eventually meet its objectives. On the positive side, the Cloud 8++ consortium has been broken up – all major players are now believed dead. The Zed.Kicker botnet appears to be dormant, but not dismantled.

On the negative side, we have lost track of Mick O'Malley once again. We believe he is the only individual who can control the botnet. I know some think he is dead, but I believe he is still alive.

For now, our first goal remains to reverse engineer the botnet to take control of it.

Our other goal is to find O'Malley, or find his body.

Nothing will be spared in this operation. We must succeed. I will lead this team until we have met our objectives.

General

CHAPTER 25.

Mick saw only blackness, and felt only numbing cold. He exhaled, and a burst of bubbles escaped. He felt which way they went, and oriented himself. He kicked his legs, stretched out his arms, and started to move.

Above him was a faint glow of light, so he swam harder towards it. He broke the surface and gulped a breath of cold air into his lungs, treading water as he got his bearings in the twilight.

He had already drifted downstream. The headlights of the pursuing vehicles stopped on the bridge above him. He dove under the water again, swimming at right angles to the current towards the far bank, trying to stay out of sight. He grabbed an overhanging branch and pulled himself out of the water.

Mick stepped on the shore and quickly made for some nearby pine trees. He did a few pushups to get his circulation going.

He shivered as he made his way along the bank, hearing more and more sirens in the distance.

Further down, he found the canvas bag he had hidden earlier. He stripped off his wet clothes and dressed in the dry ones from inside the bag. He set off walking. With a bit of luck, he would escape with his life.

Over the next five thousand kilometers he walked, rode, and sailed on his journey, Mick had one thought over and over.

Was it worth it?

CHAPTER 26.

Two months later...

Halfway between Dublin and Dun Laoghaire, Seamus Campbell got off the train and walked the short distance to the building. The Blackrock shop was Ireland's largest dealer of Moto Guzzi motorcycles, Seamus's second favorite brand of Italian motorcycles. There was a light dusting of snow on the ground that he knew would likely be melted by the afternoon.

As he walked in the door, a short man behind the counter called out to him.

"Hey, there, Seamus! You are right on time today!"

"Hey Finbar – well, I have to impress the boss, don't I?" Seamus called out as he walked behind the counter, hung up his jacket, and prepared for another day's work. He wore jeans, a green and gold team uniform shirt, and running shoes.

"Are you going to hurling training tonight?"

"For sure!" he replied.

Seamus was relatively happy these days, and had made many new friends in the small town south of Dublin. He did miss his friends and family. But on the worst nights, he thought of one particular woman.

When Seamus wasn't working at the shop, he worked on his side project: monitoring a botnet. He could see some occasional probes but so far no serious attempts had been made by anyone to wrest control of the botnet. He was also busy gathering data about the extent of the botnet – compiling information that he hoped one day could be use to completely dismantle it. He had also been painstakingly going through his personal servers to try to find evidence that the silent exploit had been used against it in the theft of his private key. He had not found anything definitive, but he did find some suspicious code that he was having a difficult time analyzing. And he did find a name in the code: nØviz.

He occasionally read articles about UBK in the press. Some were about the rollback of the U.S. Government IT contract. However, others were about new contracts involving other governments. How this could be baffled him.

Seamus had also made some contacts with the local hacker community. He pretended to know much less than he did, and so far had made a few useful friends for the future. He always kept an ear out for one particular hacker friend, but had so far heard nothing.

For now, the botnet, an Internet weapon of mass destruction, was neutralized, in the same way the radioactivity from Chernobyl was encased in a concrete tomb, but was still deadly. He had averted the zero day attack and the resulting destruction, but the weapon was still out there, and the struggle to regain control of the botnet or create a new one was far from over.

In the meantime, he planned to work on motorcycles.

# # #

ALAN B. JOHNSTON

Born in Melbourne, Australia, Alan B. Johnston holds two passports, but the same name is on both documents. He currently lives in the United States. His introduction to computers as a tween was machine language programming on a 68ØØ microprocessor. The first high level programming language he learnt was APL. During his teens, he experimented with electronics and amateur radio, talking to people all over the world on his favorite 2Ø meter band, and using amateur satellites.

He started university at age sixteen and has a PhD in engineering. He teaches and works on Internet Communication, and is the co-author of the voice security protocol ZRTP. He is the author of four non-fiction books on Voice over IP (VoIP), Internet Communication, Session Initiation Protocol (SIP), and VoIP security. He holds several patents and is a frequent conference speaker worldwide. He has traveled extensively earning more than a million lifetime frequent flier miles.

He owns several motorcycles but no Ducatis. His favorite is an old 1970s Yamaha Enduro. He is an avid dinghy sailor, but has no blue water sailing experience. He enjoys writing, having written several technical books, a dissertation, and some haiku. *Counting from Zero* is his first novel.

ALAN B. JOHNSTON

BIBLIOGRAPHY AND RESOURCES

More information and links about this book and the author are available on the Internet at:

```
https://countingfromzero.net
```

Visit us on Facebook:

```
http://www.facebook.com/countingfromzero
```

Follow us on Twitter (note there is no 'o' in from in the username):

```
http://www.twitter.com/countingfrmzero
```

If you are interested in learning more about some of the computer and Internet security topics discussed in this book, I'd suggest the following:

For more information about open source and free software ("free as in speech, not as in beer"), there is the Free Software Foundation (http://www.fsf.org).

For resources on privacy and free speech on the Internet, there is the Electronic Frontier Foundation (https://www.eff.org) and the Center for Democracy and Technology (https://www.cdt.org).

The Internet Society (http://www.isoc.org) promotes the continued development of an open, free, global Internet through standards, education, and policies.

To get an idea of the dangers of social engineering, and sound policies every organization should implement to protect against it, I would recommend <u>The Art of Deception: Controlling the Human Element of Security</u> by

Kevin D. Mitnick and William L. Simon.

For those wanting to learn the technical details of security, the classic text is Bruce Schneier's <u>Practical Cryptography</u>, which describes the Diffie-Hellman public key algorithm.

For those wanting to secure their email communication, I would recommend the GNU Privacy Guard or other open source code based on Open PGP (`http://gnupg.org`). For securing VoIP (Voice over Internet Protocol) communications, take a look at Zfone (`http://zfoneproject.com`) which uses the ZRTP protocol, and the open source project Cryptophone (http://www.cryptophone.de).

For a history of cryptography and code breaking, I would recommend Simon Singh's <u>The Code Book: The Science of Secrecy from Ancient Egypt to Quantum Cryptography</u>. It has an interesting account of the efforts of Alan Turing and others to break the German Enigma encryption during World War II, to the recent history of PGP email encryption and government attempts to control encryption.

For an interesting non-fiction account of real zero day exploits and organized crime's use of the Internet, I would recommend <u>Fatal System Error: The Hunt for the New Crime Lords Who Are Bringing Down the Internet</u> by Joseph Menn.